the Gathering

ALSO BY KELLEY ARMSTRONG

DARKNESS RISING
☙BOOK ONE☙

the
Gathering

KELLEY ARMSTRONG

HARPER
An Imprint of HarperCollinsPublishers

Library of Congress Cataloging-in-Publication Data

Armstrong, Kelley.

The gathering / Kelley Armstrong. — 1st ed.

p.   cm. — (Darkness rising ; bk. 1)

ISBN 978-0-06-179702-6 (trade bdg.) — ISBN 978-0-06-179704-0 (lib. bdg.)

[1. Supernatural—Fiction. 2. Human-animal relationships—Fiction. 3. High schools—Fiction. 4. Schools—Fiction. 5. Family life—Vancouver (B.C.)—Fiction. 6. Witchcraft—Fiction. 7. Vancouver Island (B.C.)—Fiction. 8. Canada—Fiction.] I. Title.

PZ7.A73369Gat   2011   2010032229

[Fic]—dc22   CIP

                                                                                          AC

Typography by Erin Fitzsimmons

11 12 13 14 15   LP/RRDB   10 9 8 7 6 5 4 3 2 1

❖

First Edition

For Julia

PROLOGUE

SERENA STOOD ON THE rock ledge twenty feet above the lake, singing in a voice known to bring tears to the eyes of everyone who heard it. Everyone except me.

"For God's sake, Seri," I said, "just dive already."

Serena stuck out her tongue and shifted closer to the edge, toes wrapping around it. She bounced there, blond ponytail bobbing, cheeks puffing. Then she dove. It was, as usual, an effort worthy of the Olympics, and she sliced into the water so smoothly that barely a ripple pinged across the glassy surface.

She popped back up, sleek as a seal. "Your turn, Maya!"

I flipped her the finger. She laughed and dove again.

Serena was the swimmer—captain of the school team. It's not my thing, really. This was the part I liked, just sitting on the rock ledge, bare feet dangling. I basked in the morning sun, drinking in the rich, late-summer air and the perfect view of the crystal-clear lake, the distant snow-capped mountains, the endless evergreens.

As Serena swam to the middle of the lake, I squinted over at the path, looking for a familiar blond head. Daniel was supposed to join us.

Daniel and I had been friends since I'd moved to Salmon Creek when I was five. Then, last year, there'd been a school dance where the girls were supposed to invite the guys, and Serena thought we should draw straws to see who asked Daniel. I liked him, but not the way Serena did, so I'd fixed the game so she'd win. They'd been together ever since.

As Serena swam back toward me, I stripped to my bra and panties, dropping my clothes into the bushes below.

"Ooh la la," she called. "Check out the new undies. Did some amazing friend finally take pity and buy you grown-up stuff?"

"Yes, and she'd better be right about them not going see-through when they get wet. Otherwise her boyfriend is going to see a lot more of me than she'd like."

Serena laughed. "They'll be fine. White's your color. Shows off your tan."

I shook my head at her and plaited my long black hair. I don't have a tan. I'm Native. Navajo, maybe. I'd been adopted as a baby and my mother hadn't been around to fill in any background forms.

I climbed farther up the rocks and stopped at one over-hanging the lake.

As I balanced there, Serena called, "Hey, those low riders show off your birthmark. Did you ask your parents about getting that tattoo?"

My fingers dropped to the mark on my hip. It looked like a faded paw print, and I wanted to get it tattooed so it would show up better.

"Mom says maybe when I'm sixteen. Dad says when I'm sixty."

"He'll come around." She flipped onto her back and floated. "He always does. You should do it for your sixteenth birthday next year. We'll get your mom to take us over to Vancouver, make a weekend of it. I'll get one, too. I want a nightingale, right over my boob, so when I get up on stage in my sexy dress, cut down to—"

She flailed suddenly. "Maya!"

She went under. Disappeared completely, like a hook had dragged her down.

I jumped into the water, and I hit it wrong. Pain smacked me so hard I gasped. Water filled my mouth and my nose.

I swam out in a frantic dog paddle. I could see the rings where Serena had gone under. They seemed to get farther away with every clumsy stroke I took.

I treaded water, looking around. "Serena?"

No answer.

"If this is a prank to get me in the lake, it worked," I

said, my voice quavering.

When she didn't reply, I dove. As I went under, panic hit, like it always did—my gut telling me this was wrong, dangerous, get above the surface or I'd drown.

The normally clear lake was brown, churned up dirt swirling through it, and I couldn't see.

I shot up from the water.

"Help!" I shouted. "Someone! Please!"

I dove again, blind and flailing, praying my hand or foot would brush Serena.

She's been under too long.

No, she hadn't. Serena could hold her breath forever. Last year, we'd timed her at a swim meet and she'd stayed under for five minutes before the coach ran over and made her stop.

I couldn't hold my breath even for a minute. I bobbed up again, gasping.

"Maya!"

I followed the shout to the shore. The sun glinted off the wet rocks and I blinked. Then I glimpsed blond wavy hair and a flash of tanned skin as Daniel yanked off his shirt.

"It's Serena," I shouted. "She went und—"

My kicking leg caught on something. I tried to pull, but it tightened around my ankle. I went under, screaming. Water filled my mouth as it closed over my head.

I fought, kicking and twisting, trying to grab at whatever had me. My fingers brushed something soft, and my brain screamed "Serena!" I tried to grab her, but I was dragged deeper and deeper until my feet hit the bottom. Then, whatever was wrapped around my ankle fell away.

I pushed up through the murky water. But as soon as my feet left the lake bottom, I couldn't tell where the surface was anymore. Everything was dark. My lungs burned. My head throbbed. I kept fighting my way up. Oh God, let it be *up*.

Finally I broke through. I felt the sunlight and the slap of cool air, only to go back down again. I pushed up, but couldn't stay afloat, couldn't seem to remember how to tread water. My whole body ached. Staying above was such a struggle, it was almost a relief when the water closed over my head again, peaceful silence enveloping me.

I had to struggle not to give in, had to force my arms and legs to keep churning, get my head back above—

Arms grabbed me. They seemed to be pulling me under and I struggled against them.

"Maya!" Daniel shouted. "It's me."

I didn't care. I needed him to let go of me, leave me be, let me breathe. He gripped me tighter, wrapping one strong arm around me as he swam.

I told Daniel to let me go, that I could make it to shore, just find Serena, please find Serena. He thought I was still panicking and kept hauling me along until, finally, he heaved me onto the rocks.

"Serena," I gasped. "Get Serena."

He hoisted himself up and scanned the shore and I realized he hadn't understood. Oh God, he hadn't heard me.

"Serena!" I yelled. "She went under. I was trying to find her."

His eyes widened. He twisted and plunged into the lake. I huddled there on a rock, coughing, as he swam out. I watched him dive and come back up. Dive and come back up. Dive and come back up . . .

They dragged the lake that afternoon and found Serena's body. Her death was ruled an accidental drowning. A healthy teenage girl, captain of the swim team, had drowned. No one knew how it happened. An undertow. A cramp. A freak panic attack. There were plenty of guesses but no answers.

Soon all that was left of Serena was a monument in the school yard. The town moved on. I didn't. Something had happened in that lake, something I couldn't explain. But I would. One day, I would.

ONE

I STOOD UNDER THE tree and glared up at the three-legged bobcat.

"I'm not getting you down. You're stuck until I get back from school. Maybe that'll teach you a lesson."

Fitz twisted to lick his flank.

"Not even listening to me, are you? Why do I bother?"

"Same question I ask myself every day," said a voice behind me. "It's good training for parenthood."

Dad walked down the porch steps. He was dressed in khakis and his Smokey the Bear hat.

"Ooh, big day in town for our park warden," I said. "They're even making you wear the uniform. Hayley's mom will be happy. She thinks you look hot in it."

Dad turned as red as his hair.

Mom's laugh floated out from her studio. "Maya Delaney.

Leave your father alone."

"It's true. Nicole heard her saying she loves a guy in uniform, and if Dad ever gets tired of you, her front door is open. But you have to wear the hat."

Dad made unhealthy choking noises.

Mom only laughed again. "Thanks for the warning. Now get moving. You know what happens if you're late. Daniel won't wait. You have to catch him."

"Which would be a bigger threat if the roads were better or his truck was faster."

A cold nose brushed my hand.

"Even Kenjii knows you're running late," Mom called. "Now move it."

I waved toward the window of her studio at the front of the house. When I reached the end of the drive, I turned around.

"Dad? Can you—?"

"Check on the fledglings because you overslept again?"

"Um, right. Sorry." I walked backward. "Oh, and we're going across to Vancouver this weekend for my sixteenth-birthday tattoo, right?"

He shook his head and strode toward the shed.

"Oh, sure, walk away from the conversation," I said. "How come I get in trouble when I do that?"

"You aren't getting a tattoo tomorrow, Maya," Mom called. "We'll discuss it later. Now move your butt."

Dad disappeared into the shed where I keep the wounded and orphaned animals he finds on the park grounds. I fix them up and release them if I can, or pass them onto a wildlife center if I can't. They aren't pets. Fitz is the only exception. He'd been caught by a trapper who'd never seen a bobcat on the island, and called my dad. After Fitz recovered from the amputation, I'd released him—twice—but he'd come back. He'd made it clear he was staying, if only for free food and protection from predators with all four of their limbs.

My only pet is Kenjii, a German shepherd that my parents bought when we moved to Salmon Creek and they decided a hundred-pound canine companion was a wise idea for a girl who liked to roam forests filled with bears, cougars, and other critters that might mistake her for a nice light snack.

Would things have been different if I'd had Kenjii with me at the lake last year? Serena and I always left her behind, because if we goofed around, she thought we were drowning and tried to pull us to safety. Kenjii might have saved Serena.

I think about that a lot. I think about all of it a lot. Six months of therapy hadn't convinced me I'm wrong when I say I could have saved Serena.

It wasn't the way I wanted to start my day, so I pushed the thoughts aside as we walked. It was a gorgeous fall morning, unusually dry for this part of Vancouver Island. Massive hemlocks and cedars lined the rutted trail that passed for a road. Wind had the sun dancing through swaying branches, and Kenjii tore along the path, pouncing on spots of sunlight like a puppy. The sharp breeze helped chase away the last bits of sleep, perking up my brain with the scent of cedar and rich, dew-damp earth.

It was a quiet morning, as usual. No commuter traffic out here. We're the only family living in the park. It's privately owned. The whole town is.

The St. Cloud Corporation bought the land a few years before I was born, and decided it was the perfect place for a top-secret research facility. They built the town of Salmon Creek for their employees.

Less than two hundred people live here. They get their paychecks from the St. Cloud family. They live in houses owned by the St. Clouds. Their kids go to a private school owned by the St. Clouds. Weird, I know, but I'm not complaining, because surrounding the town is a thousand acres of the most beautiful wilderness you've ever seen, and that's where I call home.

When I was five, the St. Clouds lost their park warden and they went headhunting. They found my dad, who was a ranger in Oregon. My mom's Canadian, though, from the Haida Nation. For her, the job meant coming home. For Dad, it meant the opportunity of a lifetime. For me, it meant growing up in the most amazing place on earth.

Living out here does have its challenges, though. Including transportation. Dad used to drive me to school every day, but now Daniel picks me up at the park gates in his truck— he doesn't dare drive the rutted park roads any more than necessary or the rust holding his pickup together is liable to shake loose.

Technically, the park is open to the public, but that's only because it was a condition of sale. Let's just say that the St. Cloud Corporation doesn't exactly roll out the welcome mat to tourists. The park provides minimal services. Same goes for the town itself. The St. Clouds weren't able to buy every cottage and campground between the town site and existing communities, so we do get "summer people"—campers and cottagers needing basic supplies like groceries and gas, who come to Salmon Creek to get them.

At this time of year, though, it's a rare park visitor who isn't a local. So when I heard a woman screaming, my first thought was that a female cougar had ventured into the park, hoping to get lucky.

Kenjii's ears swiveled forward. She didn't look terribly concerned, which for any other dog would suggest it wasn't a cougar. My parents bought me a big dog to protect me from the local big cats, but Kenjii had to be the only canine on the island that didn't really mind them. Bears, wolves, badgers, and foxes send her into guard dog mode. But not cats.

So, when I spotted a cougar stretched out on a thick pine tree branch near the park gates, I wasn't surprised. I can't say the same for the woman clinging to the branch above the cat. She was the one screaming. The cougar—a ragged-ear old tom I called Marv—just stared at her, like he couldn't believe anyone would be dumb enough to climb a tree to escape a cat.

There's nothing in this forest as gorgeous as a cougar—a

sleek, muscular creature nearly twice the size of Kenjii with tawny fur, a black-edged face, and light brown eyes with round pupils. They're one of the most elusive animals in the forest, too. But the woman screaming on the branch really wasn't appreciating the moment.

Marv pulled back his lips and snarled, flashing fangs as long as my fingers, which made the woman shriek louder. I stepped into the clearing—staying well out of Marv's pouncing range—waved my arms, and shouted. Kenjii chimed in, her deep bark echoing through the forest.

The woman stopped screaming. Marv looked over at me and chirped.

"Yeah, I'm talking to you, old guy," I said. "Shoo! Scat! Get out of here!"

He looked at me like I'd offended him. I shouted and waved some more, staying behind Kenjii. I'm not afraid of cougars, but I am suitably respectful of their ability to end my existence with one well-placed chomp.

As I yelled and Kenjii barked, another sound joined it—the rumble of a badly tuned motor. Then, a honk. A welcoming shout out a rolled-down window, followed by a curse as Daniel saw why I wasn't waiting outside the gates. The brakes squeaked. The door slammed. Sneakers pounded the hard earth.

It was then that Marv decided it was time to go. Daniel has that effect on people, too. He's only about five ten, but he's been the island wrestling champion twice and it shows.

Marv hopped to the ground, mustered his dignity, and slid into the undergrowth.

Daniel shook his head as he watched the cat's black-tipped tail disappear. "Haven't I told you not to play with the big kitties, Maya?"

"It was Marv."

"Again? What's that, the third time this month? I think he likes you."

"What can I say? I'm serious catnip."

The woman lowered herself to the ground. She was maybe in her early twenties. Asian. Dressed in the kind of "rugged outdoor gear" you can buy at malls in Vancouver and really shouldn't wear any place wilder than that.

She stared at us. "The cat. It just . . . left."

"Um, yeah," I said. "Most times, they do. That's a male, meaning he doesn't have any cubs to protect. Plus there's plenty of food around. I'd still suggest you return the favor and steer clear of the park today."

I walked to the front gate, opened the pamphlet box, took out the one titled "Predator Safety," and handed it to her. Then I pulled my cell phone from my backpack.

"I've gotta call this in," I said. "My dad's the warden. All cougar encounters—"

The woman backed away from me. "I don't have time."

"That cat's been hanging around. It's a problem. You need to report—"

"I will. Later."

She headed for the road and continued toward town.

"Walk in the middle," I called after her. "Cats don't like open areas."

She jogged off. Daniel hadn't said a word, which was weird. Normally he'd be the first person giving warnings and making sure she was safe. But he just stood there, staring after her, a strange look on his face.

"Yep, she's kinda cute," I said. "That'd be a whole different type of cougar, but I say go for it."

Now I got a look. Then he turned to stare after the woman, frowning.

"You know her?" I asked.

"I don't think so. Just . . . something's wrong with her."

"Um, yeah. She climbed a tree to escape a cat. She's suffering from a serious case of stupid."

"No kidding." He gave her one last look, then waved me to the truck. "Just do me a favor, okay? If you see her again, be careful."

I didn't ask what he meant. Daniel does that sometimes— he meets people and just decides he doesn't like them. Last winter, when Dr. Davidoff and his team flew in from the States for their annual visit, Daniel decided he *really* didn't like a new guy Dr. Davidoff brought and wouldn't have anything to do with him.

Mom says that's part of growing up in such a small town. You don't trust strangers. But I say it's just Daniel. Everyone has his quirks, and this is Daniel's. Most times, though, he's right. So when he says steer clear, I do.

He opened the passenger door for me.

"Such a gentleman," I said.

"No, it's sticking, and I don't want you whaling on it again and—" He stopped and peered off down the road.

I followed his gaze. The road was empty.

"Where'd she—? Damn it!" I tossed my bag in, then strode back along the truck. "If she went back in the woods, after getting treed by a cat—"

Daniel caught my arm. "Don't."

I looked up at him. He stared down the road, his face rigid, gaze distant, fingers tightening around my arm.

"Um, Daniel? Ouch."

"Huh?" He noticed what he was doing and let go. "Sorry. Call your dad and tell him. If she went back into the forest, that's her problem. We're late already."

TWO

I CALLED MY DAD on the way to school and told him about the hiker and Marv. Like Daniel said, this was the third time I'd seen the old cat in the past month. For me, that was only a little odd. I saw cougars more than anyone else we knew. Maybe they sensed I was interested in them. Always had been. Of all the animals in the forest, they were my favorite.

But a cougar that isn't afraid to get up close and personal with a human is worrisome. Treeing that hiker proved Marv wasn't only taking an interest in *me*. So I told Dad and he, in turn, had to notify the police chief and the mayor. When I was called to the office after first period, I wasn't surprised to hear that all three of them were there, looking for a full report.

The meeting room wasn't far from my class. Nothing is far

in our school. It's a single story divided in two wings—classrooms at one end, common rooms at the other, the principal's office and meeting room in the middle. There are sixty-eight kids at Salmon Creek School—and that's every grade from kindergarten to twelve.

Having fewer than seventy kids means you know everyone by name. It also means every teacher—all five of them—knows you by name and your parents by name and your pets, too.

There are more kids in the upper grades than the lower ones. When the St. Clouds built their facility, they hired staff with young families, and those kids are all teenagers now. I'm in the biggest class—the grade eleven/twelve split.

The St. Clouds give us the best of everything. That's how they lured employees into a community in the middle of nowhere—promise the best education possible for their children. Our classroom desks are all built to accommodate our laptops, which are replaced every two years. Our auditorium has theater-style seating. Our cafeteria has a chef and cloth napkins. We have a gym, but no pool or skating rink, only because the St. Clouds put those in the community center a ten-minute walk away.

It all sounds very posh. It's not really. When I say Salmon Creek is in the middle of nowhere, I mean it. We're an hour's drive from the nearest city, and half of that is on empty back roads through uninhabited forest. Since we're living so isolated, we don't feel special the way private school kids might.

We aren't here because we get amazing grades or our parents are rich; the extras were just normal. By the time we reach the upper grades, we don't even take advantage of the cafeteria chef anymore—we bring our lunches and grab a picnic table outside.

I had to pass through the principal's office to get to the conference room. I waved at the secretary—Ms. Morales. Dad was waiting by the door and ushered me inside. Mayor Tillson was at the espresso machine. He's my friend Nicole's dad. If you didn't know which was the police chief and which was the mayor, you'd probably guess wrong. Chief Carling was a tiny blonde, a few inches shorter than me, dressed in slacks and a silk blouse. The mayor was a foot taller and twice as heavy, with a bulldog face. He wore jeans and a plaid shirt that strained around his waist.

When I finished telling them everything that happened that morning, Chief Carling said, "Your dad says this isn't the first encounter you've had with this particular cat."

"The park is his territory. He's shown up more often lately, though. Getting old and bold, I guess. He hasn't made any threatening moves. I think he's just curious."

"Which is not—" Dad began.

"The point, I know," I said. "The problem is that if we relocate him, another cat will move in. A younger and potentially more dangerous one. The best thing to do would be to have Dr. Hajek tranq him a couple of times, teach him that humans aren't fun to hang out with."

Mayor Tillson smiled at my dad. "The girl knows her cougars, Rick. Do you remember when you caught her throwing sticks for one?"

The mayor retold the story, as if everyone in the room hadn't heard it a million times. It'd been just after we moved to the park. Mom had come out back to find me playing fetch with a young cougar—probably Marv.

". . . and Maya says, 'Don't worry, Mom. He's got blood on his fur so he just ate. He isn't hungry.'"

Chief Carling laughed, then said I was right—Marv had to be taught that humans and cougars couldn't be friends. "And the best way to do that would be to take Maya along. Make sure he gets the connection between her and the tranquilizer dart. With luck, that'll solve the problem. I agree that he doesn't seem to be a danger, but I don't like this sudden interest."

"Neither do I," Dad said.

"All right, then. We won't keep you any longer, Maya." Mayor Tillson rose. "I hear you have gym next. Wouldn't want to miss that." He paused, voice lowering a notch. "I hope we're going to see you on the track team again this spring."

"You will."

"That's our girl. We need our champ."

He waved at the wall of trophies. Not all mine, obviously. But there were a lot of trophies, considering the size of our school. As in academics, in sports we get the best of everything. Top equipment. Great coaches, plus expert trainers flown in a few times a year.

We can't field a team for football or hockey, so the school concentrates on track, swimming, wrestling, and boxing. In kindergarten we're encouraged to join at least one. I dislike the water, and hate hitting anyone, but when it comes to running, jumping, and climbing, I'm in my element. I'd taken last year off the track team, though. I just didn't have the heart for it after Serena died.

I left the meeting. As I walked back through the principal's office, I nearly tripped over a guy with his chair pulled over to the door, eavesdropping.

Rafael—Rafe—Martinez. Salmon Creek's newest student. Actually, our only new student in three years. Rich parents in surrounding towns tried to get their kids into our school, but they were always turned down. Rafe wasn't a rich kid. He lived with his older sister in a nearby cabin they'd inherited from a distant relative. I guess the board figured it was the right thing to do, letting him attend our school free of charge rather than spend hours on a bus every day.

Rafe told everyone he was from Texas. That was bull. I'd dated a summer guy from Texas, and Rafe's drawl was all wrong. His last name suggested he was Latino, and he kind of looked it, but his high cheekbones and amber eyes said Native to me. He was a little taller than Daniel, lean, with black hair that hung just past the collar of his leather jacket. Worn blue jeans and low motorcycle boots completed the image: American Teen Rebel.

20

It was a look we didn't see a lot at our school, and the other girls loved it. Not that Rafe needed the added cachet. Considering we'd had the same guys in our class since kindergarten, Rafe's novelty factor alone would have had the girls tripping over themselves. He was the hottest ticket in town. And he knew it.

When I bumped into him, I said a polite, "Hey," and tried to get past.

"Hey, yourself."

He grinned and, in spite of myself, I felt a little flip in my stomach. Rafe wasn't gorgeous, but he had a sexy, crooked smile and eyes that looked at a girl like she was the first one he'd ever seen. When he stood close, I swore I could feel heat radiating off him. And Rafe always stood close.

As I backed up, he hooked a thumb toward the conference room. "Barnes in there?" he asked, meaning the principal.

I shook my head. "Haven't seen him. Ms. Morales was around, though."

"Yeah, I talked to her. She says I need to talk to Barnes. Late once too often this week."

That grin sparked again, like being late for school earned him a place in the bad boy hall of fame.

"No worries," I said. "You didn't miss much."

He fell into step beside me, so close his knuckles brushed mine. "I hear you had yourself a close encounter of the wild kind."

"Um-hmm."

"Morales said you've seen more mountain lions than anyone around here. Says they practically hang out on your doorstep hoping for a saucer of milk and a scratch behind the ears."

He meant cougar—mountain lion is an American term.

"I live in the park," I said. "I'm going to see a lot of wild animals."

"Still, mountain lions . . . Never seen one myself." He slid a sidelong look my way. "Think you could fix that?"

Like hell, I thought, but just kept walking.

"Never been in your park either," he said. "What do you say I come over tonight? We can take a walk, look for big cats, watch the stars come out. . . ."

I laughed. "Do lines like that *ever* work?"

He only smiled. "Can't blame a guy for trying."

Actually I could. Rafe didn't just flirt—he charmed girls right up to the point where they fell for him, then he changed his mind. I called him a player with attention deficit disorder. That made Daniel laugh. I didn't think it was so funny.

Would I think better of the guy if he followed through and scored with every girl he could? No, but he seemed like a cat toying with a mouse—no plans to make a meal of it, just batting it around awhile, leaving it wounded and dazed, then sauntering away.

He'd taken a run at me shortly after he arrived. When I turned him down, he'd seemed to take the hint and had backed off. Had that only been a temporary reprieve? I hoped not.

"Maya?" a soft voice called.

I glanced over to see Nicole Tillson, the mayor's daughter, at her locker. She looked from me to Rafe, concern darkening her blue eyes. I mouthed "Save me," and her pixie face lit up in a grin.

She scampered over. "Oh, thank God I found you. Did you read that chapter for history? I was halfway through when Hayley called and I never got back—" Her eyes widened as if she'd just noticed Rafe there. "Oh, hey, Rafe. Do you mind if I steal Maya's brain for a minute? I seriously need it."

She tugged my arm, pulling me away before he could answer. "Okay, so the first part was on World War II, right? I got as far as . . ."

She continued babbling for another minute, then glanced over her shoulder. "Okay, he's gone."

"Thank you."

"Anytime. I know you don't like him so—" She glanced up at me. "You don't, right? I mean, I guess not, or you wouldn't have asked me to save you, but if you do . . ."

"No. Hayley can have him."

"Good. So did you bring your lunch today? If you didn't, I was thinking maybe we could all pop over to the Blender. My treat. Mom finally paid me for that extra work I did at the clinic."

We stopped at her locker so she could get the book she'd

come for. I had to help her with that. I'm only five foot five, but Nicole's at least four inches shorter, and the guys like to stick her books up where she can't reach them.

Nicole was on the swim team and in the choir, so she'd been more Serena's friend than mine. That changed after Serena died. We'd kind of taken on each other as replacement pals. It wasn't a great fit—we didn't really have that much in common—but it filled a gap.

THREE

I DON'T MIND SCHOOL. I'd like it a lot better if it wasn't indoors. Being inside just seems to sap my energy. It's gotten worse the last couple of years. I go home and I crash.

That worries my parents, but the doctors say it's a combination of hormones and my metabolism—I'm used to being outside and active, and being a teen only makes it worse. They gave me some vitamins, but I still need a nap most days.

When school ends, I get outside as fast as I can. Today I was waylaid by Ms. Morales, who wanted a firsthand account of my cougar encounter. When I finally escaped, I spotted Nicole with Daniel on the other side of the playground. He had an eighth-grader pinned to the grass, arm twisted behind his back.

"Bully!" I shouted.

Daniel glanced over and grinned. Then he let the kid—Travis Carling—go and got down on all fours so Travis could try the move on him. As Daniel gave instructions, Travis's brother, Corey, made suggestions that had everyone within earshot laughing. Travis and Corey were Chief Carling's sons.

Dark haired, over six feet tall, big, and burly, Corey was the school's second-best wrestler and boxer after Daniel. Also Daniel's best guy buddy. I could only imagine what he was suggesting Travis do to Daniel while he had him pinned. It was drawing a crowd. Corey always did. He was one of those guys who can talk to anyone—and talk his way out of trouble, which in Corey's case is a necessary survival skill.

If I had to pick the most popular guy at our school, it'd be a toss-up between Daniel and Corey. Daniel's the one everyone wants on his team—the steady, responsible leader. Corey's the guy everyone wants to party with.

As I headed toward them, I felt someone watching me. Rafe. When I looked over, he sauntered my way, grinning like I'd been the one caught staring.

Nicole said something to Corey, who looked in my direction. Daniel was on his feet now, coming to meet me. He veered toward Rafe, gaze on me, like he didn't see Rafe there. He cut right in front of him, so close that Rafe had to stop short. Daniel pretended not to notice.

As Rafe stopped, Samantha—Sam—Russo walked past and shouldered him aside with a smirk. She switched it to a genuine smile as she said something to Daniel. Sam is our second newest student. Her parents died three years ago, and she'd come to live with the Tillsons, who were her second cousins or something like that. If there was any resemblance between Sam and Nicole, though, I couldn't see it.

Sam is an inch taller than me, kind of stocky, with dark spiked hair and wide-set blue eyes. She has freckles, too, and the only time I've seen her wear makeup is when Corey teased that her freckles were "cute" and she tried to cover them up.

When she first arrived in Salmon Creek, we'd all tried to make her feel welcome. Serena and I tried harder than anyone, because we thought she was cool, in a smart-mouth, big-city way. But Sam wielded her outsider status like a shield, so we'd given up.

I still liked her. She was different. She was interesting. And we got along fine, although it'd become clear that "getting along" was the best I could hope for. The only person at our school she really liked was Daniel. It wasn't a crush, though. She didn't even seem interested in him as a guy, only as a potential friend. Daniel was nice to her, but he already had his quota of female friends.

The student she liked least these days was Rafe. He'd made one halfhearted move toward her and I have no idea what she'd said or done, but he'd steered clear ever since.

"Texas boy taking another run at you?" Daniel said as Rafe veered away and continued on.

"It'll pass."

"Want me to talk to him?"

I gave him a look. If there's one problem with having the toughest guy at school as my best friend, this is it. Daniel has a protective streak a mile wide. Sometimes, when a summer guy is bugging me, it'd be great to have Daniel barrel in and handle it. But what does that say about me? Nothing I want to say.

"You want us to take care of the guy?" Corey said in a gangster voice as he walked over with Nicole. "We could do that. Lots of places to hide a body around here. Deep caves, deep ravines, deep lakes—" He stopped short, then smacked me between the shoulder blades. "So, how's the almost birthday girl? Getting ready for her big party? Sweet sixteen and never been—"

Daniel cut him off with a sputtering laugh. "Believe me, Maya's definitely been kissed."

Corey gave a devilish grin. "Oh, I wasn't going to say *kissed*."

Nicole blushed furiously, and I laughed.

Across the playground, Rafe had been waylaid by Hayley Morris, another member of our swim team and singing group. Like Serena and Nicole, she was petite and blond— we used to joke that this was a requirement for joining. Hayley was not a friend. She was, however, Rafe's number one admirer. She was also the first of his not-quite conquests and the only one who hadn't taken the hint when he moved on.

She'd planted herself in front of him. He eased back more politely than I would have expected, just shifting until she was out of his personal space. She got right back into it. He moved back. She moved forward. It was an oddly formal little dance, and I was watching it when Daniel said, "Maya?"

"Hmm?"

"Ready to go?"

"Anytime you are."

"Can I get a lift to the community center?" Nicole asked. "I want to squeeze in some swim practice before Ms. Martin comes by for my singing lesson."

Corey frowned. "That's a lot of practice, Nic. Are you sure you'll have time to do your homework?"

"Of course. I do homework right after—" She caught his expression and blushed as she realized he was teasing her.

"At least she *does* her homework," I said.

Daniel turned to Nicole. "Sure, I'll give you a lift. You ready, Maya?"

"Doesn't look like Maya needs a ride today," Corey said.

I followed his gaze to see my dad barreling down on me, scowling in a way that really didn't suit him at all.

Daniel mouthed, "Call me," and headed for his truck, Nicole trailing.

"In the car," Dad said, pointing to the Jeep at the curb. "Now."

"What did I—?"

"I said *now*, Maya."

He strode off, leaving me tagging along like I was five, every kid still in the school yard watching. Mom was in the passenger seat. She rolled down the window, smiling, then saw my expression.

"What's wrong?" she asked.

"No idea," I said. "He won't tell me."

She moved the seat forward for me to squeeze in the back. "Rick, what—?"

She laughed, then I saw Dad's grin as he slid into the driver's seat.

"Payback for this morning," he said. "You embarrass me; I embarrass you."

"Oh, that's mature," I said.

"Keeps me young."

"So, did you bump into Mrs. Morris today? I hear Mr. Morris is away at a conference." I waggled my brows at him in the rearview mirror.

"Enough, you two," Mom said.

"What's with the ride?" I said. "You missed me so much you couldn't wait for me to get home?"

"Don't answer that, Rick." Mom looked back at me as Dad pulled away from the curb. "We need to pick up some things in the city, and we thought we'd go out for dinner."

By "city," she did not mean Vancouver. When I tell online friends that I live on Vancouver Island, they start asking questions about the city of Vancouver. I guess it makes sense that it would be on the island with the same name.

It's not. It's across the strait, and while it's barely thirty-five kilometers away, the water flowing in between means we only cross for special occasions.

The city we were heading to was Nanaimo, on the eastern coast. With just under a hundred thousand people, it was hardly a major urban center, but on an island almost five hundred kilometers long, with a population of under a million—half of them living in Victoria at the southern tip—you take what you can get.

"I can pick the restaurant, right? Since Saturday is my birthday and apparently we aren't going to Vancouver to get my tattoo. Not that I'm bitter about that or—" I stopped as I glimpsed a familiar face out the window. "Hey, there's that hiker from this morning. Did you ever catch up with her?"

"No, and I really do need her to file a report. Hold on."

Dad pulled over to the curb as a group of kids passed. He peered out the window. "Where'd she go?"

"Right there, behind Travis Carling."

Dad opened the door and got out. The kids went by . . . and there was no one else on the sidewalk. I rolled down the window.

"She was right there." I pointed. "In front of the library."

The library was part of the community center, which took up most of the block, meaning there was no way the woman had ducked around it. Dad walked over and tried the library doors, but they were locked—it was open only three days a week.

"I think it's time for a drug test," Dad said as he came back to the car.

"I'm serious. I saw her."

"Maya's right," Mom said. "I noticed her before the kids went by. I don't know where she went, but she *was* there."

"She doesn't want to tattle on the cute kitty," I said. "Don't worry. Just hand her the papers while she's cornered again by a hundred and seventy-five pounds of *snarling* kitty and she'll change her mind."

FOUR

I T TOOK US FIVE minutes to get out of Salmon Creek. Without exceeding the speed limit. When I tell people that I live in a place with fewer than two hundred people, they don't really get what that means. They say things like, "Oh, I'm in a small town, too," and I look up theirs to see it has a population of six thousand.

Two hundred people means Salmon Creek doesn't get on most maps. It's not even a town—it's a hamlet, with only six streets—the downtown strip and five courts of about ten houses each.

There are three shops downtown. There's a decent grocery, but if my mom needs anything more exotic than white mushrooms and dried herbs, she has to grow it in our greenhouse. There's a hardware store, but if you want something unusual, it has to be ordered from the city. Then there's the

Blender, our only restaurant, owned and run by Hayley's dad. Good food but don't expect sushi.

Kids in other small towns complain about needing to go to the city to find a mall. We can't even buy clothing here. Well, we can, but it's carried by the hardware store; and unless your fashion sense runs to coveralls and rubber boots, you'd better plan a trip to Nanaimo.

The last building we passed on the way out of town was the medical research facility. That might sound like a huge hospital-sized place, with helicopters landing on the roof at all hours, but it's just a boring-looking building, two stories tall, about the size of a small office complex. It looks innocent enough, like you could walk right through the front doors. And you could . . . you just wouldn't get much farther.

Security is supertight in there. Every door has a key card lock and some have access codes, too. I know because I've been in it. Everyone has. One problem with running a top-secret facility is that it makes people curious. So every year there's an open house. Most of us kids stopped going as soon as our parents let us. It's an afternoon of hearing talks on their drug research and being toured around labs full of computers and test tubes. Drug research may be big business—big enough to build a town to protect it—but it's killer dull.

I'd be a lot more interested—in a negative way—if they were doing animal testing. If they are, it isn't here. Same with subject groups; they don't ever visit Salmon Creek. The helipad on the roof is only for flying in other doctors—like Dr.

Davidoff and his group—and corporate bigwigs from the St. Cloud company, who want to keep tabs on where their money is going.

So Salmon Creek is a small, quiet place. Maybe I'd be itching to get out if I remembered living somewhere else. But most kids are fine with Salmon Creek. We get used to driving an hour to the city. Our parents have carpooled monthly trips for us since we were young. Almost all of us plan to go off to college or university, and not many intend to return, but we're happy enough living here until then.

When we finally got to Nanaimo, we parked at the harbor front. There's a ferry up the coast that will take you over to Vancouver across the Strait of Georgia. You'd be able to see the city from the harbor if there weren't islands in the way. Well, in theory you could, though at this time of year we usually get fog, and sometimes you can't see even those nearby islands, despite them being close enough to swim to if you're really good. Serena swam out to Protection Island once and we—

I shook off the memory.

Canada might be famous for its winters, but that doesn't apply here. Vancouver Island is temperate rain forest. We get rain, not snow. This year, our dry summer was holding on, and the occasional memo about small wildfires in the interior was making Dad nervous. Nobody else was complaining, that was for sure, and it was nice to look out and see all the islands, not a curtain of fog.

We walked along the marina docks. It was a gorgeous afternoon, the sun shining off the water, boats lined up at the floating Petro-Can station to fill up before heading out to sea. An engine whined as a seaplane took off.

We crossed Front, then cut along a tiny street before coming out on Commercial. I scanned the street, a mix of local and tourist shops, about half of them devoted to food.

"Can we get a snack before we shop?" I asked. "I'm starving."

Mom shook her head. "You can grab a chocolate bar, but we need to be someplace before five."

"No, that's okay," Dad said. "Go ahead." When Mom gave him a look, he said, "If she'd rather get something to eat, let her. There's always next year. Or the year after that . . ."

I stopped walking. "Okay, what's up?"

When neither said a word, I peered down the street of shops and saw a sign that caught my eye: Sacred Ink.

"Oh my God," I said. "Seriously?" I grinned and grabbed Mom's arm. "Seriously?"

"Yes. You're getting your tattoo."

I threw my arms around Dad's neck. "Thank you!"

"Hey," Mom said. "I'm the one who had to persuade him it wasn't going to turn his little girl into a streetwalker."

"I never said that," Dad said.

"No?" I said. "Cool. Cause I've decided to skip the paw print. I'm thinking of a tramp stamp with flames that says

'Hot in Here.' No, wait. Arrows. For directionally challenged guys."

Mom grabbed Dad's shoulders and steered him away from me. "She'll get exactly what we agreed on. Now go hang out in a guy store and we'll call when we're done."

"This is so cool," I said loudly as Dad walked away. "Have you met the tattoo artist? Is he hot?"

"He's a she," Mom said.

"Is she hot? Cause I'm still young, you know. My sexual identity isn't fully formed."

"Your father can't hear you anymore, Maya." Mom sighed. "Poor guy. Why can't you be a normal teenage daughter who'd sooner die than say the words 'sexual identity' in front of him?"

"You guys raised me right. You should be proud."

I picked up my pace, but Mom said, "No need to run. Your appointment isn't for another twenty minutes."

I slowed to let her catch up. "So how'd you get Dad to agree? Did you play the cultural card?"

"Of course not. That would be wrong."

I grinned. "You did, didn't you?"

Dad's quick to defer to her on that part of my upbringing. If she'd told him that tattooing was a part of Native culture, he would have backed down.

Mom's background, though, is as different from mine as English is to Irish. That makes it tough on her. She wants me to be aware of my roots, but she isn't really sure what they are, so she teaches me what she knows instead.

My Haida grandmother lives in Skidegate on the Queen Charlotte Islands north of us, and we're really close. She's a lot more into the traditions than my mom is. I love hanging out with her, working at the cultural center, and helping with the festivals. But sometimes I feel like one of the tourists. I felt the same way when I was twelve and we visited a Navajo reservation. And I felt the same way when we went to visit Dad's extended family in Dublin. I'm aware of my background, and I'm proud of it, but I don't really feel attached to it. Maybe that'll change someday.

I wasn't surprised when we got close to the tattoo studio and I saw a Haida raven painted on the sign. Inside, I could see more native art . . . and a shocking lack of skulls, Celtic crosses, and dragons.

"Cool," I said.

"The owner is a young woman who graduated from Emily Carr," Mom said. "Not exactly the kind of art they had in mind, I'm sure."

"Is she Haida?"

Mom shook her head. "I believe she's a member of the Scots tribe."

In other words, Caucasian. That could earn her some ill will among Natives if she used their designs in tattoos, but Mom would say it was no different than a Russian tattooing Celtic knot work. As long as she'd studied the art and understood its meaning, Mom would be fine with it. Grandma would disagree. They'd respect each other's opinions, though, and Mom always said that was the important thing.

Mom continued. "I chose Deena because she specializes in traditional tattooing, which I think would work best for what you want."

I needed a free-form tattoo, not one done with a stencil. It can be a whole lot harder to find someone who can do one, unless you want it looking like a prison tat. There wasn't much risk of that here. The studio looked like a combination doctor's office and art gallery, all clean lines and cool colors.

There was no one in the front room. When Mom opened the door, a woman's voice called, "Just a minute!"

I walked over to a sign that read TRIBAL TATTOOS. In smaller print, it said, IF YOU DON'T KNOW YOUR TRIBAL TATTOO, PLEASE DON'T ASK ME. THE BEST WAY TO HONOR YOUR HERITAGE IS TO LEARN ABOUT IT YOURSELF.

A voice floated over from the next room, "Nothing worse than getting a Cherokee facial tattoo and discovering your grandmother was really Assiniboine."

Mom greeted the young woman, who didn't look a lot older than me. She was about my height, with reddish-brown hair. Freckles dotted her round face. She introduced herself as Deena.

"You get a lot of that?" I asked, pointing at the sign.

"Unfortunately, yes. That's the problem with having a shop in the tourist district. People with some Native blood come in here, wanting to recognize that part of their heritage, which is wonderful; but if you aren't even sure what your heritage is, you've got a long way to go before you ink yourself with it."

"So no Kokopelli for me," I said. "I guess I'll have to go with the unicorn."

Deena laughed. "Yes, your mother tells me she thinks you're Navajo."

"She's not," said a quavering voice from the back room. An old woman appeared. "That girl is not Navajo."

"Aunt Jean," Deena murmured under her breath. "I'm working. Please don't—"

"You're not Navajo." The woman jerked her chin at my mother. "So your daughter isn't Navajo."

I could see my mom struggling not to snap back, "You aren't either." Mom has issues with the whole "respect for elders" part of her culture. She did raise me to show respect— just not the blind sort she'd grown up with.

"My daughter is adopted," she said evenly.

"That's not what I mean. The Diné do not give up their children."

She was right. The U.S. Indian Child Welfare Act overrode state adoption laws, giving tribes the right to overturn legal adoptions if the new parents weren't part of their nation.

"This is my great-aunt Jean," Deena said. "She's a folklorist. Lived with the Navajo for . . . how long, Auntie?"

The old woman ignored her and kept staring at me.

"She's the one who got me interested in native traditions."

A note of desperation crept into Deena's voice as she hurried on. "I was fascinated by her work, and I'm thrilled that she's come to live with me as her *health declines.*"

She emphasized the last words, and Mom nodded, taking this to mean we were seeing signs of dementia. My great-grandfather has that, so we know what it's like.

"Why didn't the Diné want her?" the old woman asked.

"I was left at a hospital in Portland," I said. "I'm obviously Native, but there's no way of telling what tribe. My grandmother has friends who are Navajo and they said I look Navajo. Doesn't mean I am, but unless my bio parents come forward, no one's ever going to know for sure."

"Your mother didn't want you either?"

Mom stepped in front of me. "I think we should leave now."

Deena leaped in with apologies, then turned on her aunt and reminded her that this was her place of business. I could tell Mom wanted to leave, but when the old woman retreated to the back room, she calmed down.

I talked to Deena about my tattoo. Then Mom handed me my bathing suit and I went into a side room to change. I could hear Deena trying to distract Mom by talking about a university friend who'd studied Mom's work at Emily Carr.

Mom's an architect who specializes in designing homes that fit into the natural landscape, and she's well known for it. Talking about her work was a good call, and by the time I came out, she was back to her usual self.

Deena had me stand on a chair so she could get a better look at my birthmark.

"It used to be darker," Mom said. "It's faded as she's gotten older, and she wants to keep it."

"In other words, make it as natural looking as possible," Deena said.

I nodded. "Just tattoo over what's there. I don't want to change it or make it look more like a paw print or anything."

"No reason to," Deena said, her fingers tracing the edges. "It already does. Remarkable."

"What is that?" came the old woman's voice, so low I barely heard her. I turned to see her in the doorway staring at me.

"It's a birthmark, Auntie. Looks like a cat's paw, doesn't it?"

The old woman muttered something I didn't catch. Deena tried to smile, but it was strained. "We don't speak Navajo, Auntie."

The old woman's gaze met mine and in it I saw fear and disgust. "I said, '*Yee naaldlooshii.*'" She turned to my mother. "That's why the Diné didn't want her. She's a witch."

Mom didn't say a word, just set her jaw like she was locking it shut and handed me my clothing. I hesitated, but one look in her eyes told me not to argue. As I pulled on my clothes over my bathing suit, Deena apologized again and begged her aunt to leave. Neither my mom nor Deena's aunt paid any attention, Mom fuming, the old woman glowering and mumbling under her breath.

When I was dressed, Mom ushered me to the door. I took one last longing look at a display of tattoos, then followed her out.

FİVE

WE WALKED A FEW doors down before Mom turned
to me, deflating. "I'm sorry, Maya. I know you
were really looking forward to getting that tattoo."

"It's okay." It wasn't okay. If I had to wait, Dad might
change his mind. There was no way I could go back to that
shop, though.

Mom looked around, distracted, her gaze finally settling
on Bubble Tea Stars. "You were hungry, weren't you? Let's go
get you something to eat and I'll call your dad."

I wasn't hungry anymore, but I followed her in. She
phoned Dad, saying only that there'd been a problem and I'd
need to get my tattoo another day.

"We'll go to Vancouver next weekend," she said when she
hung up. "Make a special trip of it."

Exactly what Serena had suggested just before she died.

Her last words. I blinked back a prickle of tears and turned to peer into the ice cream freezer.

"I'm really sorry, Maya. I shouldn't have lost my temper. She was obviously senile and I overreacted."

"Do you know what that word meant? The one she called me?"

She shook her head. "No idea. I don't even know if it's Navajo. She may have lived with them, but she's white. The language is nearly impossible for an outsider to learn."

"Calling me a witch, too." I shook my head. "At least give me a chance to earn it first."

Mom tried to smile and surveyed the menu blankly, like we hadn't been in here so often the counter girl had recognized us and said hello. Mom finally ordered an herbal tea with lemongrass. I got lychee bubble tea—cold milky tea with tapioca balls.

"You said you were hungry," Mom said. "Maybe a sandwich?" She pointed at the Vietnamese submarines. "You like those."

"I'm okay."

"Ice cream, then," she pleaded, like if I didn't eat, she'd know I'd been permanently scarred by the old woman's words. "They have Nanaimo bar. You love Nanaimo bar ice cream."

"Sure, I'll take a bowl."

When we sat down, she was quiet for a minute, then said, "What that old woman said, about you, the adoption . . ."

I sighed and set down my spoon. "My mother left me in

the hospital because she cared enough to want a better life for me. She must have had a good reason for not going through traditional adoption means. Maybe her family opposed it. Or maybe no one knew she'd been pregnant." I looked at her. "Did I get that right? Because I've heard it, oh, only a million times."

"Just checking. As you get older, your feelings might change."

"Nope." I slurped up a few boba balls from my tea. "I'm happy right where I am. And being abandoned is cool, in an old-fashioned gothic kind of way."

That was a lie. Sure, other kids thought it was cool. I didn't. I had no interest in meeting my birth mother, not because I'd felt she'd "abandoned" me or didn't want me. I'd been a baby. She hadn't known me long enough to reject me personally. She'd just rejected the general idea of having a kid, and I'd won the adoption lottery with my parents.

Abandoning me had been inconsiderate. I'd said that to my parents once, and they'd laughed. It was a strange word, I know, especially from an eight-year-old. They'd then given me the whole spiel on how my mother was a good person blah, blah.

What I meant was that she should have left a note detailing my family background and medical history. If I'm curious about anything, it's my family. Was I Navajo? Did I have grandparents? Brothers? Sisters? And, even more important, was there a history of medical problems? I suppose that's a weird thing to worry about, but I blame growing up in a medical research town.

When I was little, my grandmother used to tell me this story about how I came to live with my family. She said my real mother was a cougar who'd had a late summer litter. She'd been an old cat and knew the signs that it would be a long, hard winter and her cubs wouldn't all survive. So she'd begged the sky god for mercy and he turned her smallest cub into a human girl and told the cat to take her into the city. She'd left me at the hospital, but before she went, she'd pressed her paw to my hip, leaving me a mark to remember her by.

That, she said, explained not only my birthmark but also my love of animals and the forest. Even as a kid, I knew it was only a story. Still, that's exactly how I felt, even now—like I'd just appeared, from nothing, with no background, no history.

I was still thinking about that when Dad showed up. He didn't get mad like Mom had. She always jokes he's the only Irishman born without a temper. He was upset, though, and confused, not understanding how any person could lash out at a stranger like that. He was mostly just worried about me and how I was taking it, and because I didn't want him to worry I went through the whole reassurance routine again, insisting I hadn't been scarred for life by the mutterings of a senile old woman.

We left shortly after that, no one being much in the mood for dinner out. By the time we got home, the sun was dropping behind the house, setting it off in a glow of sunset. I love our house. My mom designed it, getting permission from the St. Cloud company to take down the cabin they'd built for the last warden.

Coming up the drive, you can't see it at all. It blends right in with the forest, like it's been there forever. It's a two-story modified log cabin, with huge windows and skylights, so when you're inside, you feel like you aren't. It smells like the forest, too, even with the windows closed in bad weather.

Both stories have wraparound decks. Right now, there was someone sitting on the bottom one—Daniel with Kenjii stretched over his feet as he played a game on his DS. Beside him was a duffel bag.

As we drove in, he stood.

"Got your text," he said when I climbed out. "How much did it hurt?"

"Not at all," I said. "Apparently, I can't get a tattoo because I'm a witch."

"I could have told them—" He stopped. "Oh, you said *witch*."

"Ha-ha."

"You're serious?"

"Kind of. I'll explain later."

"Hello, Daniel," Mom said.

"Hey." He nodded to my dad, then gestured at his duffel. "This okay?"

He didn't say, *My dad's drunk again and I need a place*

to stay. He didn't need to.

Mom said, "Of course it is."

"You still have your key, don't you?" Dad said.

Daniel shrugged. "Yeah, but it's nice out." Even if it was pouring rain, he'd have waited on the porch. Daniel's funny about stuff like that. He has this rigid sense of right and wrong, and even if he has a key, he wouldn't go inside until we were there.

We put Daniel's duffel in the spare room. He stays at least once a month, sometimes for a couple of days, so it would make sense to just keep some stuff here, but Daniel refused. I think he keeps hoping that this will be the last time he needs to stay with us. It never is.

We went outside so I could check on the animals. On the side porch Fitz stretched out in the last sliver of sunlight.

"Dad felt sorry for you, didn't he?" I said. "That's great, but you're not going to learn if we keep getting you out of trees."

Fitz only lifted his head, yellow eyes slitted, and yawned. Daniel laughed and crouched beside him, scratching behind his tufted ears, then under the ruff around his face. Fitz rolled onto his back and Daniel rubbed his stomach.

"Uh-uh," I said. "If you get—"

"Scratched, it's my own fault, I know."

A cat scratch is bad enough, but a bobcat is twice the size of your average tabby. When he takes a swipe, there's blood involved.

Fitz was on his best behavior with Daniel, though. He usually is. He can sense Daniel likes animals. That's how we met. A week after we moved in, Daniel brought us an injured squirrel. The old warden had taken in wounded animals, and Daniel had figured that was part of the job. As for what a five-year-old was doing riding his bike deep into a predator-laced forest, well, that says something about the level of parental care in the Bianchi household.

When he'd brought the squirrel, I'd asked my dad if we could look after it. After some talks about conservation and how the goal was to release the animals—not make them into pets—my parents agreed. That was how I discovered my passion for rehabilitating wildlife. It was also how I made my first friend in Salmon Creek.

As Daniel played with Fitz, I sat on the grass, stretching out my legs and closing my eyes. I swore I could feel energy filling me. I inhaled the smells of the forest, the sharp tang of long grass, the sweet perfume of the trees. As I relaxed, I realized how tense I'd been since leaving the tattoo studio. I could say I was just disappointed, but what the old woman said bugged me, as much as I tried to shrug it off.

As I rested, Kenjii circled the house. She gave Fitz a respectful berth—having been on the receiving end of his killer claws many times—and lay down beside me, head on my knee.

I petted her awhile and then asked Daniel what had happened this time. He shrugged and said, "The usual," which meant his dad got drunk and started in on him. Not physically. I think Daniel would have preferred that. Violence was something he understood, something he could deal with. This wasn't.

Daniel's mom had taken off three years earlier. She'd never really been there much anyway—always vague, distracted, caught up in her studies at the lab, no time for Daniel and his two older brothers. The one who really missed her was her husband. That's when the drinking went from "a case of beer on the weekend" to "dead drunk by ten most nights." It was just Daniel and his dad now—his brothers were in college.

Sometimes when Mr. Bianchi drank, he ignored Daniel, which was fine. But sometimes he didn't. He said stuff. Not the usual "you're lazy/stupid/worthless" insults either. These were . . . ugly. He'd say that Daniel wasn't his son. That Daniel was a mistake. That he was a freak, an abomination, evil.

Once, after Serena died, I was over there, and his dad started in on me, calling me a freak, too, and saying that I killed Serena to get Daniel. Daniel coldcocked him. Then he took off to my place and stayed for two weeks. He went back, though. He always does.

His dad had apologized. *He* always did *that*—told Daniel he'd been drunk and he didn't mean it and Daniel should never tell anyone what he'd said. Which showed how little he knew his son. Whatever happened in that house stayed in that house, and I kept my mouth shut, too, even if sometimes I thought I shouldn't.

"He's been worse lately," Daniel said after a while.

I looked over. He was toying with Fitz now, dragging a long piece of grass over the porch as the bobcat chased it. Daniel was looking the other way, and all I could see was a sliver of his face. I didn't need to see his expression, though. Just hearing his tone, seeing the set of his broad shoulders, the way his bare arms tensed, muscles bunching, I knew what his face would look like: lips tight, dark eyes distant and sad. That's the part he didn't like me seeing—the sadness, the shame.

I moved to sit on the edge of the deck. Kenjii slunk over. Fitz gave both of us a *watch your step—he's playing with me* look. Daniel kept trailing the grass over the deck, leaving seeds behind.

I wanted to reach out to him. Put my arm around him. Rub his back. Do something that said, *I'm here.* But I never did. Couldn't.

After Serena died, there'd been long days and evenings, just the two of us, grieving, and sometimes he'd hug me, and that was fine because I knew it was just comfort. But I didn't feel like I could do the same back without a really good excuse or he might take it the wrong way.

It's not just because of Serena. Obviously, I don't want to be the slut making a move on her dead pal's boyfriend. But more than that, I don't want to do anything that might make him uncomfortable staying here when he needs a place. I'm pretty sure I could give him a hug without him misinterpreting it, but I can't take that chance.

So I sat, and said nothing. After a minute he slid over beside me. Fitz grumbled, then stalked off, with a halfhearted swipe at Kenjii, as if this were her fault. We watched as he disappeared into the forest.

"Hunting time," I said, because I couldn't think of anything else.

"He does a good job of it," Daniel said.

"As long as he can catch his dinner off guard." Missing a back leg meant Fitz could walk fine—he just couldn't run, either after prey or away from predators.

"And as long as he doesn't climb a tree to get it."

I gave a soft laugh and pulled my knees up. After another moment of silence, I said, "You said your dad's getting worse?"

"Yeah. I'll be glad when he goes on that business trip tomorrow. Bet you will, too. Birthday party time."

He jostled my shoulder and I forced a smile. After a minute he cleared his throat and said, "He had a teleconference with the St. Clouds last week. I think he told them he wants to leave Salmon Creek."

I looked over sharply. "What?"

"Lately, when he's drunk, he goes on about how he wants out, how he's trapped. Trapped in Salmon Creek because of me and because of his contract with the company. Once he sobers up, he never wants to talk about it. Then he had this meeting."

"How'd it go?"

"Bad. I think he tried to get out of his contract. They told him no. He should have known that. Everyone's contract is tight for security reasons. You remember how the whole town council had to lobby the St. Clouds to let Serena's folks go after . . . well, *after*."

I nodded. From what I understood, it hadn't been much of a fight. Mayor Tillson and everyone took their case to the St. Clouds, who'd given Serena's parents a generous severance package. For that kind of thing, you really needed a good reason. You couldn't leave the project halfway through and take your expertise to a competitor.

"So now he's mad," I said, "which means he's drinking more."

Daniel nodded.

"Well, he can't blame you for that."

Daniel tossed a stick for Kenjii.

"He doesn't blame you, does he?"

"Yeah, he does. Who knows why. Finally, tonight, I just had enough. I told him *I* wasn't holding him back. As far as I'm concerned, he can go. I'll take care of myself. Not like I don't do that already. He flipped out. He called me an ungrateful brat and came at me, and I—I—"

"Hit him again?"

"I—I think so. I mean—" He exhaled and rubbed the back of his neck, eyes closing as he grimaced. "I must have. I just don't—"

His gaze went distant, the way it had that morning, staring after the hiker, and when I looked into his eyes, I saw nothing.

"Daniel?"

He shook it off. "Yeah, I hit him. I just got so mad that I didn't even realize . . . Well, you know."

"Your boxing instincts kicked in. He came at you and you hit him without realizing it."

"Right. Exactly." Another exhale, this one sounding like relief. "Anyway, he's fine. Just seriously pissed off, which is why I'm here."

"You could stay here," I said softly. "If he does leave."

He rubbed his arms, like he was getting cold. His gaze was down, but his jaw was set in that way I knew well, ready to refuse. Only he didn't want to refuse. He wanted to know that if it came down to that, his dad leaving, he could stay here. I could see that worry and that need wearing away at his pride until finally he grunted, "Yeah. Okay."

After another second, he got up, and said, "Let's feed the animals."

SIX

WE PUT KENJII IN her dog run. If I go in the shed while there's a predator in residence, it makes her anxious. And when she gets anxious—whining and scratching at the door—it really doesn't help the sick animals inside.

As we left the dog run, Daniel said, "Don't mention that stuff to your parents, okay? I'm sure Dad's just talking crazy again."

"No need to mention it until there's a reason to."

"Yeah."

"You need a jacket? It's getting cool."

"I'm good."

The shed is really a specially built wildlife rehabilitation building, designed by my mom. The roof is glass. It's in the shade, so we don't barbecue the critters, and there's plenty of ventilation.

The shed is temporary lodgings. I don't take any animal that has a good chance of recovering on its own, because no matter how careful I am, sometimes rerelease isn't possible, and the animal has to go to the wildlife center outside Victoria.

Right now, the shed housed one snake, two fledglings, and a marten. The sharp-tailed snake was a young one that had been stepped on by a hiker, who'd recognized it as a rare species. The fledglings were orphaned bald eagles. The marten—a cat-sized predator that looks like a long-haired weasel—had been shot by a moron teenage tourist playing big-game hunter with a crossbow.

We started with the snake, dumping in a couple of live slugs. Serena used to argue that killing one creature to save another made no sense. We'd have long debates about that. Not arguing, just working it through. I agreed she had a point, but the snake was rare and the slugs weren't, so it made sense from a conservation view.

But if you pushed her argument even further, you could say that no predator should be saved, because even if I feed them roadkill and hunter leftovers, they'll kill other animals when they get out. Then there's the argument for letting nature take its course with every living thing, and so we should leave wounded animals to their fate. I don't mind it when people say stuff like that. I just don't happen to agree.

After the snake, we fed the fledglings. Again, I dropped the food in, using gloves. Hand-feeding them is only done in an emergency. With the birds, letting it fall into the nest also mimics the way Mama Eagle would do it.

"They look ready to leave soon," Daniel said.

I nodded. "Dad said we might take them to the wildlife center next week."

The birds were almost ready to fly, meaning they had to go to the center, because I wasn't equipped to help them learn that. Someday I would be, but for now I stuck with nursing duty.

"This guy looks ready to go soon, too," Daniel said as he peered into the marten's cage. "Wow. Has it really only been a week?"

"Less. Believe me, she has a long way to—"

I stopped. The marten had woken and reared up against the side of her cage, nose wriggling madly. When she saw me watching, she chirped, then started racing laps as she waited for food.

Daniel laughed. "Someone's definitely feeling better."

"That's not—" I peeled off the gloves. "That's not possible. It should take days before she's even walking."

"You're just too good a nurse. You need to go visit your grandma, let your dad and me take over, slow things down."

It's true—the animals don't heal as fast when I'm not around. That sounds like bragging, but we saw it every time

I went away. Daniel knows how to do all the stuff. So do my parents. But when I'm gone, the healing process slows.

Dr. Hajek, the Salmon Creek veterinarian, says some people are just natural healers. She sometimes calls me into town to help with pets that're in a lot of pain—I calm them down so she can do her thing, and in return she volunteers her time with cases of mine that need serious medical attention.

Still, as good as I am, there was no way the marten should have been racing around her cage. When I said that to Daniel, he only shrugged.

"Obviously she wasn't as badly hurt as you thought. Hate to break it to you, Maya, but you can be wrong."

"Dr. Hajek did the diagnosis." I leaned over the cage. The marten reared up again and chirruped at me. "That bolt went into the right haunch and—"

I stared at the marten's haunch. The skin was bare, where Dr. Hajek had shaved it. Underneath, the only sign of injury was a pale scar crisscrossed with dark stitches. When I'd checked the marten yesterday morning, I'd thought she was healing fast. But the wound had still been there.

I reached into the cage.

"Um, Maya?" Daniel said. "Gloves? Those teeth and claws are like needles. You're the one always telling me . . ."

I didn't hear the rest. It was as if my hand was being pulled into the cage against my will. The marten didn't even flinch, just sat there and waited, dark eyes on mine, calm and trusting.

I touched her wounded flank. Pain ripped through my leg and I stumbled back.

"Maya!"

Darkness enveloped me. I inhaled the scent of pine needles. My leg throbbed. My heart raced so fast, I panted for breath.

"Pop goes the weasel!" a boy yelled.

Another guy laughed. Footsteps pounded the dry earth so loud they sounded like an oncoming locomotive. A single thought filled my head. *Escape.* I pulled myself along, dragging my injured leg over a carpet of dead needles—

"Maya!" A warm hand grabbed my chin. "Come on, Maya."

I gasped and blinked. I was sitting on the floor. In Daniel's lap. I bolted to my feet so fast, I elbowed him in the stomach.

"Thanks," he wheezed. "Next time I'll let you hit the floor."

"What happened?"

"You fainted." The corners of his mouth twitched. "I believe *swooned* is the correct term. It's not nearly as romantic as it sounds, you know. More like a deadweight collapse. With drool."

I wiped my mouth and looked around, still getting my bearings.

Daniel's voice softened as he stepped closer. "Are you okay?"

I nodded. He asked what happened, but I couldn't tell him, because I wasn't really sure myself. I just stared at the marten, watching me now, head tilted. When I wrenched my gaze away and went to get her dinner, I realized my hands were shaking. Daniel took the meat from me, donned the gloves, and fed the marten.

With his back to me, he said, "So I spilled my guts already. Your turn. If you won't tell me what happened just now, at least tell me what happened at the tattoo place."

I did. I was tempted to joke that his dad was right—apparently I *was* evil—but he wouldn't appreciate that.

When I was done, he stood there, his broad face screwed up in disbelief. "So this old lady, who's never met you before, sees your birthmark and says you're a witch?"

"Sounds like something from a TV movie, doesn't it?" I hummed a few bars of suitably sinister music. "Should have been a fortune-teller, though. The teenage girl goes to the fortune-teller, whose gypsy grandmother says she's cursed."

"Maybe that was it. Like one of those reality TV shows. You got pranked."

"In Nanaimo? Must be a low-budget Canadian production."

"Is there any other kind?"

I laughed and took out a little more meat for the marten, who spun in her cage, chirping. At least someone didn't think I was evil incarnate. Not if I had food anyway. I dropped it in.

Daniel said, "If the woman has Alzheimer's or whatever,

her niece should keep her out of the studio before she scares off more customers."

"I know."

I closed the marten's cage. She narrowed her eyes and chattered, scolding me for not giving her more.

I shook my head. "We can't have you getting too fat to run when we let you go."

"We're done talking about it, then?" Daniel said as I shut the food locker.

I shrugged. "Nothing more to talk about. It wasn't exactly high on the scale of enjoyable life experiences, but I can deal with it."

"You just fainted, Maya."

"That has nothing to do with—"

"No? Good. Then you won't mind me telling your parents, so they can get you to the clinic tonight and check you over."

"I'm fine," I said as I double-checked my charges. I couldn't hang out and play with them after they were fed— minimal human contact was the goal, however tough that was sometimes.

"I fainted because I missed dinner and I'm starving. And, yes, maybe I'm kind of stressed. But my parents are already worried about what that woman said about my birth mother. You know how they get about that. They'll decide it's opened up a Pandora's box of conflict over my adoption and my racial identity and blah, blah, blah. I really don't want to spend the next week on Dr. Fodor's couch, thank you very much."

"All right, then. I'll forget it for now, but if you pass out again . . ."

"I'll tell someone."

"And you'll make sure you aren't in here by yourself. Get your mom or dad to help you. Say you're worried about the fledglings imprinting on you or whatever."

"Yes, sir."

We headed out the door. I'd turned to lock up when Daniel's hand clamped my shoulder.

"Don't move," he whispered.

I followed his gaze to a light-brown form crouched on a rock, barely visible in the thick twilit woods.

"It's just—" I was about to say "Fitz" when I saw the long tail swishing.

"Dad!" I shouted. Then even louder, "Dad!"

I backed up and slammed into Daniel. "Move toward the house."

"The shed—"

"Is probably what he wants, so he won't follow us to the house. *Damn* it. This is exactly what I was worried about. He's too used to people." I nudged Daniel backward. "Nothing here for you, Marv! Get going!" Then, "Dad!"

The cougar rose, readying itself for the leap. Its head appeared through the cover of shadow and I saw its face . . . and its two perfectly good ears.

It wasn't Marv.

The cat leaped. Daniel grabbed my arm and whipped

me behind him so hard I flew off my feet. I hit the ground as the house door slammed and Dad shouted. I saw Daniel stumble back. Saw the huge tom in flight, on target to hit him. I screamed and jumped up. Daniel twisted to run. The cat caught him in the back and knocked him off his feet. Huge canines flashed, heading for the back of Daniel's neck, the killing blow.

As I covered the last few feet, I heard the rifle fire. Heard my dad shout, "Maya!" Heard my mother's shriek. Felt the bullet whiz past me. I kicked at the cougar's head. My foot connected, knocking it sideways, teeth snapping together harmlessly.

The cat turned to me, lips pulled back, teeth flashing, eyes slitted as he snarled. I kicked him again. My parents shouted for me to move aside so Dad could take the shot. Only, if he did, he stood a chance of hitting Daniel, and I wasn't letting that happen.

"Go!" I shouted. "Get off him!"

The cat had Daniel pinned face-first to the ground. Daniel lay still, playing dead as I kept shouting at the cougar and my parents shouted at me. The cat snarled again, and I braced myself, ready to run if those powerful hind legs bunched for flight. But he made no move to come after me, just snarled and spat and stayed over Daniel.

Rage boiled up in me. Maybe it was shock, but it felt like pure fury. I screamed at the cat, looking him square in the eye, and when I did it was like everything else disappeared.

The world seemed to dip and darken, and I smelled wet earth and thick musk and fresh blood. The wind whipped past, like I was running. Running so fast the ground whizzed beneath me, the wind cut across my skin. Exhilaration filled me. My muscles sang, and it was the sweetest—

The sudden scream of a cougar jolted me back to reality. The big cat was still staring at me. Just staring. Another scream. I turned to see a second cougar charging toward us. A cougar with a ragged ear.

The younger cat jumped off Daniel and spun to meet Marv. They hit so hard the ground vibrated. I grabbed for Daniel, but he was already on his feet, reaching for me. He pushed me ahead of him as we ran for the porch, the cats snarling and growling and yelping behind us.

My dad pulled us onto the porch, then lifted the rifle.

"Rick, no," Mom said, passing him the one with tranquilizer darts instead.

When he hesitated, she said, "The kids are fine."

He still hesitated, like he didn't care, just as long as he made sure it never happened again.

"Dad, please," I said.

He looked at me, then took the tranquilizer gun, aimed, and fired. The dart hit the younger cougar in the flank. He let out a yowl and attacked Marv with fresh fervor, then in midtwist, toppled over. Marv grabbed the unconscious cat by the neck and shook him. When the other tom didn't react, Marv chuffed and looked at us, like he expected applause.

Instead, he saw the barrel of a rifle. With one chirp of indignation, he galloped toward the woods. Dad fired, but Marv veered at the last second and disappeared before Dad could shoot again.

Daniel was okay. He had some puncture wounds where the cougar had dug in his claws, and he'd definitely be bruised and battered tomorrow, but he'd avoided a bite, which was the main thing.

He argued that he didn't need medical attention, but Mom drove us into Salmon Creek, calling ahead to make sure one of the doctors would be at the clinic. Dr. Inglis met us there, which surprised Mom. Dr. Inglis is the head of the research lab, and doesn't usually work at the clinic, but she said she'd been out with Dr. Lam, and when he'd gotten the page, she decided to come along.

While Dr. Lam looked after Daniel, Dr. Inglis chatted with me. She'd heard this was my second cougar encounter today, and wanted to know all about it. She made it sound like personal curiosity, but I knew it wasn't. She was making sure I was doing okay, that I didn't need the services of Dr. Fodor to deal with the trauma.

One drawback to living in a medical research town is that they're paranoid about health, both physical and mental. The adults get off easy. Not the kids. Sneeze twice in a row and the teacher calls the school nurse. Drop out of a sport or let your grades fall and you're whisked off to Dr. Fodor's couch.

They especially monitor the teens, as if hormonal surges could make us spontaneously combust at any moment.

The worst is when Dr. Davidoff comes to town. I hate Dr. Davidoff. We all do. He's creepy, with cold hands and awkward, lame jokes. But he's the St. Clouds' top doctor, so every year, he brings a team to visit the lab. And, since they have world-class doctors on hand, it's time for every kid to get a complete physical. Oh joy.

My parents are big on eating natural food, getting lots of exercise, and staying healthy, but even they find the town's obsession a bit much. Still, they don't knock it, not if it means I get the best care possible. I suppose that's the point. The town keeps its employees happy by keeping their kids healthy. Since they have the resources right there, it's an easy benefit to provide.

Dr. Lam cleaned Daniel's wounds and gave him painkillers for tomorrow. Then Dr. Inglis listened to his version of events and made sure he wasn't traumatized before she called Chief Carling to report it. Out here, wildlife attacks are like gunshot wounds in the city—every one needs to be recorded.

Dad took the tranquilized cougar to Dr. Hajek's. The tom had been tagged, so we needed to find out where he was from and whether he could be returned. She had the facilities to hold him; we didn't.

The cat had come for the shed. I was sure of that. No matter how clean I keep it, it carries the scent of the rabbits and fawns I've housed there; and new predators to the area often check it out, hoping for a well-stocked food larder. Once they realize they can't get in, they usually leave it alone.

As for why the new tom was in our park at all, he was clearly checking out territorial prospects. The island isn't overpopulated with cougars, so Marv doesn't see a lot of challengers. As he gets older, though, they're bound to increase. This only proved how quickly a younger and more dangerous big cat would move in if we relocated Marv.

I felt bad for the old guy. He'd come to our rescue and how would he be repaid? Hunted and tranquilized to teach him a lesson about getting too friendly with humans. Yet as romantic as it is to think Marv had been protecting us, it was far more likely that he was simply protecting his territory. Still, I'd feel guilty when Dad did it, and, to be honest, I'd miss my encounters with the old cat.

SEVEN

I HAD A ROUGH night. Between being verbally attacked by a total stranger and physically attacked by a cougar, I'd need a skin of granite not to let it affect me.

I dreamed about the old woman and the cougar, and those were definitely nightmares. But I also dreamed of what I'd felt when that cat looked me in the eye. What I'd smelled and felt and seen.

I dreamed of what had happened in the shed with the marten. My blackout. No, not a blackout. A vision of what had happened to the animal.

I'd talk to Mom about it later. I always went to her with things like that, because she wouldn't go all Native mystical on me and talk about vision quests and whatever. Not that Dad or Daniel would do that—they'd been around us long enough to know better. But still, well, I'd just be more comfortable talking to Mom about it.

It's like my love of nature. Some people say it's because I'm Native, and I know they're not trying to stereotype me, though sometimes I really wish I was into model airplanes instead. I love animals and yes, I'm Native, but as my teachers would say, correlation doesn't imply causation. I have a park ranger for a father and an environmental architect for a mother. They met at a rain forest conservation rally and have raised me out in the woods. It'd be bizarre if I *didn't* turn out the way I did.

But what had really happened tonight? With the cougar, it was obviously adrenaline with a chaser of shock, and maybe a little post-traumatic stress thrown in for good measure. One best friend had died in front of me last year. Another almost did tonight.

I could rationalize it while I was awake, but once I fell asleep, I was running again, ground and wind whooshing past. I smelled the musk of animals, the tang of the earth, and blood. I smelled blood and it made me run all the faster, heart speeding up not with fear but something else, something that gripped my belly like . . . like hunger.

I bolted upright. Sweat poured down my face, and I gasped for breath as my heart pounded. My legs ached like I really had been running.

I pushed off the covers, got out of bed, and went to the window. I stood there in the moonlight, hands pressed against the cool glass as I scanned the forest, looking for . . . I don't know what I was looking for, only that I was looking and I was aching and I wanted something. Wanted it so bad.

The window was open a crack, and I could smell the rich, loamy night, just like in my dream. I bent to open it farther, then crouched there, my heart galloping. I let the cool air and the scents wash over me and, gradually, my heartbeat slowed and the sweat dried and I was left standing there, confused and shivering, until I went back to bed, pulled up the covers, and fell asleep.

"You could have stayed with my mom today," I said as Daniel navigated the potholes and ruts. "You've got to be hurting."

"Nope. Don't feel a thing."

"Tough guy," I said.

"No, well-medicated guy. You really think I'd let you go to school without me? I'd show up tomorrow and hear that I got pinned running from a cougar, only to be saved by you rushing in and staring him down."

"Um, yeah, that's pretty much how I remember it."

"Exactly why I'm going. To get *my* version out first."

I laughed. "Not a chance. But I will include the part about you throwing me to safety. The girls will love that. Especially Nicole."

Daniel gripped the steering wheel, his gaze straight ahead.

"So it's still a no, then?" I said. "Look, if you aren't interested, I'll stop teasing you, but you did say she's cute . . ."

"Yeah."

"And it's been over a year." Not just a year since Serena's death, but a year since he'd gone on a date. That was starting to worry me. "All I'm saying—again—is ask her if she's going to my party. Yes, obviously she is, and obviously, as the host, you're not asking her for a date, but it would just . . . open the possibility, you know. Let her know you might be interested, and see how things go. No pressure."

"We'll see."

We pulled in the parking lot to see Corey talking to a girl who looked, from the back, like Sam. As we drove closer, though, I could see her dark hair was sleek, not spiked, and her clothes had colors, which meant they'd never be found in Sam's wardrobe. Then I caught a glimpse of her face and realized it was our elusive tree-climbing hiker.

Corey waved us over. He said something to the woman and she turned, smiling. That smile evaporated when she saw us. Her gaze darted about, like she wanted to make another escape. She settled for pasting on a big, phony smile.

"Hey, guys," she said. Then, to me, "Does your dad still want that report, because I was super-busy yesterday. I can try to squeeze it in today."

"That's okay," I said. "He's got other problems right now."

"Another cougar," Daniel said to Corey. "I saved her."

"A mountain lion?" the woman cut in. "What happened?"

"This is Mina Lee," Corey said. "She's a reporter doing a story on Salmon Creek."

"Cool," I said. "What paper?"

"It's an American one," she said, as if kids from hick-town Canada wouldn't recognize the name. "We're doing a series on unusual small towns, and this one certainly qualifies. I'm particularly interested in getting the point of view of young people like you. Your opinion of this place must be a lot different from your parents'."

When we didn't react, she leaned forward, conspiratorial. "It can't be easy living out here. Two hundred people . . ." She shook her head. "It must be so isolating."

"It is." Corey turned to Daniel. "If there were more kids here, I wouldn't need to hang out with you. And we wouldn't need to hang out with girls. Even if they are hot girls, and, well, being such a small town, there's not a lot of competition for dates, so they're stuck with us and—" He looked at Mina. "I like isolated."

Mina studied us, trying to figure out if we were making fun of her. Honestly, unless it was a rainy Saturday night and no one had wheels to drive into the city, we didn't mind living here. I could tell that wasn't what she wanted, though, so I played along.

"It can be a bit much," I said. "No Starbucks. No clubs. No Aéropostale. Hell, we have to drive an hour just to hang out at the mall. Epic inconvenience."

73 ﷽

The guys struggled to keep straight faces as they nodded.

"And then there's the"—I lowered my voice—"medical research."

Her eyes glinted. *Bull's-eye.*

"How do you feel about that?" she said. "Living with such secrecy and under such intense security. I mean, they built an entire town to hide their work."

"I worry that they're hurting bunnies," I said.

"We aren't supposed to talk about the medical stuff." Daniel looked around, mock-anxious. "We get in a lot of trouble for that."

Mina nodded. "I understand. But I'd love to chat. Privately."

She set a time and place for us to meet her after school, then handed me her card and told us to bring along any other kids who wanted to talk.

EIGHT

As she walked away, Corey rubbed his temple, grimacing.

Daniel glanced at him. "You got your—?"

"Headache meds? Yes, Dad. I'll take one when I get inside."

I handed him Mina's card. "Your mom will want this."

"I texted her before you guys showed up. Even snapped a photo. She'll pass it on to Mayor Tillson and Dr. Inglis."

Dr. Inglis was as much a part of town politics as Chief Carling and the mayor. Mina Lee wasn't the first "reporter" to come sniffing around Salmon Creek. From the time we were little, we'd been told how to deal with them.

As far as we knew, no actual reporter had ever come to cover Salmon Creek. We might be an unusual little town, but we're definitely not worthy of a feature in an American newspaper. We were, however, worthy of attention from activists and competing medical companies. Over the years, we'd had a few activists posing as reporters, searching for evidence of animal testing or stem cell research. Of a bigger concern to the St. Clouds, though, were the corporate spies.

Drug research is a huge business, with potentially huge profits. Imagine how much you could make if you developed a cure for cancer. Or even the common cold. The St. Clouds built Salmon Creek so they could develop new drugs without rivals peering over their shoulders. But that doesn't mean their rivals don't occasionally send spies to see what they're working on.

Still, it doesn't take us long to sort out the troublemakers from the tourists. An alert about Mina Lee would go through Salmon Creek before lunch, shutting down all her potential sources of information.

I told the guys I'd catch up with them later. I had to go in early and prep Mrs. Morris's classroom. No, I'm not a teacher's pet. There's a rule at our school that if you aren't on a sports team, you need to do extra work. Being temporarily off the track team meant I was on teacher-helper duty two mornings a week.

"Watch out for Rafe," Corey said. "I saw him in the smoking pit."

"Phony," I muttered.

"She thinks he's not a real smoker," Daniel explained.

"He's not. Half the time he doesn't light his cigarette. The other half he takes a couple of puffs and puts it out. It's part of the bad boy package."

Corey grinned. "Been paying attention, have you?"

"Maya *always* pays attention," Daniel said. "She notices everything and has an opinion on it, which she's not afraid to share as frequently and as loudly as possible."

Corey laughed.

"Watch it," I said as I walked away, "or I'll share my *opinions* on what happened last night."

"Hey, yeah," Corey said. "So what did happen?"

I left Daniel to explain and went around the school the back way, past the smoking pit. Yes, we had a smoking pit, which is completely weird for a private school owned by a medical company. Kids smoke, though. It's a given, and the more adults try to stop it, the more kids are determined to do it. So the school board designated a smoking pit right beside the furnace room, where the rumble makes it hard to talk. Then they enacted a town bylaw prohibiting the sale of cigarettes to anyone under twenty. Of course, kids can get them elsewhere, but only the most determined bother.

I was almost at the door when Rafe skirted a crowd of ninth graders and slid in beside me, unsmoked cigarette dangling from his hand.

"Yes, I had another wild encounter last night," I said as we walked toward the entrance.

"Really?"

"That's not what you wanted to talk to me about?"

"No."

"Damn."

He only laughed and grabbed the door for me. We went through. He walked beside me, so close I could smell woodsmoke on his jacket. I thought of warning him that there was a ban on campfires with the dry weather, but that sounded snotty. I'm sure he knew. I'm sure he didn't care.

I tried to forget he was there. But I could smell the smoke on his jacket, hear the clomp of his boots in the empty hall, even hear him breathing. I could feel him there, too. That sounds weird. I don't know how else to describe it, though. I was just really, really aware that he was walking beside me.

When we turned the corner, he veered so that his hand brushed mine, and I jerked away.

"You really don't like me, do you?" he said.

"I don't know you well enough to say that."

"Easily fixed. What are you doing after school?"

I shook my head as I stopped at my locker. He leaned against the one beside it.

I started my combination. "I suspect I could spend every evening this week with you and I wouldn't know you any better than I do right now."

"Sure you would. Anything you want to know, I'll tell you."

"That's the key word, isn't it? What I *want* to know. Not necessarily the truth."

His lips twitched with what looked like genuine amusement. "Are you calling me a poseur? I should be offended."

"You could prove me wrong." I stuffed my bag in, took out my binder, then gestured at the cigarette in his hand. "Smoke that."

"In here? I think that's against the rules."

"Which shouldn't bother you at all, if you're the rebel you pretend to be. But that's not what I meant. We'll go outside. I just want to see you smoke the whole thing without coughing."

"Are you saying I don't smoke?" His brows lifted, then he leaned down so close to my ear I could smell toothpaste. "Maybe, as a guy who changes schools a lot, I've discovered that the best place to meet kids is a smoking pit."

I paused, hand still on my lock, thrown by his honesty. His grin sparked and I knew that was exactly the point. I snapped the lock shut and headed for the classroom. He fell in step beside me.

"So, what are you doing after school?" he asked.

"You don't give up, do you?"

"Nope, so you might as well surrender now."

"And that's exactly what *will* make you back off, isn't it?"

He arched his brows, as if he had no idea what I was talking about.

"You like the chase," I said. "But once you get a girl, you back off before you can collect the prize. Kind of missing the point, I think."

"Huh. You're right. Tell you what, go out with me and you

can show me how it's done."

I'd walked right into that. I headed to the empty class-room, set my books on my desk, and opened the blinds for Mrs. Morris.

Rafe sat on the edge of a desk. "You're right. I chase hard, but once I get to know a girl, I realize she's not right for me." He met my gaze, his eyes earnest and soulful. "I guess I haven't found the one I'm looking for."

I sputtered a laugh. "And you think I might be it. The girl you've been yearning for. Dreaming of. Your soul mate." I laughed even harder and shook my head. "Please tell me that line doesn't actually work on—"

"Rafael . . ." said a voice from the door. "I should have known. Cornering girls in classrooms so they can't run away. Desperate. And kind of pathetic."

As Sam walked in, every trace of good humor drained from Rafe's face. The look he gave her sent a chill through me. And I don't chill easily.

"I'm talking to Maya," he said, his voice so low it was almost a growl.

"Um, no, you're stalking her."

His whole body went rigid at that. His gaze flitted my way.

"We were just talking," I said. I didn't mean to defend him, but there was something about the way Sam lobbed her insults that got my back up.

"Well, I need to talk to you now, so . . ." She flicked her fingers at Rafe. "Shoo. I saw a bunch of eighth graders outside. They're probably more your speed."

Rafe looked at me. "Is she harassing you?"

Sam choked on a laugh. "Me? Seriously? Dude, you're the one doing the harassing, and I'd suggest you give it a rest before Daniel rips you a new one. Which would be fun to watch, but I'd hate to see him get into trouble for taking out trash like—"

"Okay," I said, lifting my hands. "Enough. Rafe? I'm fine. I need to talk to Sam. I'll see you in class."

As he left, Rafe shot Sam the kind of look you'd give a rabid dog. What had she done to him? Maybe she'd spooked him with her crazy bitch routine, only he didn't look spooked. He looked pissed.

While I cleaned the board, Sam settled onto a desk and stomped her boots on the chair, dirt showering the seat. "What a freaking loser."

"What's up, Sam?"

"I saw you guys talking to a woman in the parking lot. Nicole said she's a reporter, asking questions about us. How we all got here, if any of us weren't born here. Nic says she's really interested in the ones that weren't. You, me, Rafe . . ."

"Probably hoping we'll be less attached to the town and more likely to spill secrets. Why? Do you have outstanding assault warrants somewhere?"

"Ha-ha."

Actually, it wouldn't surprise me at all if Sam had a juvie record. She was even quicker with her fists than Daniel and, unlike him, she didn't try to hold back.

"So did she say anything to you?" Sam asked.

"About you?"

"About any of us. The ones who weren't born here."

Which wasn't what she meant at all. I could tell by the way her gaze shifted to the left. I walked over and lowered my voice.

"Are you in trouble, Sam?"

"What?" She slid off the desk. "No. God, I can't even make an innocent comment without you jumping to conclusions. If you start telling people this chick is after me—"

"You don't need to threaten me, Sam, because you know I don't spread stories. Chief Carling has already been told about this woman, so you won't need to worry about her much longer anyway."

She looked alarmed. "Corey called his mom?"

"Um, yeah. Standard procedure for anyone poking around, which you'd know if you didn't sit through every assembly with your iPod blasting." The bell sounded, and I moved to my desk by the window. "I'm sure they'll call another assembly today, and tell us how to handle it . . . again."

When Sam reached her desk at the back, she hesitated, then said, "About Rafe. I'm sure you're just being nice, but be careful."

"Did he do something?"

"Not yet, but he's trouble. Some girls go for that. You're not one of them. You're smart. Just . . . stay smart, okay?"

I nodded. Then the door banged open, and kids streamed in.

NINE

I WAS RIGHT ABOUT the assembly. It came during last period. Really, you'd think by now, the town could trust us older kids enough to just say, "Hey, there's one of those fake reporters in town. Here's her picture. You know the drill." But apparently, under the age of eighteen, our memories have short expiration periods.

If there's anything worse than being confined to a small auditorium with everyone in the school, it's being confined there at the end of the day, when I'm desperate for fresh air and open skies. The crush of bodies, their stifling heat, the smell of them as deodorant began wearing off, even the sound of everyone breathing and coughing . . .

"Go," Daniel whispered at the halfway mark. "Anything new, I'll fill you in."

As I passed Mrs. Morris, I motioned that I was going out

to use the washroom. I'm sure she knew better, but she just smiled and waved me on. We aren't a school with a truancy problem. Let's be honest: Where would you go if you skipped class? No mall. No coffee shop. No hangout where the person running the place hasn't known you from childhood . . . and knows you should be in class.

The school is on the edge of town. Hell, most of the *town* is on the edge of town—you can't walk far in any direction without ending up in the forest. That's where I went.

As I started along the path, I noticed a young, dark-haired woman. But not Mina Lee. This one was taller than me, with long black hair that curled over her faded denim jacket. Native or Latina. She was watching me and making no effort to hide it. Mina Lee's partner? If so, she needed lessons in subtlety even more than Mina did.

When I headed her way, she started grinning and rocking on her toes, like she was fighting an urge to run toward me. She looked about nineteen, but her grin belonged on the face of a five-year-old. She was bouncing like a five-year-old, too.

When I got a better look at her face—high cheekbones, sharp nose and chin, and slightly slanted amber eyes—I realized this had to be Rafe's older sister. I'd never seen her before. Few people in town had. She was supposed to be an artist. Shy and reclusive, Rafe had told everyone. One look at this girl, so eager to say hello she could barely stand still, and I knew that was a lie. Surprise, surprise.

"Hello," I said.

She launched herself at me so fast I didn't have time to get out of the way before she had her arms around my neck, hugging me like a long-lost sister.

"Um, hi . . ." I said, giving her a quick hug back, then stepping away.

"I shouldn't do that, right? Sorry. I couldn't help it. I've been waiting so long." She resumed bouncing on her toes. "I'm so happy to meet you."

"I'm . . . happy to meet you, too. I'm Maya."

"I know. I'm Annie." She bounced there, grinning and staring at me. Her eyes were wide and childlike, and as I looked in them, I had a pretty good idea why Rafe was keeping his sister a secret. She was . . . I guess *mentally challenged* is the right term.

"Rafe's right. You are pretty. I like your hair." She reached out and stroked a lock hanging over my shoulder. "I wish mine was straight. I used to straighten it, but it never really worked. I don't think I was doing it right. Rafe tried to help, but—" She giggled. "He's not a good hairdresser."

I couldn't help smiling at that image.

"So you live in the Skylark cottage?" I said. "That must get lonely."

"Sometimes. But it's okay. There's so much forest to run in." She closed her eyes and lifted her face to the sun, her smile rapturous. "It's wonderful."

"You like the forest?" I asked.

She opened her eyes and they shone with a light that

made her beautiful. "I *love* the forest."

"Me, too."

She laughed. "Of course you do, silly. It's in *our* blood."

I guessed she meant Native blood. Like with Rafe, I couldn't really tell her heritage, but I supposed that answered my question. I was going to ask what tribe she was, when her eyes went wide.

"Uh-oh. I'm in trouble now," she said.

I followed her gaze to the back door. Rafe was bearing down on us, his expression set somewhere between annoyance and anxiety.

"I'm going to get a stern talking to," Annie whispered, her tone saying she wasn't the least bit concerned by the prospect. When Rafe got within ten feet, she launched herself at him the same way she had with me. Instead of hugging him, she grabbed him in a headlock and ruffled his hair.

"I didn't break the rules," she said as she danced away. "She came over to me, and she talked to me first."

"She's right," I said.

"Okay, just . . ." He took her gently by the wrist. "We have to go, Annie. Say good-bye to Maya."

"She doesn't need to—" I began.

"Yes, she does."

He led Annie off before I could argue. I glowered at his retreating back. Was he embarrassed by Annie? All the hair-styling in the world wouldn't make him a decent brother if he forced her to stay locked in a cabin all day. Maybe that was how he'd been raised, but the next time he came sniffing around, we were definitely having a chat about this.

As I stormed back toward the school, I heard running footsteps behind me.

"Maya!" Rafe called. "Hold up a sec."

Seems we were having that chat sooner than I expected.

"I need to ask you a favor," he said.

I nodded, too pissed off to open my mouth.

"Don't tell anyone about Annie, okay? Please? You saw— Well, you saw she's got some problems, and I'd really appreciate it if—"

"If I let you keep your mentally challenged sister a secret? Kept her from wrecking your street cred? God, you're a piece of work, Rafael Martinez. I thought Sam was being harsh on you this morning, but she wasn't nearly harsh enough."

As I ranted, his face hardened. By the time I finished, it was like granite, his eyes cold chunks of amber.

"Are you done?" he asked, voice as frosty as his eyes.

"No, I haven't even begun. I was planning to talk to you later, offer to take Annie to lunch, let her meet people, but obviously that's not going to work, so I'll move straight to step two. Talk to my parents."

I walked away before I could see his reaction.

He called after me, "How old am I, Maya?"

I turned. "How the hell should I know? Whatever you've told the school, I'm sure it's a lie anyway."

"I'm sixteen, just like you. Or like you will be tomorrow,

from what I heard. My birthday was last month."

"Congratulations." I started walking again. "I'll send you a card next year, if you hang around that long, which I doubt."

"You don't need to doubt it. I'll be leaving for sure if you tell anyone about Annie."

I wheeled. "Are you threatening to take her—?"

"Legally, I can't take her anywhere. I'm sixteen, Maya. Barely sixteen. She's nineteen. Who's the guardian here?"

I paused, then said, softly, "Oh."

"Yeah, *oh*. Annie and I never knew our dad. Our mom died last year when Annie was eighteen. Before the accident. So she got custody of me."

"Accident? It's brain damage?"

The look in Rafe's eyes, the grief . . . It hurt just to see it, and he turned away fast, mumbling, "Yeah. It's brain damage. Point is that if anyone finds out, I'm off to a foster home and she's off to an institution. Which neither of us wants."

I stepped toward him. "I'm sorry. I just . . ." *Jumped to conclusions. Big surprise.* "I'm sorry."

He turned back and ran his hand through his hair. "Yeah, well, I know it looked bad. It *is* bad. I definitely don't want her living like this. The school thinks I'm seventeen, with my birthday early next year, so at worst, we'd have to wait that long."

I didn't know what to say to that. It was like when he admitted why he pretended to smoke—his honesty threw me. This time, though, he didn't seem to be trying to win points, which threw me all the more.

He was trusting me with things I hadn't earned his trust for, which only made me realize he didn't have anyone he *could* trust with stuff like that, not in Salmon Creek, and I felt bad for him, which I was sure he wouldn't want. . . .

"I meant what I said," I said finally, "about spending time with Annie. Not in town obviously, but maybe we can go for a walk or whatever. She said she likes the forest. I could show her stuff."

"She'd like that." He looked over at me. "Thanks."

My cheeks heated. I looked away and mumbled, "Sure." Then I asked, "Are you coming to the party tomorrow?" because it was, at the moment, the only change of subject I could come up with.

"Daniel's party?" Rafe looked confused, as if he couldn't imagine why I'd think he was going to the party of a guy who obviously didn't like him.

"Well, it's at Daniel's place, but it's really—"

"Your birthday party. I know." He kept giving me that look, and I didn't blame him—I was as unlikely to invite him as Daniel was.

"Everyone goes," I said. "The whole class."

"Yeah, I know. Hayley asked if I was going, but I kind of figured that didn't exactly count as an invitation. Unless I went with her, which I'd really rather not."

I had to laugh at his expression. "Don't blame you. But you can now consider yourself officially invited by the birthday girl. It's an easier way to meet people than hanging out at the smoking pit. Healthier, too."

That got a smile from him. Not that lazy grin I'd seen so often, but something as different from his usual self as that ice-cold anger I'd seen him show to Sam and, later, to me. A crooked smile. Hesitant. Not quite shy, but close enough to do more to my insides than that sexy one he tossed around so casually. When I felt that, I felt a faint pang of panic, too—something in my gut that said falling for Rafe Martinez was a bad idea. When he said, "I'll see," in a tone that said he wasn't likely to show up, I was relieved.

"It depends on Annie," he said. "It's Saturday, so she'll expect me to stick around."

"Understandable," I said. "Have a good weekend, then, and I'll see you Monday."

I hurried off before he could reply.

TEN

"SO, NO TATTOO YET," I said as I sat on the rock, legs dangling over the edge. "Mom wants to take me to Vancouver for the weekend but . . ."

That was our plan. I don't want to do it without you.

I couldn't say that, not even sitting here alone, talking to the lake, pretending Serena was still here, still swimming, still singing, forever swimming and singing.

I hardly ever came to the lake anymore. When I did, it was to talk to her, which seems weird, since this is the place she died. But it was the place she loved best, too, and if I sat very still and closed my eyes, I could hear her laughing, hear her singing.

Her voice haunted this place even more than her memory, and usually I couldn't take the reminder. But this was a special day, my sixteenth birthday, when we should have been in Vancouver, getting tattoos and bugging my mom to let us drive the car, then sneaking out at night to flirt with college guys.

"Mom still feels bad about what happened at the tattoo place," I said. "I wish she wouldn't. I just want to forget it." I hugged my knees to my chest. "That's weird, isn't it? That it's bugging me. Since when do I care what other people think? I do, I guess. But you always knew that."

I shifted again, the rock cold under me. "It's like this splinter that won't come out, and I keep picking at it and it only gets worse. Then there are the dreams. I had them last night again. I don't want to tell Mom and Dad, because they'll hike me back to Dr. Fodor, and he'll say it's post-traumatic stress, that seeing Daniel with that cougar brought it on again. What's the point of talking to a therapist if I know what he'll say?"

I caught a faint whiff of smoke on the breeze. Campers? I'd have to mention that to Dad so he could find and warn them.

The distraction helped and I stretched out again, reclining on the rock as the sun reappeared.

"I got my birthday presents this morning," I continued. "Mom did a blueprint for a tree house for Fitz." I smiled, imagining her laugh. "Seriously. It's got this set of ramps, so he can climb up, then walk down. Only problem will be building it. We'll need to wait for Walter to come back next spring." Walter was Dad's seasonal helper and the town carpenter.

"Dad's taking me into town this week to get my learner's permit. He says he's due for a new Jeep next year, so when I get my novice, he's going to buy the old one from the St. Clouds, which means I'll be able to drive Daniel to school. He'll love that, won't he?"

I laughed, but it trailed off into silence. After a moment, I said, "He's doing well. Daniel. He got back on track—" Faster than I did, I was going to say, then realized that didn't sound good. Serena wouldn't want him moping around, but she wouldn't want to think he'd forgotten her already, so I said, "He's still not dating. I think he should try but . . ." I shrugged. "He will when he's ready."

I flipped onto my stomach and looked down at the still water. "Speaking of Daniel and my birthday, he's up to something. I texted him this morning, asking if he wanted me to come over and help get the place ready, and he said no, it was under control." I imagined her answer and laughed. "Yeah, definitely up to something if he's turning down cleaning help. Better not be pranking me, because he knows I'll give as good as I get and—"

"Maya?"

I scrambled up as a figure appeared at the edge of the woods. Nicole. I waved and she stepped through into the clearing, gym bag slung over her arm.

"Please don't tell me you're going swimming today," I said.

She blushed. "I know, I practice too much."

"Um, no. I mean swimming . . . in a lake . . . in October."

"It's not that cold. And the pool we're going to next month is always freezing, so I thought it'd be good for me. But now that you mention it . . ." She gazed out over the lake and shivered.

"Uh-huh," I said, and we both laughed.

"I heard you talking," she said as she came closer. "Who's up there—?"

She stopped as she realized I was alone. Then she looked at the lake and her cheeks colored. "Oh. I-I'm sorry. I'll just, um . . . I'll see you tonight."

"Hold up," I said as I scrambled off the rock. "I was just leaving. My mom will have lunch ready soon. Join us. There's always lots."

I caught up and we walked in awkward silence for a minute before she said, "Daniel asked me to the party this morning."

When I glanced over, she blushed again. "I mean, obviously, I was invited. But he called to make sure I was coming, and I thought maybe he wanted help, but he said he was with the guys today, so I thought, you know, he was just making sure or something." Another bright flush. "It probably doesn't mean anything, but it was nice."

I nodded. "He said he might ask you."

Her face glowed, and I felt a little guilty. Mom says I shouldn't play matchmaker. If it's going to happen, it's going to happen. But if I can help make things happen—whether it's getting a couple together or organizing a fund-raiser or being captain of the track team—then I don't see the point in sitting back and doing nothing.

I thought Nicole would be a good fit for Daniel. Not a love-of-his-life match, but someone who could help him get back into dating, someone who really liked him and would be happy just to hang out with him, take things at his pace, understand if it didn't work out.

"I hear you invited someone, too," she said.

"Huh?"

She grinned and elbowed me. "Forgotten already? I met Rafe in the store last night and asked if he was going tonight, and he said that you invited him."

I opened my mouth to say it wasn't like that, then shut it. If Rafe said I invited him, then he wasn't lying. No more than I'd been when I said Daniel had considered asking Nicole. It just wasn't the way it sounded.

"I told Daniel about it when he called," Nicole said. "I was just going to razz him about it, but he seemed surprised."

That was putting it mildly, I was sure. I should have mentioned it—I just hadn't figured Rafe would take me up on the offer. He probably still wouldn't, but I should have told Daniel anyway.

"Daniel's fine with it," she continued. "You know how he is. If you're cool with it, he is, too." She kicked a tree branch off the path. "Anyway, Rafe's not so bad. Hayley doesn't think so anyway. She— Oh."

When she hesitated, I said, "What is it?"

"Just, well, if you're going with Rafe, and Hayley finds out I knew about it . . ." A deep breath. "I'll have to tell her. She'll be really mad if I don't." Another pause. "And she'll be really mad if I say you invited him."

"Which has nothing to do with you."

"I know but . . . maybe I just won't tell her."

Fair or not, Hayley would take it out on Nicole. If any of the kids had a problem with small town life, it was Hayley. You can't be a convincing mean girl without an entourage. Stuck with a meager selection, she'd decided to convert Nicole. I hated how she treated her—best friends one day, ordering her around the next. Nicole didn't seem to like it either, but with Serena gone, I guess she'd decided Hayley would have to do, since I didn't seem to be interested.

I looked out at the lake. I could use a girlfriend. A real one I could talk to, not just someone to hang out with. How could I push Daniel to replace Serena in his life when I wasn't ready to?

When would I be ready to?

I didn't know. Just not yet.

Nicole came to my place for lunch, then we hung out, but it was awkward. I was used to being with her as part of a group, and it wasn't long before she "remembered" a singing lesson, and I spent the rest of the afternoon with my animals.

When Dad took me to the party that evening, I still hadn't

shaken my mood. If anything, it'd gotten worse. I couldn't stop thinking about Serena. Couldn't stop thinking this was my second birthday without her. The first party, though. She'd died at the end of August and even by October, I hadn't been ready for a party without her. Now I realized I still wasn't.

We were halfway down the wooded road to Daniel's place when Dad pulled over to the side.

"You don't look like a girl heading to her sixteenth birthday party," he said.

"It'll pass. I'm just . . ."

"Serena?"

I nodded. My eyes filled and I pushed my palms against them. "Great. I knew I should have bought the waterproof mascara."

Dad pressed a tissue into my hand. I carefully wiped my eyes, then flipped down the visor mirror.

"You look beautiful," he said.

"You're parentally obligated to say that."

"True."

I made a face at him, then adjusted my seat belt, and said, "Carry on, Jeeves."

"Jeeves is a valet, not a chauffeur."

"We can't afford both, so you're stuck with double duty."

He stopped in front of the house. The windows were dark.

"Oh, please," I said. "Not the surprise party thing again."

"Better work on your surprised face."

I opened the door. "No final words of warning?"

"I trust you."

I sighed. "That'll be my epitaph someday. So trustworthy. So honest. So boring."

I headed up the walk. Like all the houses in Salmon Creek, the Bianchi home is owned by the St. Clouds. This one is two stories with four bedrooms, one for Daniel's parents and one for each child. No matter what your job is, your house is just big enough to fit your family comfortably. They're all nice, though, not cookie-cutter military base houses. The Bianchi place is modern Victorian, with gabled windows and a big front porch that cries out for a swing. Yet there's no swing. Never has been.

The front door was locked. All part of the show, given that I knew where the key was. I unlocked it and let myself in.

"Oh my, no one's here," I called. "Could I have the wrong day? Maybe they all went someplace else to party without me."

Silence. I walked into the living room. When no one jumped out and yelled "surprise!" I started to get concerned. I wandered through the empty, silent house, finally ending up in the dining room where brightly wrapped gifts were piled on the table.

"Okay, guys, so where are you?"

I noticed something on top of the pile. A papaya. I groaned. That was my classmates' old nickname for me. Maya

Papaya. Original, I know.

There was an arrow carved in the papaya, pointing to the screen door.

"Follow the papayas," I muttered, shaking my head. "Guys, guys, guys . . ."

I headed for the door.

ELEVEN

I FOUND ANOTHER PAPAYA in the middle of the yard, pointing to the path leading into the forest. As I walked, I alternated between looking for papayas on the ground and for classmates overhead. Given how many times I'd jumped out of trees or off rocks and scared the crap out of my friends, I figured payback might be coming.

But there was no sign of anyone—just papayas, a half dozen of them leading me along the path. Then I stepped out into the clearing at the base of a rock face that rose fifty feet in the air. I'd seen this particular cliff many times, but today it was different. Today it had toeholds and cuts carved out and stone protrusions drilled on. A belay and pulley hung from the top.

"Oh my God," I whispered.

"Happy birthday, Maya," a voice said behind me.

I turned as Daniel stepped from the trees.

"You like?" he said.

I ran over and threw my arms around his neck.

"I think that's a yes," Corey said, off to my left.

"Hey, we helped, too."

That was Brendan Hajek, the veterinarian's son, who'd become captain of the track team after I'd bowed out last year. He was Daniel's height and slender with light brown hair worn to his shoulders, usually tied back, like it was today. There'd been a time when he'd ask me to school dances, and whenever he did, I was really tempted to say yes despite my rule against dating town boys. Brendan was quiet and sweet, and between track and a love of animals we had a lot in common. But I had my "summer boy" rule for a reason—I wouldn't risk my friendships by dating my friends. Eventually, he'd stopped asking. Now he was dating a girl a few towns over.

I gave both Corey and Brendan a hug, which I think shocked the hell out of them, but neither complained. The others streamed out of the forest. Even Hayley had come with her younger sister, Brooke, and Brooke's boyfriend. Like I said, Hayley and I don't get along. I like Brooke, though. It's not her fault her sister is a bitch.

I said a quick hello to everyone, then hurried to the climbing wall and stared up, barely resisting the urge to start jumping up and down, screaming like a game show winner.

"You always said this rock face would be perfect for climbing," Daniel said as he walked up behind me.

"If only it had more cracks and crevices," I said.

"And now it does."

I grinned up at him until Nicole grabbed my arm and said, "Come and try it out."

As she pulled me away, I glanced back at Daniel. "How long did it take to build?"

"Too long," Brendan said. "And we weren't even around for most of it."

"We've been at it since six this morning, finishing up," Corey said. "So we'd really appreciate it if you girls could grab us some cold beers . . ."

"Are you going to show us how it's done, Maya?" Brooke said. "I'll never make it all the way up, but I'd love to try. I'm sure Hayley would, too."

"Um, no," Hayley said. She turned to me. "I can't believe you still do stuff like this. Are you ever going to grow up?"

"I still do it," Corey said.

"Because you're a guy. Girls don't climb walls. Not real girls, anyway. Just tomboys whose closets are filled with tank tops and jeans and sneakers. Who still consider braids and ponytails high fashion. Who wouldn't know how to apply makeup on a dare."

"Knock it off, Hayley," Daniel said.

I was wearing makeup. Just not a lot. I had my hair down, too, and although I *was* wearing jeans, they were my fancy ones, paired with a new fitted tee and ankle boots. It might have been the T-shirt slogan that she objected to—BRUNETTE

IS THE NEW BLONDE—but I didn't buy it to set her off.

"Am I the only one around here who thinks Maya has a hidden Y chromosome?" Hayley said.

"If she does, she's hiding it pretty good," Corey said, giving me a lascivious once-over.

Hayley scowled at me and opened her mouth to say something else. Daniel started to cut her off, but Corey beat him to it.

"Lessons later," he said. "First, we need to see if this girl is as good a climber as she thinks she is. Challenge time. A race to the top. Maya versus anyone who dares take her on."

"That'll be a short list," I said.

Corey grinned. "Not when they hear the prize." He turned to the others. "Anyone who beats our Sweet Sixteen gets to kiss her. The lineup forms behind me."

Brendan got behind him. Daniel grinned at me and joined. The other guys filed in.

"Oh my God," I said. "What are you guys? Twelve?"

"No," Brendan said. "Just really, really immature."

"In other words, typical guys," said a voice.

Sam stepped out from behind Hayley and Brooke and cut in line behind Daniel.

"I'll skip the kiss," she said. "But as the designated bad girl, I can't resist the urge to show up the good girl."

"So what do I get when I beat everyone?" I said.

"*When?*" Corey shook his head. "Do you need a wide-load

sign for transporting that ego? Fine. Beat all of us and I'll kiss you."

"Speaking of egos . . ."

"Beat us and we'll install more holds over there." Daniel pointed to a tougher and higher section of the rock face ten feet down, then looked at me. "How's that?"

I smiled. "Game on."

Nicole and Brooke took the path up to the top, so they could referee. Hayley stayed at the bottom.

Between the natural crevices and bumps, and the newly installed ones, there were more than enough for two people to climb side by side.

Corey went first. I beat him easily. Brendan was a little tougher, but I still made it to the top before he was much past the halfway mark. Neither had any real climbing experience—they just counted on their general athletic prowess to pull them through.

Next up was the only real threat. Daniel. He'd been climbing with me for years. I was the natural—I was faster and more agile—but he had double my upper body strength and that counts for a lot.

Daniel did a test run first. Brendan and Corey complained about that, but he was right—I'd gone up twice now, which gave me an advantage. If I was going to win, I wanted to do it fairly.

Daniel belayed back down as I got into position. His feet hit the ground with a thump, then he looked over at me.

"Ready?"

"Always."

Nicole did the countdown from the top. I started fast, reaching the halfway mark head and shoulders above him. But that's when things got tricky, the holds and grips a little farther apart, and he had the advantage. By the three-quarter mark, he'd caught up.

"Better kick it up a notch," he said, as he drew alongside me. "I know you really want those extra holds."

"And I'm sure you really don't want to make them. But don't forget the second part. You win, you gotta kiss me. Might be better to stick with the holds."

He laughed and heaved up to the next grip, pulling away now. I grabbed another and found toeholds first, shooting a couple inches above him, the advantage lost a second later when his longer arms found the next grips as I was still getting leverage. I kept my face forward now, climbing in earnest for the first time since we'd started.

A hiss and boo from below told me I was in the lead. Then a grunt from beside me. A sharp intake of breath and I knew he was pulling up. The crowd cheered. I looked up to see Brooke leaning over the side, ropes in hand, urging me on. Only three feet to go. I could see Daniel out of the corner of my eye, his chin level with my nose, just a scant inch advantage, but I knew it was enough and as soon as he grabbed that top ledge and heaved himself up—

A grunt. Daniel wobbled and the grip slid out of his hand. He dropped only a few inches, but by the time he'd recovered, I was pulling myself over the top. Brooke and Nicole were cheering. The others below called up good-natured boos.

I took a breather as I hung off the ledge. I could hear Daniel panting beside me, but I didn't look over.

There was no way he'd lost his hold on that grip. He'd let go. Given me the win at the last second as he realized what was coming if he'd won. A kiss he didn't want.

The ego bruise lasted only a moment. Was I surprised? No. How awkward would that have been? Neither of us wanted that kiss. As always, Daniel had done the right thing and, if I'd been in his place, I'd have done the same.

After a moment, I grinned over at him. "Loser."

"The rope slipped," he said, tugging at it, like he was testing the belay system.

"You just keep telling yourself that. It'll keep you busy while you're building those new holds."

"You still need to beat everyone else. You haven't won yet."

"Just keep telling yourself that, too."

He laughed and gave me a shove. I returned the favor, sending him swinging, then belayed down before he could retaliate.

The next challenger was Sam. She was strong enough to climb and obviously had some experience, just not enough to give her a serious shot at victory. She took the defeat well, though, just teasing me in a surprisingly good mood.

The other guys were easy wins. Everyone was joking about a rematch with Daniel and ribbing the guys about losing a kiss and gaining a weekend of work, when a familiar voice drawled, "Is the game over? Or is there room for one more?"

TWELVE

RAFE WALKED OUT OF the forest. The leather jacket was gone, replaced by a tattered denim one. Instead of boots, he wore sneakers that looked as old as the jacket. As he walked toward us, his gaze was fixed on me like he didn't notice anyone else there.

"You're late," I said.

"Yeah, had some trouble getting away. Then I figured I was at the wrong place until I saw the gifts and followed the papayas."

He stopped in front of me and smiled—his real smile, the crooked one that made my breath flutter. To my left, Daniel rocked forward. He didn't say anything, just stayed poised like that, watching for trouble. Rafe didn't seem to notice. His gaze stayed locked on mine, crooked smile fainter now, but his eyes still shimmering.

"So did I hear right?" he said. "Race to the top? Winner gets a kiss?"

"Maya's done seven climbs in a row," Daniel said. "You can race me."

"But I don't want to kiss *you*."

The others laughed. Rafe didn't even look at Daniel when he answered, just kept watching me with a smile that now held a hint of challenge.

"If she says no, she forfeits the new grips," Corey said. "She had to defeat all comers. That was the deal."

"I'm the one who offered," Daniel said. "So it stands as is. He's late."

"I am. So it's up to Maya. She's already won. I'm just the bonus round."

He grinned then, but it was a different kind of grin, a mock arrogance that made me laugh and shake my head.

I looked into his eyes and saw the challenge sparkling there, and I hadn't even decided what to do when I heard myself saying, "You're on."

As Rafe walked over to the dangling harness, he stripped off his jacket, earning him giggles and whispers from the girls and grunts from the guys, who weren't nearly as impressed. Rafe skipped gym whenever he could, so I'd assumed he wasn't the athletic type. I was wrong.

He wore an old T-shirt with the sleeves torn off, and his lean muscles moved under coppery skin. He had a tattoo on the inside of his forearm—a small one that looked like raven wings. When he turned around, I caught the faint edge of another tattoo on his shoulder peeking from under his shirt.

He glanced over, like he'd sensed me looking. When I didn't turn away, he grinned and mouthed something I didn't catch, probably didn't want to.

Brendan helped Rafe into the harness. It took a while, the process punctuated by Rafe's questions. Then he stood at the base of the rock face, saying, "You put your toes here, right? And you grab those things that stick out?"

The others laughed and yelled, "Quit while you're ahead!" Daniel relaxed and rolled his eyes at me. I rolled mine back, but not for the same reason.

When we were finally in position, the others pulling away, I whispered, "Poseur."

Rafe glanced over, brows arching. "Keep calling me that and I might get insulted."

"Stop earning it and I'll stop saying it." I faced forward as I tested my rope and waited for Daniel to get to the top.

"Are you implying that I know how to climb?"

"Are you implying that I'm stupid enough to think you'd challenge me if you didn't? Of course, you can't be that good if you need to slow me down by pretending you don't know what you're doing."

He was about to shoot something back, when Daniel leaned over and called, "Ready?"

Rafe motioned for him to wait a second, then whispered, "How about we up the stakes? I win, you talk to me."

Now it was my turn to raise my eyebrows. "I'm afraid to ask what you mean by *talk* . . ."

"Exactly that. I win, I get thirty minutes of your time tonight."

"To charm me and lie to me and pretend to be whoever you think I want?"

"Nope. Tonight it's me, in case you haven't noticed. The real Rafe Martinez. A special one-night appearance."

"And if I win?"

He grinned. "Then you get to spend thirty minutes with me, lucky birthday girl."

I laughed and motioned for Daniel to start the countdown.

Rafe still pulled the "I don't know what I'm doing" routine, starting slow and cautious, hoping I'd second-guess my assessment and take it easy. I didn't. He realized that when my foot reached his shoulder level. By the midpoint, he'd shot up to my waist, but his muttered curses told me he'd underestimated how good I was—or overestimated how good he was—and it was clear he wasn't going to catch up in time. So I stopped.

Daniel leaned over and mouthed, "What are you doing?" Below, the others yelled, a cacophony of shouts and cheers and jeers. Rafe reached up, his bracelet hitting the rock with a ping. I glanced at it. A worn rawhide band with a cat's-eye stone. I could see his tattoo better, too, as he pulled himself up, and I recognized the symbol. A crow mother kachina. Hopi.

As he drew up alongside me, he cocked one brow.

"You really *want* that kiss don't you?" he said.

"No, I just want to see what you can really do."

He smiled then, a blaze of a grin that made me forget I was hanging twenty feet above the ground.

"All right then," he said. "No holds barred. On my count?"

I nodded.

"One, two, three . . ."

We took off. I kept my face to the wall, throwing everything I had into the climb, certain I'd pull away to victory. But he stayed alongside me, his grunts and labored breathing telling me he was trying just as hard.

I struggled to concentrate, but all I could hear was his breathing. It was weirdly relaxing, like the ticking of a metronome, and I found myself moving faster, smoother, the rock seeming to glide under me, hands and feet finding the notches and grips automatically, like climbing a tree, that blissful feeling of going higher and higher, the earth and everything earthly vanishing below me, the air getting thinner, the world quieter as I pulled away until—

My hand hit the top ledge and I jolted out of it, and looked over to see Rafe beside me, sweat dripping down his face, eyes glowing, face glowing, his gaze locked on mine again, lips parting to say something—

A jerk on my harness made me look up sharply as Daniel adjusted the rope, preparing to let me belay down. The look on his face told me who'd won.

"Damn," I said. "Seriously?"

"By a fingertip," Rafe said. "You need to grow longer arms."

Before we'd even hit the ground, the others crowded around, asking who'd won. I waited for Rafe to claim the victory. He didn't. So I told them.

"Because she let you catch up," Sam said. "I wouldn't count that as a win."

"Which is why I didn't say I won," Rafe said, as he undid his harness.

"Still counts," Corey said. "Give the guy some room so he can collect his prize."

Daniel rounded the bend in the path, picking up speed, like he was coming to rescue me from my obligation. When he caught my eye, he slowed.

Rafe shucked his harness and took mine. He set them aside and I braced myself, but he only called over to Daniel, "That's an amazing wall. Sometime I'd love to know how you did it."

Daniel nodded, still watching Rafe warily.

"Um, your prize . . ." Corey said. "If you aren't going to take it, I'd be happy to play stand-in."

"I'll collect it later," Rafe said. "Without an audience."

"Uh-uh," Corey said. "No rain checks."

Rafe only shrugged. "I can ask for one. If Maya doesn't want to honor it, that's her choice."

Daniel grunted and collected the gear. He didn't say anything, but I knew Rafe had scored a point.

Sam strolled over from where she'd been standing at the back of the group, gaze fixed on Rafe like a mugger spotting an easy mark. He stiffened. Being the sort who doesn't find brawls an entertaining addition to her birthday parties, I decided action was needed. Sam wasn't here to help me celebrate my big day. She wanted something, and if she got it, she'd be less likely to pick a fight.

"So, guys," I said. "Since I've been doing the family thing today, I haven't heard what happened with that fake reporter chick. Anyone spoken to her since yesterday?"

"I did," Brendan said. "I was walking home after school, cutting through the forest after I split with Corey, and she just happened to be taking the same path. Following me, I think. Anyway, she wanted to talk. So I did."

"You're not supposed to," Brooke said. "You know that."

Brendan gave her a look. "I'm a big boy."

"And she was kind of cute," Corey said, elbowing him.

"No, but I wanted to get a better handle on her game."

"Good idea," Daniel said. He waved for us to start back to the house and for Brendan to keep talking.

"All she wanted to talk about was us—the high school kids. She kept saying she was working on an article and wanted to slant it that way, what life is like for teens in Salmon Creek. She asked a lot about the extracurricular stuff, which was weird."

"Like what?" I asked.

"Which sports we did. Which clubs we had. Why we had those ones. Who was on each team. She took notes for that part—dividing us up by what activities we were in."

"Looking for cliques," I said. "Trying to make us sound as if we're just like the kids in city schools. You have your choir girls and your wrestling guys . . ."

"I guess so. After that, she started asking about the medical stuff."

"I hope you shut your mouth," Brooke said.

"Yes, but the questions she was asking were weird. About us again. How often did we get checked out? Did we get any special shots? Were we on special diets?"

"Oh my God," I whispered. "We're lab rats. They're experimenting on us. Building super wrestlers and singers who can take over the WWE and *American Idol*. The first steps to world domination."

"I think that'd be *Canadian* Wrestling Entertainment and *Canadian* Idol," Daniel said.

"Okay, the first very, very small step toward world domination."

"And that's exactly what you two can tell her," Brendan said. "She was asking who I'd pick for 'class leaders.'" He finger-quoted the phrase. "I was about to tell the truth and say that'd be me, but then I realized she was looking for someone to pester with more questions, so I nominated you guys."

"Thanks." I glanced at Sam, who was following the conversation with obvious frustration. "Did she single out anyone in particular? Not to speak to but just in general?"

"Well, she asked about Serena and—"

"Serena?" I said, Sam forgotten. "What about her?"

Brendan glanced at Daniel. "Um, nothing specific. Just reporter stuff. You know. Anyway, then she asked—"

"Was she interested in Serena's death?" I said. "Could that be what she's investigating?"

"Course not. I mean, maybe as a side story, but umm . . ."

He glanced at Daniel again and when I turned, Daniel's face was averted, but I knew what had passed between them. A look from Daniel warning Brendan to get the hell off the subject before I was in no mood to enjoy my party. He was right, of course. My heart was already pounding double time.

I took a deep breath. "Did she ask about anyone else?"

"Oh, everyone," Brendan said, rushing on. "Names, friendships, hobbies. She was really interested in our hobbies. When we talked about the teams and stuff, she asked why Rafe and Sam aren't on any. I said Rafe just moved here, and I don't know what he's into."

"And me?" Sam said.

"I said you're antisocial."

"Thanks."

"She asked whether you were good at any of the school's specialties—singing, track, swimming, wrestling . . . I said all I know is you like to hit people."

She flipped him the finger.

"What? It's true. Then she asked if they let girls on the boxing team and I said Mr. Barnes tried to get you on it, but you weren't interested. Then—get this—she starts asking if you've got a hate-on for certain people."

Sam looked worried, almost alarmed, but when she saw me watching, she tried to hide it and said, "So what'd you tell her?"

"That you're an equal opportunity hater. You pick on all of us. Except Daniel. I think you're sweet on Daniel."

Sam punched Brendan in the side. She made it look like a play punch, but I heard it connect, and he gasped.

"Anything else?" I asked.

"That's when she started in on the medical stuff and I said I had to leave," Brendan said, still sounding a little winded. "So, Rafe, you gonna join us on the track team? You're in good shape and, without Maya this fall, we're short a member."

Rafe glanced over with a "Hmm?" He'd been walking beside me but had tuned out the conversation, gaze drifting over the forest, fingers tapping his leg, like he was bored already.

When Brendan repeated the question, he shrugged and said, "Not really my thing."

"You have to join something," Hayley said. "They're

just cutting you some slack because you're new. How about swimming?"

That got a chuckle. "Definitely not my thing."

Conversation turned to the swimming team and an upcoming meet, and Rafe's gaze returned to the forest, like he was looking for an escape route.

I eased over, close enough to murmur, "Go on."

"Hmm?"

"*This* obviously isn't your thing either." I slowed to let the others get ahead. "You showed up. Good enough. Go on. Enjoy the rest of your night."

"Trying to get rid of me?" He managed a smile that barely touched his eyes. "Or trying to get out of our deal? I won thirty minutes of your time, remember."

"You can have a rain check on that, too."

He searched my face. "Are you mad because I didn't take the kiss? It wasn't an insult. I have every intention of cashing that check. Just not with all your friends watching."

"I appreciate that."

"Yeah?" Another searching look. Then he smiled. "Good."

"Doesn't mean I'll accept the chit when you cash it. But you scored points for chivalry."

"Yeah?"

I nodded. "Hayley was *very* impressed."

He laughed. "Just what I need."

"Did I hear someone say my name?" Hayley said, slipping over between us.

"That was Rafe," I said, as we headed into the yard. "He said you're just what he—"

Rafe coughed, covering the rest. I grinned and jogged to catch up with the others.

THIRTEEN

B Y THE TIME WE got inside, Rafe had done a disappearing act. I thought maybe he was just getting away
from Hayley, but he didn't show up for pizza or gift
opening or the obligatory cake ceremony.

I should have been relieved. I'd given him permission to
leave. I didn't want anything to do with the guy, right? Maybe
that was true yesterday; maybe it'd even been true this morning, when Nicole said he might be coming. But now, when he
actually took off, what I felt was anything but relief.

Still, I wasn't letting that spoil my party. The pizza was
great. The gifts were good, if you exclude the dollar store
dream catcher from Hayley. I got books and silver jewelry
and funky T-shirts. Corey and Brendan had helped build
the wall, of course. The materials and the equipment came
from Daniel, meaning I needed to start thinking of an

amazing gift for him next year.

After cake, we sat around the kitchen, talking. That's when the kids who weren't part of our circle drifted off for the night. Once they were gone, Corey brought out the booze. Well, a twelve-pack of beer. That's Daniel's house rule. One pack of Lucky and when it's gone, it's gone. No one drove to the party, so no one would be driving home. And because it was Daniel setting the rules, no one broke them. No one dared.

When we party with summer kids, the new cottage renters sometimes joke about hiding the booze from me. I'm Native, so I must drink. But I don't. My friends think that's because I'm being stubborn and contrary. Not true. The point of drinking seems to be to lose control, and that's definitely not my idea of a good time.

By the time the beer came out, there were only seven of us left. Daniel, me, Nicole, Brendan and Corey, of course. Hayley stayed, too, as usual. So did Sam, which was new. Hell, having her come to our parties at all was new. Daniel didn't care. It's not like she'd tattle on us about the beer.

After breaking out the booze, the next step was breaking into couples. As long as no one tried to use his room, Daniel was fine with people sneaking off to find a quiet place. He was taking some baby steps in that direction himself with Nicole, sitting on the love seat in the living room. Corey and Hayley disappeared first. They were a "couple of convenience." Had been since eighth grade. Neither was really into the other, but if there wasn't anyone better around, they'd pair up.

Brendan's girlfriend had to work, so he sat with me. Just talking, mostly about track. I think he was looking forward to giving back the captain's position. Some people don't like taking charge. Can't fathom that myself.

Sam stayed with us, which was awkward, trying to include her in a conversation she had no interest in. We changed the subject, to be polite, but she seemed happy just to sit there, chugging her beer.

When she went to get another one, Brendan said, "Did you notice how many were left?"

I pointed at my glass of Coke.

"Right," he said. "You wouldn't know. But I think it was down to a couple, so I'd better grab one."

That left me on the sofa, inspecting my nails, trying not to glance over at Daniel and Nicole, deep in close conversation on the love seat.

A thump on the sofa made me jump. Rafe vaulted the back of it, and landed beside me.

"I thought they'd never leave." He stretched out his legs, hit the coffee table, and sent my drink shaking. "Whoops." He grabbed it. "Yours?"

I nodded. He reached over me to put it on the side table, then wedged his beer bottle between his thighs.

"Sam and Brendan, huh?" he said. "Now that I wouldn't have guessed."

"They just went to get a beer." I motioned to his. "Or fight over the last one."

I stopped myself before I asked where he'd been. That would imply I'd been disappointed that he'd left. So I just nodded at his drink again and said, "Did anyone tell you house rules?"

"When it's gone, it's gone. No BYOB. No dope." The corners of his mouth quirked.

"Yes," I said. "I'm sure we're very quaint compared to your big city bashes."

"Wouldn't know. Never been to one." When I gave him a look, he said, "Big parties, sure. Just not big cities. Growing up, we were strictly small town, usually rural."

I must have looked skeptical, because he said, "I'm being me tonight, remember? All truth, all the time. The big city crap is just that."

"Okay, then." I twisted to face him. "If you're being honest, what about the accent? If that's supposed to be Texas, you really need to work on it."

He laughed. "You accusing me of using a fake drawl? Don't you think it's sexy? Every other girl up here does." He grinned, a little of that old arrogance seeping back in, but in a way that didn't seem as bad as usual. He leaned forward, voice lowering, though Daniel and Nicole were too far away to hear us over the music. "It's real. A *real* mongrel mess. Part Texas, part Arkansas, part New Mexico, part wherever else Mom felt like living. We moved around a lot." He eased back a little, still close enough that our legs touched. "What about you? I heard you weren't born here either."

"Oregon," I said. "We moved when I was five."

"And is it true what I heard? You were found on the steps of a church? Wrapped in swaddling clothes? With a secret necklace that will unlock your true destiny when you turn eighteen?"

I laughed. "That would make a much better story. No church, necklace, or swaddling clothes. But, yes, 'foundling' is the correct term. Very Dickensian."

Rafe was about to say something, when he noticed Daniel watching us. He leaned over and whispered, "Any chance I can get my thirty minutes without the chaperone?"

I glanced at Daniel. He mouthed, "Want me to get rid of him?" I shook my head. Nicole followed the exchange, then stood, plucking Daniel's sleeve and saying something I couldn't hear. Daniel hesitated, then nodded. They got up and headed toward the kitchen.

As they passed, Nicole leaned over the end table and whispered, "We're going outside. Get some air." She winked. "And leaving you two alone."

"Thanks," I said.

They left, but the music was still booming, and Sam was heading back in through the dining room, which promised an even bigger problem.

"Want to go someplace quieter?" Rafe asked.

I nodded. He took my pop and his beer and followed me out. There was a back TV room and that's where I went first. All seemed quiet until I pushed open the door, and found

Hayley and Corey making out on the couch . . . and not completely dressed. Before I could shut the door again, Hayley jumped off Corey and yanked down her shirt. She started to snarl something at me. Then she saw Rafe standing at my shoulder.

"Hey, Hayley," he said. "Corey."

The look she leveled on me was lethal. "You bitch," she said. "You scheming little—"

I closed the door fast.

"Thanks, guys!" Corey yelled.

"Sorry!" I called back.

"How about outside?" Rafe whispered. He caught my look and said, "Just on the porch or something."

"I think that's where Daniel and Nicole went. I have an idea."

I led him upstairs. As I pushed open the door to Daniel's bedroom, I said, "It's a way station not a destination."

Rafe chuckled. "Damn."

I went in, leaving the door ajar, and headed for the window. It usually opened easily. Before Daniel dared to march out the front door with his bag packed, he'd take the window exit and ride his bike to our place. It'd been a while since we'd gone out to sit on the roof. We used to—the three of us—but since Serena died, whenever Daniel suggested it, I changed the subject.

The house had been painted this summer and it seemed like the window hadn't been opened since. I whaled on it, then looked over to ask Rafe for help. He was standing in front of Daniel's dresser, holding our drinks as he looked at the photos shoved in the mirror frame.

"You guys really *have* been friends a long time." He pointed the beer bottle at one. "What are you there? Six?"

"About that."

He grinned. "I like the pigtails."

He leaned in to look at a few others. Someone yelled something downstairs, and I said, "Come on," suddenly realizing I really didn't want to be found with Rafe in Daniel's bedroom, however innocent the explanation.

Rafe took his time, still checking out the room. He gestured at a pile of textbooks on the floor.

"What's he use those for? Weight lifting?"

"If you showed up in class more often, you wouldn't be asking that. Daniel's not a dumb jock."

"No kidding." He leaned over to read the titles. "Pre-law? Please tell me those belong to his older brothers."

"An uncle. They're Daniel's now. A little outdated but . . ." I shrugged.

He looked at me like he thought I was kidding. Everyone in town joked about Daniel taking over Chief Carling's job, and when he was little, even he thought he wanted to be a cop. Then he spent a year in cadets and realized paramilitary careers weren't for him.

Daniel had his own very firm ideas of right and wrong, and didn't like following anyone else's. So he'd set his sights on law. It wasn't a sure thing. Daniel was a solid A-minus student, but he really worked for those grades. Harder than I did, which made me feel bad sometimes.

I finally got Rafe over to the window and held the drinks while he yanked it open. Then I handed them back and told him to wait.

"Can I ask where we're going?" he said.

"Up."

He grinned. "Should have guessed. After you then."

FOURTEEN

FROM THE WINDOW, I swung over to the porch roof. I took
the drinks from him, set them down, and climbed onto
the main roof. By the time I was there, Rafe was on
the porch roof, holding the drinks up to me. I grabbed them
and he clambered up. Then I stood, carefully, and walked to
my usual place—the flatter roof on the storage space above
the garage.

Rafe sat beside me. I handed him his beer and looked out
into the dark forest. As I inhaled the smell of it, I closed my
eyes and relaxed, but I didn't feel that usual slow stream of
energy seeping in. Maybe it was too late for that and I was too
tired. If anything, the energy seemed to be flowing out, leaving me blissfully relaxed, even a little light-headed.

When I glanced over at Rafe, he was staring into the
night, sipping his beer, looking just as calm, happy even.

Neither of us said a word, but it wasn't an awkward silence. Just . . . nice.

After a few minutes, he said, "Better not let my thirty minutes slip away, huh?"

"I'm not wearing a watch."

His grin sparked at that, and I felt this tingle in my gut, a slow heat, as if there was more than Coke in my glass. I glanced away and took a gulp. It didn't help. I felt weirdly disconnected. Like when a summer boy sneaked rum into my Coke on our first and last date. I knew what booze tasted like now, though, and my pop was fine.

"So, you wanted to get to know me . . ." he said.

I laughed, and the fuzzy feeling evaporated. "Um, no, I don't think I ever said *that*."

"Close enough. Here's your chance. Ask me anything and I'll reply with relative honesty."

"Relative?"

"I'm the mysterious new guy in town. You like that. You just won't admit it. So, yes, relative honesty. Ask me anything."

"Fine. What's the scariest thing you've ever done?"

He laughed. "Wow. Straight for the jugular." He took a deep breath. "Okay. Scariest thing? Scariest thing I've ever gone through was my mom dying. But you said scariest thing I've *done*. That would be coming here. I'm used to moving, like I said. But this was different. I'm not a legal immigrant, obviously, but we needed to get away, and we knew we'd inherited this cabin, so we had to take the chance and hope nobody asked too many questions."

"You had to get away because of Annie. Because you were afraid she'd lose custody of you."

"Partly, and partly . . ." He chugged his beer, as if shoring up his nerve. "The scariest thing I've ever done was coming here, and the dumbest thing I've ever done was the reason I had to."

After a minute of silence, I said, "Are you going to tell me or was that just a tease?"

I expected a smile. Instead, he drained the rest of his beer in one long, almost desperate swallow.

"I took money from the wrong people," he said.

I stiffened, certain he was pulling his bad boy crap again. But he'd gone very still, watching me, his eyes anxious, like he wished he could take the words back but was glad he couldn't.

I'd asked for honesty. He'd given it, more than he should, because he wanted to earn my trust, wanted it badly enough to offer this. I wondered why, but I couldn't seem to hold on to the thought, couldn't seem to care as that lazy, drifting feeling returned.

I knew he was waiting for me to say something. But what? I was dying to ask what he'd done, but even for me, being that blunt crossed a line.

"So I was wrong," I finally said. "You *are* a bad ass."

He laughed at that, a long whoosh of relieved laughter,

the spark returning to his eyes. "That's right. I've earned my rep the hard way. I'm as bad as they come."

He leaned in, until his breath tickled my hair. "Seriously? That's the worst thing I've ever done, as well as the dumbest. Otherwise, I'm strictly minor league."

He lifted the empty beer bottle. "First drink I've had in about six months. I've been drunk once in my life. It was after my mom died. I went to a party, and I started drinking, and I didn't stop until I woke up covered in puke. Which, let me tell you, is a serious turn-on for girls."

"I bet."

"I've smoked pot once." He leaned in again and whispered, "You'll notice a lot of firsts and lasts in this confession." He set his empty bottle aside. "I was fourteen, in a new place, trying to make friends. Annie caught me. Dragged me away and said if she ever caught me doing that again, she'd tell Mom, who was sick then, so it was the last thing she needed. I found new friends."

He shifted, getting a little closer but subtly, like he was only restless. "What else? I've shoplifted. Small stuff, years ago. Another new school, more bad choices in friends. You'll notice a lot of that pattern, too. I almost broke into a house once. A guy told me this other kid swiped his iPod and he wanted me to get it back. I almost fell for it. At least he bothered lying to me. Most times, kids just figured I'd be happy to help them do something illegal."

"Because you look like the type?"

"Yeah, but not in the way you mean. A lot of the places we went—small towns and that—were very white. You're lucky here. I mean, I'm sure you get some problems, but you're . . ."

"Sheltered."

"I didn't mean it like that."

"It's okay. I know I am. When I leave Salmon Creek, there's a distinct change in tone." I motioned to his arm, now covered by his jacket. "I saw your tattoo. Hopi, isn't it? The crow mother?"

"Very good. Yeah, Mom was Hopi. Annie and I got the tattoos after she died."

He went quiet, then snapped out of it and tugged his jacket sleeve up to give me a better look. It was a gorgeous tattoo. Before he pulled the sleeve down, I touched the cat's-eye bracelet.

"I like that," I said. "From a girlfriend?"

"Looks like something a girl would give a guy? Right idea, wrong person. It was from my mom. Last gift before she died." Again that quiet grief threatened to fall. Again he shook it off. "Anyway, so, yes, Mom was Native and my father was, apparently, Latino. So kids would try to get me to commit their criminal acts for them, either figuring I'm a dumb Indian who needed money for booze or a dumb Mexican who needed it for dope. Either way, they were sure I was dumb enough to do something illegal." A pause, then a crooked smile. "And, apparently, they were right."

Another minute of silence. The question was hanging

there: *What did you do?* Instead I said, "Are you . . . okay?"

"You mean, are we in danger of federal marshals barreling through the woods with a warrant for my arrest? Nah. It wasn't like that. I just . . . After our mom died, we didn't have as much money as she thought we did, because Annie and I had sneaked into her savings to get stuff for her. Medicine, food she liked, whatever. It wasn't bad at first. Annie was working. Two jobs sometimes, and selling her sculptures on the side. Mom was a carver, and Annie got the artistic genes. I wanted to quit school and work, so she could concentrate on her art, but she wouldn't let me. She helped me get a part-time job, though, so I felt better about it."

I thought of the girl I'd met. Tried to imagine her as the big sister who'd dragged her brother away from pot-smoking friends, wouldn't let him quit school, took care of him. It sounded like he was talking about a completely different person. I guess, in some ways, he was.

"And then the accident happened," I said.

"Yeah. The damage . . . it took a while to develop. At first Annie could work, but then, not so much. She's just . . . she's not interested in stuff like that anymore. Out here, she'd be happy to wander around the woods all day, find a stream when she's thirsty, eat berries when she's hungry, nap when she's tired."

"So you needed money."

He nodded and looked out over the forest. "Annie knew

we needed money. She still understood that. She met these guys and they offered her some, and the old Annie—she would have told them to go to hell, but she's not like that anymore and . . ." He kept his gaze straight ahead, face hard. "I got there just in time, and I—I didn't want to ever have to worry about that again. So there were these other guys, drug guys. A buddy of mine was a runner for them. I got him talking, found out they were doing a deal and had money to pay for it, so I . . ."

"Helped yourself."

"Yeah. Seemed easy. And it was. Only I found out later why it was so easy—because those guys were connected and no one else was stupid enough to rip them off. Until I came along." He smiled, but it faltered and finally fell. "And, having won thirty minutes of your time, I think I just gave you thirty minutes of reasons to run the other way as fast as you can."

"I don't run away."

He looked at me, startled, and what I saw in his eyes was so raw that my breath caught and all I could do was sit there, staring at him, that weird floating feeling trickling through my veins.

"That wasn't what I meant to talk about," he said, his voice low. "I really wanted to impress you, Maya."

"You did."

I leaned forward and kissed him. His eyes widened, then

his lips parted and he kissed me back, mouth warm and firm against mine and that floating feeling washed over me and through me, and it was so amazing that when it ended, I just stayed there, my face so close to his I could feel his breath, see those incredible amber eyes, and that was *all* I could see, all I *wanted* to see.

We hung there, face-to-face, just staring, then he said, "Yes?" and I said, "Yes," and he kissed me again, and it was no awkward, hesitant, first-date kiss. It started at third date, deep and hungry, bodies colliding, and I'd like to say he started it but I honestly wasn't sure.

This tiny voice in my head screamed "Slow down!" but it was so small and so faint that I could barely hear it and I didn't want to. All I felt was Rafe's mouth on mine, his arms around me, his body against me, and I didn't care about anything else. It was like jumping from a cliff, a terrifying, exhilarating, mind-blowing rush, and I didn't want it to end, didn't care where it led, only wanted to follow.

I could feel his heart beating, and I could hear it, pounding. I even swore I could smell him, just him. The world seemed to spin and fade, and I drifted in and out, and that voice kept saying that something was wrong, something was very wrong, but I didn't care.

One minute we were sitting up, making out. The next we were lying on the roof, and I was on top of him, and I didn't know how I got there. I was kissing him and then, all of a sudden, I wasn't. He was holding my face in his hands, poised above his, as he panted softly, his pupils so huge I could drown in them.

"Hate to ask," he said, struggling for breath. "How much did you drink?"

"Nothing. Just Coke."

"Oh."

He held me there another moment, searching my gaze, his breath coming in soft puffs, fingers in my hair, looking like he was struggling to hold me there, away from him. I strained against his hands, and he said, "Okay," hesitantly, like he wasn't sure it was okay. Then he kissed me again deep and hard, like he didn't care if it was okay.

Only it wasn't the same now. His hesitation kept playing in my head, and that little voice got louder until finally I heard myself saying it aloud, "Something's wrong."

"It's all right," he murmured. "I won't try anything. Just this, okay?" His mouth lowered to mine. "Just this."

He kissed me, and I realized he was on top of me now and I didn't remember that happening. I pulled away, saying louder, "Something's wrong." He blinked, hard, like he was clearing his head, and I was suddenly really aware of him, on top of me, holding me down and I panicked, struggling up so fast my elbow caught him in the chin, and he fell back.

I looked around. Everything was hazy. I struggled to my feet, blinking hard, feeling like I'd just stepped off a merry-go-round.

"Maya?"

Rafe's voice seemed distant and distorted and I said again, "Something's wrong," but the words came out mumbled and thick.

I looked down at my empty Coke glass. I remembered Rafe handing it to me at the sofa. Remembered him offering to carry it.

"Oh God," I whispered.

He stepped toward me. I stumbled back, and he lunged to grab me, calling "Maya!" as I scrambled down the roof. The world kept spinning and I couldn't focus, couldn't think, could only see Rafe coming at me, lips parted in words I didn't hear. I inched back until I was at the edge. Then I crouched and jumped and as I did, I realized what I'd done, saw the ground rushing up and then—

Thump. I landed in a crouch, gasping as pain slammed through my legs. I blinked hard, certain I was hallucinating. I couldn't possibly have leaped off a two-story roof and landed on my feet. I heard a shout and saw Rafe dangling over the edge. He hit the ground and turned toward me. My heart jammed into my throat and I stumbled back, saying, "No!"

"Maya?"

Sam jogged around the corner. I stepped toward her, but my legs wouldn't hold me and I went down, landing on all fours, hearing the thump of running feet from both sides, Rafe and Sam.

"Stay away from her," Sam said, then yelled. "Daniel!"

"I didn't—" Rafe began. "Whatever happened, it wasn't me."

More running footsteps. Heavy. Daniel.

"Maya?" The footsteps picked up speed. "What's going—?"

"My drink," I whispered as Sam crouched beside me. "Something in my drink."

A bone-crunching crack. Then a thump as Rafe hit the ground beside me. I scrambled back. Nicole helped me to my feet, and pulled me out of the way as Daniel bore down on Rafe, his face livid.

"Get up," Daniel said.

Rafe stayed down, lifting his hands. "If Maya's been dosed—"

"If? *If*? Are you saying she's faking it?"

"No. Obviously something happened. I mean maybe her drink was spiked. But I had nothing to—"

"Get up!"

Rafe didn't. Sam stepped behind him, blocking his escape.

"Go ahead," Sam said. "Stomp him."

Daniel continued forward. "Get up, you son of a bitch."

"Screw that," Sam said. "Hell, if he does get up, I'll hold him for you."

"Stay out of this," Daniel said.

"Just leave him," I said, my voice still thick, the

world still tilting. "Let him go."

Daniel didn't seem to hear me and kept bearing down on Rafe. I staggered forward to stop him, but now it was Corey taking my arm and pulling me back.

"Daniel," I said. "Don't—"

Branches crackled. A blur burst from the forest. It charged so fast all I could see was that blur. Then it jumped between Rafe and Daniel.

A cougar. Not Marv or the new tom, but a female, planted between them, facing Daniel, lips curled back. She let out a snarl. I jerked forward. Corey caught me and held my arm.

I'm not exactly sure what happened next. I faded again, everything sliding in and out of focus, no matter how hard I struggled to stay alert, heart pounding at seeing that cougar so close to Daniel, the house and safety too far away.

I remember the cat snarling. I remember Daniel backing up. And I remember Rafe, lying on the ground, saying, "It's okay. It's okay," over and over in this calm voice, completely calm, like he didn't even *see* the cougar. The cat backed up, getting closer and closer to Rafe and he didn't move a muscle and I remember thinking, "She's protecting him," which was crazy, but that's what I thought.

Then the world blinked, and my legs gave way. As I went down, Daniel ran toward me, and I opened my mouth to shout for him not to turn his back on the cat, but she was already twisting away.

I don't remember anything else.

No, that's a lie. I remember one more thing. I remember the cougar turning away and I remember what I saw on her flank. A dark patch of fur in the shape of a paw print.

FİFTEEN

I BLACKED OUT AFTER that. I came to a few minutes later, but the rest of the night is fuzzy. I couldn't seem to stay awake and kept drifting off.

Someone had dosed my drink, and everyone was sure who'd done it. Everyone except me.

I kept replaying the evening. Rafe *had* handled my drink. More than once. He'd been the one to suggest we go someplace quieter to talk. He'd been the one to suggest we go outside. So he was the obvious choice.

Except that once he'd gotten me alone, he'd done what he promised—talked. I'd kissed him first. He'd made sure it was okay before continuing. He'd asked how much I'd had to drink. He'd hesitated. And maybe that was all part of the setup, so later if I regretted what happened, he could say that I'd taken the lead and he'd just followed.

Maybe he did do it. I wasn't ruling that out. I wasn't sure I believed it, though, certainly not enough to call Chief Carling, which is what Daniel wanted to do.

It was strange. I remember sitting there, talking, but it was like I was watching someone else saying things I'd never say. I didn't defend Rafe. But I wouldn't let them call Chief Carling or even my parents. If it had been anyone else sitting there, I'd have been the one leading the charge, insisting the victim take action.

Two years ago, a summer guy—a grown-up—had cornered Nicole in the woods, and if Serena and I hadn't found them and scared the guy off, I'm sure she would have been raped. She hadn't wanted to tell anyone. I'd talked her into it, then escorted her to Chief Carling and sat with her while she told her parents. Now, having her there, listening to me refuse to report it . . . It felt wrong.

But reporting it felt even more wrong. If I accused Rafe, they'd find out about Annie. If Rafe *had* done it, then I would have to tell someone, because he might do it again to another girl, but if I wasn't totally sure it was him . . . I couldn't say anything unless I was sure.

I was in no condition to make a decision. I had witnesses, so it wouldn't matter much if I reported it now or in the morning. I wanted the night to think about it. Daniel wasn't happy with that, but he finally agreed, and I called my dad to come and get me.

॰॰   ॰॰   ॰॰

I dreamed of the cougar. I kept seeing that mark on her flank. Kept seeing her in front of me, looking at me, and I was mesmerized by her eyes. Then it wasn't her eyes at all, but Rafe's, looking into mine as I kissed him. Then we weren't kissing, we were scaling the climbing wall. Then it wasn't the wall, but the roof, climbing across the roof, jumping off the roof, flowing back and forth, the roof and the wall, flipping between them until both were gone and I was back in the dream of two nights before, that amazing run.

This time, I wasn't alone. Rafe was beside me, and as we ran, a subtle shift brought me lower and lower, until I wasn't running on two legs but on four. I looked down at the ground blurring beneath me. Beneath my paws.

I jolted upright in bed, gasping for air, heart pounding so hard it hurt.

Yee naaldlooshii.

I knew that word. As I sat there, doubled over, panting and shaking, I kept hearing it over and over, and I *felt* that I knew it. Somewhere, somehow I knew it.

When I caught my breath, the feeling passed. Of course I knew it. I'd heard the old woman say it and hadn't been able to forget it.

Look it up.

How?

My gaze shifted to my laptop. I shook my head. There's a reason the U.S. Army had used Navajo for codes in WWII— because it was almost impossible for anyone to decipher. I knew about a half-dozen words and struggled with them. I had no chance of spelling this one right.

Try.

"No."

I said the word aloud, startling myself. My heart pounded again. My hands trembled as I clutched the covers.

Afraid of a word? How stupid was that? I was just stressed out from the party and the dreams, and it was too late to fire up my laptop. Our connection out here sucked anyway. I would look it up tomorrow, at Daniel's place. Having him there would help put it in perspective.

That settled, I laid back down and fell back to sleep . . . right into a fresh dream.

This time, I saw the cougar again, the one with the mark on her flank. Only she was chasing me. I ran through the forest, trying to get away. She was right behind me. Then I heard Rafe, his voice echoing through the forest.

"Maya, stop!" he shouted. "Don't run. It won't help."

I kept running.

"Please!" he yelled. "You're only making it worse. Stop running away. You can't run away. Accept it."

Accept *death*? Never. I ignored him and ran until my lungs burned, and still the cat was right on my heels, one leap away from ending my life.

Finally I saw my salvation. The lake. As I raced up the rocks, Rafe shouted to me again. I saw him, across the water, motioning and yelling.

"Maya, don't! Please. Listen to me. Whatever you do, don't jump—"

I jumped.

Icy water closed over my head. I pushed to the surface and swam, not stopping until I was in the middle of the lake. Treading water, I looked around. The cougar was back on the rocks, pacing and yowling. Rafe was on the other side.

"Get out, Maya! This doesn't help. It isn't safe."

I ignored him. This *was* safe. This—

Fingers closed around my ankle and yanked me under. I fought, but a hand grabbed my other leg and I kept going down, gulping water as I screamed. I could hear Rafe's voice, faint and distorted as he shouted, and I could hear the cat screaming, her cries blending with my own.

As the hands pulled me down, I realized what he'd been telling me. Stop running away from the truth. The truth that followed me everywhere, like the cat—

I woke up gasping and sputtering, still feeling icy water filling my lungs. I hacked and coughed until Mom came to my door. I told her not to worry, I was fine—and huddled under the covers until she was convinced.

I threw off the blanket as soon as she was gone and lay there, nightshirt pulled up around my midriff as I panted. Even the remembered chill of the water wasn't enough to cool me as my heart raced.

A dream. Just a crazy dream, merging the experiences

of the night—the cougar and Rafe—with the issue I'd been trying to avoid all day. Serena's death.

When she died, I told myself I'd find out what happened. In the year since, what had I done? Sat around and grieved, and waited for the answer to drop from the skies.

Her death had been ruled an accident. No one was looking for another explanation. No one *wanted* to look. Did that include me? Was that what the dream really meant—my conscience telling me to stop hiding from her death and do something about it?

Brendan said Mina Lee had asked about Serena. She must really have checked out Salmon Creek to know a teenager died here last year. If she was investigating the medical research, did she think it had something to do with Serena? That seemed like grasping at straws, but it might mean she'd looked at the circumstances surrounding Serena's death and seen possibilities no one here had.

I needed to talk to her. I wished I hadn't given away her card. Still, it wasn't like she'd refuse to speak to me. I just needed to find out where she was staying. I'm sure Corey could get that from his mother.

With that solved, I relaxed enough to drift off and I stayed asleep until past ten. Even on Sundays I can't do the sleep-until-noon thing because of the animals. I'm usually up before nine, but my alarm didn't ring, which meant my dad must have turned it off and fed the animals for me.

I took my time getting up. Although I'd decided what to do about Serena, I hadn't made any decisions about being dosed last night. I should tell my parents. If anyone else was in my situation, I'd insist on it, badger her until she did, but if I told them and said "I don't know who did it," then I couldn't come back later and accuse Rafe.

But how was I going to decide whether or not to accuse Rafe? Break into his cabin and search for drugs? He wasn't stupid. He'd have gotten rid of the evidence.

I thought about it while I showered and dressed, and I was still thinking about it when Mom knocked.

"Someone's here to see you," she said as she came in.

I hoped it was Daniel—I really needed to talk to him. But Mom wouldn't call Daniel "someone."

I remembered what Brendan said about Mina Lee wanting to talk to me. Please let it be her. "Is it a woman?"

"No. It's the new boy. Rafael."

Mom said it slowly and had this weird look on her face, kind of concerned, and I wondered if she'd heard that I invited him to the party. I wouldn't doubt it, the way gossip travels in this town. If she had, then she'd have thought it was just me leading the charge to make the new guy feel welcome. But if he was here on a Sunday morning, maybe it was more than that, and if so, why hadn't I mentioned him?

All I could think was "Rafe's here. Oh God, what is he doing here?" My heart pounded and it felt like terror but it felt like excitement, too, and that scared me even more.

"Maya?"

"I suppose it's about the party." Which was the truth. "Just give me a sec to brush my hair."

SIXTEEN

MOM SAYS THAT WHEN she was little, her grandmother used to brush her hair a hundred strokes to make it shine. Well, if that works, my hair must have been blinding by the time I finally got downstairs.

I wished I was someone who could say "I'm not feeling well" and hide out in my room. But I had to face him.

As I went down those steps, I was angry and confused, and outraged that he'd show up at my house. But it wasn't anger making my heart race. I kept thinking of the dreams and thinking of last night and thinking of how he'd made me feel. That scared me because I needed to be totally objective about this.

I found Rafe in the living room, looking out the front windows, hands stuffed in his pockets. His hair looked like it'd been finger combed and could probably use a wash. He wore the same clothes as last night.

He didn't do it. He isn't guilty.

No, I just didn't *want* him to be guilty.

I stepped into the room. His head tilted, as if he'd heard me and he turned. He saw me there and he stepped forward with a spark in his eyes that made my insides flip and an inner voice scream, "I can't do this!"

The smile disappeared fast, gaze dipping as he mumbled, "Hey."

"You wanted to talk to me?"

He nodded. "Can we . . . ?" He looked around and I knew he was going to say "Can we go somewhere and talk?" then realized how that would sound, under the circumstances.

"We can step out on the porch," I said, then called. "Mom? We're on the back deck. Is Dad out there?"

"Somewhere."

Rafe nodded. He got the message. When I whistled for Kenjii after we went outside, I was probably overdoing it, but I wasn't taking any chances.

We sat on the edge of the deck. Kenjii tried positioning herself between us, but that was a bit much so I nudged her down. She sat at my feet, watching Rafe. I almost hoped she'd growl at him or give some sign that she distrusted him. She didn't.

I was about to speak when a yowl cut me off. Rafe jumped. I looked up to see Fitz in his favorite tree, staring at me, yellow eyes slitted, like I'd been the one who'd put him up there.

"Hold on," I said.

I walked toward the tree. Seeing Fitz, Rafe swung into my path.

"That's a lynx," he said.

"No, it's a bobcat, and he's going to keep yowling until I get him out of that tree."

"Get him out?" Rafe said. "I really don't think—"

"It's okay."

I grabbed the lowest branch and swung up. When I glanced down, Rafe had his hands on the limb, like he was ready to follow.

"Stand back," I said. "He doesn't like strangers."

"So he's a pet?"

"I don't keep wild animals." Which was true.

Rafe stood there, gripping the tree. "Maya, I really don't think—"

"I'm serious. Unless you like the ripped look for that jacket, get out of the way."

I shimmied along Fitz's branch. Rafe climbed onto the bottom limb and stood.

"Maya, seriously. Don't—"

I grabbed Fitz. He harrumphed, giving me hell for taking so long. I hefted him up, which is not easy with a twenty-pound cat. Then, holding him by the scruff of the neck, I lowered him toward Rafe. Fitz's three legs shot out, claws extended. He spit and snarled.

Rafe backed up fast. Then he looked at me, crouched on

the branch, holding a spitting, three-legged bobcat. And he laughed. Laughed so loud that Fitz let out a chirp of surprise and started struggling. I leaned down as far as I could and dropped him onto Rafe's branch.

The branch dipped and Rafe nearly went flying.

He motioned at the stump of Fitz's rear leg. "Former patient?"

I nodded. "He can climb up fine, but getting down is another story. My mom designed a tree house for him. Once it's made, I can stop doing this."

Fitz jumped down and the branch bobbed again. Rafe heaved himself up, face coming nearly to mine, then he stopped and he looked at me, and it was like the last twelve hours vanished and we were back on that roof, before everything happened, staring at each other, my heart tripping.

He smiled, and it was that crooked, sexy-shy smile again, and I forgot about backing out of the way. Forgot why I *should* back out of the way. He lifted himself up until we were face-to-face, then closed his eyes and leaned forward. That's when my brain clicked on and I jerked back fast enough to make the branch dip.

His eyes flew open, and he saw the look on my face and his gaze dropped as he mumbled. "Sorry."

I lowered myself to stand beside him, just out of reach.

"I didn't do it," he said.

"And you'd admit it if you did?"

He swore. I glanced at the house. If my mom looked out,

she could see us. If I screamed, she'd hear me. If we talked, though, she couldn't listen in. Good.

I sat beside him, legs dangling.

"That's the problem, isn't it?" he said, sitting, too. "I can say it wasn't me, but I'd say that even if it was. I've been up all night, trying to figure out how I can prove it. I can't. I had access to your drink. I wanted to be alone with you. Whatever that drug did to you, I'm the one who benefited. No one else."

I couldn't argue with that, but he looked at me, like he was hoping I would.

"I wouldn't do that, Maya. Sure, you don't know me that well, but you said it yourself—I get a girl and I back off before I can collect the payoff. I don't need to dose girls." He stopped. "That sounded unbelievably arrogant, didn't it?"

"Kinda. But if you're trying to say that only guys who can't get girls drug them, you're wrong. It's not always about that. You're new in town. You're trying to fit in, make an impression. You've heard I don't go with local guys. You've probably heard I don't make out with near strangers at parties. Maybe that's the impression you wanted to make. The cool stud who can get any girl."

"Sure, if I want Daniel making an impression of my head in the nearest wall. If he caught me kissing you and he wasn't convinced it was your idea, then I'm on his blacklist. Which means I'm on his friends' blacklist. I'm on your friends' blacklist. I'm on the blacklist of everyone who doesn't want to piss off you, him, or your friends. In this town, that seriously limits my social circle."

He had a point.

He continued, "Yeah, I've done dumb things, as I admitted last night, but think about it—if I dosed you and got you alone, would I have started rambling on like I did?"

Another good point.

"Yes, I know your reputation," he continued. "So when we started heating up, I knew something might be wrong. That's why I asked if you'd been drinking. Even when you said no, I wasn't sure, but, hell, of course I *wanted* to think you were just that into me."

Definitely a valid point.

"And, let's be totally honest. If a guy gives a girl a roofie, he's not looking for a make-out session. If my hands weren't wandering by that point, they weren't going to."

He shifted on the branch. "I wish I could prove I didn't do it, Maya, but I can't. I can only say that it doesn't make sense. I'd risk getting the crap beat out of me by Daniel, becoming a total social outcast, and maybe even getting arrested and losing Annie. As much as I like you, one make-out session isn't worth that. And I *do* like you, meaning one make-out session definitely isn't worth that if it'd be the last one I'd ever get."

He looked at me, like he was expecting to see something in my face, and when he didn't, he frowned. "I do like you, Maya. You get that, right?"

"Why?"

His frown deepened. "Why what?"

"Why do you like me?"

He laughed. "Do you want a list? Smart, pretty, funny—"

"That's not what I—" I shook my head. "Never mind."

It sounded like I was fishing for compliments. But something about this bugged me. Hot new guy comes to school, checks out all the girls and decides I'm the one he really, really wants. It was the ultimate fantasy, which meant there had to be an angle I was missing.

Maybe it was as simple as him wanting the girl who didn't want him. I didn't know. But it bothered me. And what bothered me even more was this little part inside me that didn't really care *why* he was interested, was just happy that he was.

I jumped out of the tree and got two steps away before Rafe followed, catching my sleeve and saying, "Maya?"

I turned.

"You don't believe me, do you?" he said. "About the dosing."

"No, I do."

He grinned that mesmerizing grin and when I didn't move, his fingers wrapped around my elbow and he tugged me behind the tree. Before I knew it, my back was against the trunk, and he was in front of me, lips coming down to mine.

I sidestepped fast. "No."

His lips quirked in a smile. "What? You want dinner and a movie first now?"

"You think that's funny?"

The smile vanished. "Course not. I just—"

"Think we should be able to jump back to where we were, because maybe I was dosed and maybe we went a little further and a lot faster than I like, but it's still where I *wanted* to go. That's what you think happened, isn't it? I wanted it—I just couldn't admit it."

He stepped back and ran his hands through his hair, and I knew that's exactly what he thought. But he said, "I don't know what happened."

"Neither do I. That's my point. I have no idea how much of it was me, and how much of it was the drug."

He stepped in front of me again, hands sliding around my waist. "Let's find out, then."

I backed out of his grasp. "You aren't getting this, are you?"

"No, Maya, I'm not."

"Then I think you should leave."

He sighed. "Now what did I do?"

"Nothing. I just . . . I need you to back off." I softened my tone. "I'll talk to you at school tomorrow, okay?"

"But I'm here now."

"What? Are you on a schedule?"

"Course not." He stepped toward me. "I like you, Maya."

"You keep saying that."

"And it's a problem? I don't get this. Do you expect me to just wait until you figure things out?"

"No. I expect that if you're interested enough, you'll wait; and if you aren't, you won't. Your choice."

"And it doesn't matter to you one way or the other."

"I never said—"

He waved off my protest, and strode into the forest. The crackle of twigs continued until his footsteps receded into silence.

I stood there, staring after him long after he'd gone. Finally Kenjii came over and nudged my hand. I patted her head and walked back toward the house.

"Maya?" Mom called as she stepped onto the porch and looked around. "Is Rafael still here?"

I shook my head. She squinted, trying to see my expression, but I stayed in the shadow of Fitz's tree.

"You should come in and have some breakfast," she said.

"I'm not hungry," I said. "I'll check on the animals."

SEVENTEEN

I N THE EXCITEMENT OF the cougar attack, then my party, I'd forgotten about the marten, but when I went back into the shed that morning, I couldn't deny that the wound was completely healed. Even the scar was white now, as if the injury were weeks old.

The right thing to do would be to examine her leg, then let her go. But after what happened the last time, it took ten minutes before I could bring myself to touch the marten. When I did, nothing happened. I checked the wound and picked out the stitches. The marten just lay there, calm and patient.

I don't release animals here. That encourages them to stick around. Even with Fitz, I'd let him go on the other side of the park. But he'd found his way back, and after a second relocation failed, I'd given up.

I had a cat carrier for transporting the small animals to

their release points. I made sure the cage had been cleaned out last time—I'd learned my lesson after having nearly given a rabbit heart failure by putting it in a carrier filled with fox hair.

Before I reached into the marten's cage, I was so busy trying to mentally distract myself that I'd forgotten to glove up. As my hands went around the marten, the room swirled into darkness. I smelled damp earth and wet grass. Heard the scream of an eagle and my heart beat faster, legs pumping as I ran, the grass lashing me. Then—too late—I smelled it. Humans. I tried to veer for a tree, but something hit my back leg, pain—

I jolted from the vision. As I stumbled back, I looked around frantically, terrified that I'd dropped the marten. But she was still in her cage, head cocked in confusion.

The door opened and a voice said, "Hey."

I spun. Daniel stood silhouetted in the doorway. I glanced at the carrier, then the marten. I waved Daniel back out and followed.

We walked to the porch, where Fitz lay stretched out on the railing. He hopped off and strolled over as we sat down. I said nothing for a moment, my mind still back in the shed.

Daniel cleared his throat. "Your mom said Rafe was here. Proclaiming his innocence?"

"I think he's right."

I tensed for the outrage. Daniel just waited for me to explain. I didn't detail every point but emphasized what I figured would be the best evidence to prove it to a teenage guy—that Rafe hadn't tried anything more than kissing.

"*Nothing?*" Daniel said.

I shook my head. "It was just kissing. And he asked if I'd been drinking. If I'd said yes, I think he would have stopped."

Again, I waited for the outburst. Was I crazy? *Clearly* Rafe was the one who dosed me.

Daniel nodded. "Yeah, I think you're right. I don't like the guy, but . . ." He shrugged.

"Your bad-guy radar isn't pinging?"

"No," he said, almost regretfully. "I'm not convinced he did this either, and if you agree . . ."

"I do. But who else could it have been?"

"Well, I might have an idea, which is why I'm willing to give Rafe the benefit of the doubt, and part of the reason I came over. Nicole stopped by this morning to see if I needed help cleaning up. I think what she really wanted was to tell me something about last night. When I was in the kitchen, getting you a drink, Hayley was hanging around. She could have slipped something in while I was grabbing my beer."

"Nicole said that?"

"Not in so many words. I had to really work to even get her to admit she'd seen Hayley near your drink."

"Didn't want to tattle on her friend."

"Exactly. But when she got to thinking about it, it made sense. Hayley works at the clinic with Nicole sometimes, and she says Hayley has sneaked into the drug room before.

Nicole figured she's been getting Ritalin or Demerol, so she kept her mouth shut."

"Only there are other drugs in there, too. Hayley's jealous because Rafe's taking an interest in me. Rafe left the party, so she thought she could slip roofies in my drink and I'd hook up with Brendan. She could tell Rafe about it, and he'd change his mind about me."

"Then Rafe shows up again and it backfires."

I nodded. "Hayley *is* the most likely suspect, but it's not enough to tell Chief Carling. I just need to keep my eye on her."

"We both will. I'll tell the guys, too."

"Good. That's settled." I stood. "Let's grab some food. Then I need to talk to you."

Daniel got up. "About you and Rafe . . ."

"There is no me and Rafe. Surprise, surprise."

I turned to go, but Daniel snagged my arm.

"You liked him," he said.

I exhaled. "Honestly, I don't know. Yes, I invited him to the party, and I'm sorry about not warning you—"

"It was an open invitation. Everyone knew that. Sure, I was surprised. I didn't think you were interested in him."

"I wasn't. Not that way. Just . . . something happened at school Friday and—" I shook my head. "The less I think about Rafe, the better, so let's eat. Then afterward—"

I want to talk about Serena. About how she died. I need answers.

The words formed in my head, but wouldn't complete the journey out. Was bringing Daniel in on this the right thing to do? It was the natural thing—he was my best friend and I could use his help. But was it selfish? What if he was happy with the answers he had, if dragging him into some amateur investigation would only remind him of her and—

"Maya?"

"S-sorry. I just . . ." I shook my head. "Never mind."

"You wanted to say something."

"It's okay. I changed my mind."

He pulled back, barely a fraction, but I knew he was hurt.

Why was it so easy to do that these days? For both of us. He wouldn't want to talk about something, and I'd be hurt. Or I wouldn't want to talk about something, and he'd be hurt. Or he'd invite me along with the guys, and I'd analyze every nuance of his voice and expression, worrying that he really didn't want me along, was only being polite. Or, like the other night, I'd want to comfort him, but would be worried about how he might misinterpret that.

It never used to be like this. Maybe that's just part of having a close friend of the opposite sex. As a kid, you don't think anything about it. Then you're a teenager, and you can't help but think about it.

I don't want to lose our friendship just because we're older now, but sometimes I swear I can feel Serena there and—

"Something happened in the shed." I blurted it without thinking.

"What?"

I laughed uneasily. "That didn't sound good, did it? Cue the ominous music." I shook my head. "Never mind. It was silly."

I tried to walk away, but he caught my arm and when he turned me to face him, his expression sent a chill slithering down my spine. It was concern, yes. But behind that, rage simmered.

"Was it Rafe?" he said, his voice so low it was almost a growl. "Did he try something this morning?"

"What? No." When he didn't look convinced, I said, "Come on, Daniel. If he tried anything, do you really think I'd protect him? Give me a little credit, please."

"Sorry." He released my arm and the anger faded. Then he blinked. "The shed. Do you mean like what happened the other day? When you passed out?"

I hesitated. Part of me wished I'd never mentioned it, but a bigger part was glad I had. I told him everything.

When I finished, I waited for his reaction. Was I afraid he'd laugh? Worry about my mental health? I knew better. I knew Daniel.

He listened without interrupting. Then he quietly processed it, sitting beside me on the deck, ignoring Kenjii and Fitz as they approached.

"Okay, the healing thing seems weird," he said finally. "But I think it seems weirder to you than it does to me. You're good at healing animals. Who knows why? If you're getting even better at it, well, it's not like you're *hurting* them. It bugs you, though, so I say hold off on releasing the marten. We'll take it to Dr. Hajek and see if there's a scientific explanation. Chances are she'll just say the same thing she always does. Some people have a gift. You obviously do."

He stretched his legs, getting comfortable now. "Same goes for the visions or whatever they are. You're more freaked out about them than I am." He paused. "Well, no. I'm a little freaked out, but only because they seem to come with a sudden lack of consciousness, which could be dangerous. Remember what I said about getting your parents in there with you? That goes double now."

"And otherwise I should just ignore the fact that every time I touch an animal, we do a body swap?"

"Not a body swap. You're seeing memories, I think."

"You know what I mean."

He stretched out farther, leaning back on the porch now, face gathered in thought. It was a minute before he spoke again. "It could be temporary. Maybe stress related. If it's not, I guess you'll have to learn to handle it. It could be part of the healing power. Imagine how helpful it would be if you actually saw what happened to the animals when they were hurt."

"Uh-huh. Visions. That strikes you as just a normal extension of a healing gift."

He sighed. "I don't know what you want me to say, Maya. Does it seem strange? Yes. Do I think you're going nuts? No.

Maybe I should be taking this more seriously but . . ." He shrugged. "It doesn't seem serious."

He meant it didn't *feel* serious. That was what mattered for Daniel. What did his gut instinct tell him? He wouldn't say that, because it sounded all touchy-feely, but it was the way he processed things. Healing an animal in less than a week and seeing visions of its trauma seemed seriously weird to me. If it didn't to him, though, how could I argue with that?

"Like I said, the passing-out part does worry me," he continued. "You might want to visit the clinic about that."

"Just don't mention the visions if I want to stay off Dr. Fodor's couch."

"Exactly. Now, let's get some food. There's something I need to talk to *you* about."

EİGHTEEN

I'M PERFECTLY CAPABLE OF cooking lunch. Well, making sandwiches or popping something in the microwave. Daniel could do the whole operating a stove and mixing ingredients routine. Mom insisted on making lunch, though. Dad insisted on supervising, asking me to set the table, pour drinks, et cetera.

Normally, not their style, but they were worried about me and knew I didn't react well to hearing "I'm worried." They were using meal prep as an excuse to make me hang out in the kitchen with them.

The conclusion, I believe, was that I might have been upset by something to do with Rafe or the party, but I was fine now. Well, maybe not completely fine, but enough for them to back off, which they did, letting us take our lunch outside.

"I found this shoved under our front door this morning," Daniel said after we settled on the porch.

It was Mina Lee's business card. My pulse sped up. I forced myself to sound casual as I asked, "You think we should meet? Figure out what she wants?" I paused, as if considering it. "That's not a bad idea."

"Turn it over."

I did. On the back, she'd written the name of a library in Nanaimo, a Dewey decimal reference code, and a page number.

"Huh?" I said.

"Exactly. I called her. No answer. Called again on the way here and her phone's either turned off or she's out of range."

"Which isn't that strange out here. We should call Corcy. See where she's staying."

"He already told me. She's at the Braun place."

I stood. "Well, then, let's go talk to her."

Daniel cast a pointed look at my grilled flatbread. Then he glanced up, squinting as if he were avoiding the sun, but I knew he wasn't. He was studying me, just like my parents had done.

I pretended to stretch, then sat back down. "After we finish eating, I mean."

He wasn't fooled, but he let it slide. Another bite of his sandwich, then he nodded. "I think we *should* talk to her. First, though, I want to check out that book."

"Drive all the way into Nanaimo to find a book, when

she's staying ten minutes away?"

He shrugged. "I'm curious. Got a couple of things to pick up in the city, too. We can go out for dinner, make a day of it."

"Dinner?"

"Sure." He peered at me again. "No rush, right? She's not going anywhere. And it's not like we have anything important to ask her."

"No. Course not. I just . . . I'm not really in a city mood today. After last night, I kind of wanted to hang out in the park, recharge my batteries. You know me."

He nodded. "Sure. You do that. I'll go to Nanaimo, then talk to Ms. Lee after, and fill you in on everything tomorrow."

I hesitated. I could do an end run around him and hike to the Braun place while he was in Nanaimo. Maybe it was a conversation better conducted when he wasn't around anyway. He'd find out, though, when he went to see her. Then I'd have to explain why I'd gone to see her, plus admit I'd done it behind his back.

"Actually, can I change my mind?" I said. "A trip to the city might be the best thing for me." A thought struck. "I'd like to go back to that tattoo studio, too, see if I can talk to the old woman. I should just forget it, but it's going to keep bothering me until I find out what she was talking about."

"All right. Eat and we'll go."

In British Columbia teens can get their learner's permit at sixteen. With that they can drive—as long as they have an L magnet on the vehicle and a licensed driver in the passenger seat. At seventeen, they can move up to their novice license, which needs an N magnet but no other driver.

Daniel was still sixteen, which meant he shouldn't be driving without an adult. He did, obviously. It's not like Chief Carling was going to pull him over. That's the way it worked in Salmon Creek—prove you're responsible and no one cares if you're driving early or having a beer in the backyard.

When we went into the city, though, Daniel borrowed Brendan's N magnet for his truck. Totally illegal. That didn't bother Daniel, which might seem weird, considering he's normally the one making sure the rest of us stay in line. But his rules weren't always the same as the ones the authorities laid out. Which is probably why he'd make a better lawyer than a cop.

When it came to driving, he just took extra care. He figured that made him a lot safer than the twenty-year-olds whipping past in their jacked-up trucks; and since my parents were fine with him taking me to Nanaimo, they obviously agreed.

When we got to the tattoo studio, it was closed. I should have figured that, being a Sunday and off prime tourist season. I peered through the window at the dark interior.

"You really wanted to talk to her, didn't you?" Daniel said.

"I know it sounds crazy. It's just—"

"You want answers. Let's get them."

He waved for me to follow. There was a diner beside the tattoo studio and a café beside that. Lots of restaurants here, over half of them specializing in caffeine. It's the West Coast—we love our coffee shops.

He surveyed the two, then waved me to the café. He held the door for me and an elderly couple who were leaving, then followed me.

Inside, he scanned the customers and staff as if looking for someone he knew. Sizing them up. It was a knack he had, like picking out people who might be a threat. After a few seconds, he prodded me to an older woman behind the counter.

As soon as she saw him, she smiled, eyes crinkling, like he reminded her of her grandson or a cute boy she'd gone out with in school.

Daniel ordered a couple of muffins, then said, "We were just over at the tattoo place. We saw it was closed today."

She frowned. "You kids aren't thinking of getting one, are you? I know they're popular, but it's not something you should be doing at your age."

"No, nothing like that," Daniel said. "We were actually looking for the artist's aunt."

"They both live over the shop. Just go around back, look for the delivery sign, and head up the stairs. The apartment door is at the top."

꘍   ꘍   ꘍

Two minutes after Daniel knocked, Deena's aunt peeked out the window, saw me, and let the curtain fall. Daniel kept knocking, getting louder, until finally the woman yanked open the inside door, her hand darting out to lock the screen.

"What?" she said.

I'd rehearsed what I was going to say. Polite, respectful, deferential. When she locked that screen, though, the speech flew out of my head and I said, "What did you mean, calling me a witch?"

"Exactly what I said. Now go away." She started to close the door.

With one wrench on the screen door handle, Daniel snapped the lock. He yanked the door open and caught the inside door before the old woman could close it.

"We're not coming in," he said. "I just want you to answer my friend's question. You insulted her, and you owe her an explanation. She says you called her something else."

"*Yee naaldlooshii.*" The old woman's lip curled as she said it.

"What does it mean?" I asked.

The old woman snorted. "Why do you care? Obviously it won't mean anything to you. You don't know your language. You don't know your heritage. The Diné shunned you. Sent you away to be raised by strangers."

"She asked what the word means," Daniel said.

"And I said—"

"She asked what the word means."

Daniel's voice took on a rumbling tone he used when someone wouldn't listen to him. The old woman's gaze rose to his as if drawn there against her will.

They looked at each other for at least five seconds. Then she made a strange noise, deep in her throat, and when she spoke, she spit out the word, like she couldn't help herself.

"Skin-walker," she said. And slammed the door.

NINETEEN

W E WALKED TOWARD THE Harbourfront branch
library, just across the road and down the street
from the tattoo studio. A guy was playing his gui-
tar out front as tourists barreled past, eyes averted. I dropped
a toonie in his hat. Daniel did the same, the two-dollar coins
clinking in the empty hat.

We sat down. I took out my muffin from the café and got
one bite before Daniel said, "I take it you know what a skin-
walker is or we'd be in the library looking it up. And I take
it you're upset about it because you haven't said a word since
we left that apartment."

"Not upset. Just feeling dumb for not figuring it out on my
own. A skin-walker is a Navajo witch, which is exactly what
she called me. It's not a good witch. Or something they dress
up as for Halloween. For some, skin-walkers are really out

there, cursing people. The tattoo artist said her aunt used to live with the Navajo. A folklorist. She would have heard all the stories. At the time, I'm sure that's all they were, but now, with the dementia or whatever, she's confused and thinks they're real."

"Are skin-walkers a kind of shape-shifter? Like were-wolves?"

I nodded. "They're supposed to be able to take on different forms, usually coyotes and wolves."

"So this woman, who used to study those legends, knows you're Navajo, sees what looks like a paw-print birthmark, and thinks you're a skin-walker."

"I've never heard of them being marked, but maybe she has. A regional version of the legend. Anyway, I have my answer so I can stop worrying, which is good, because I have more than enough to worry about these days."

"You want to talk about it?"

"Not much to say. It's just a bunch of things hitting at once and it's like they're feeding on each other, making them all worse. The tattoo place problem. The cougar problem. The Rafe problem."

"You're really upset about him, aren't you?"

"I'm really *confused* about him. So let's talk about happier subjects. You said Nicole came over this morning." I bumped his shoulder and grinned. "I take it that means last night went well."

He stared down at his untouched muffin.

"Or not," I said.

He put the muffin back in the bag. "Yeah. It didn't. I mean, it was fine. We talked. We . . ." He shrugged. "I gave it a shot, but it's not going anywhere, Maya. I know you think I'm still hung up on Serena. I'm not." He glanced over. "I'm really not. I miss her and I wish to God I could have—"

His voice caught and he looked away. The bits of muffin in my stomach turned to lead pellets.

"It was me," I said. "I'm the one who saw her go under. I'm the one who could have saved her. If I'd brought Kenjii . . . If I'd learned to swim better . . . If I hadn't panicked, thinking I was drowning . . ."

"No," he said firmly. "Whatever happened out there, we did our best. I know you did and you know I did, and we're not going to get into it again. We're not. Okay?"

I tried to look away, but his gaze skewered me.

"I know you feel guilty and you know I do, but that has nothing to do with me dating again. It *doesn't*."

I nodded.

"I miss Serena and I wish she was still here, but even if she was, I'm not sure—" He swallowed hard. His jaw worked. Then he said, slowly, "It's not going to happen with Nicole, Maya. She's cute and she's nice, but that's . . ."

He shifted, rolling his shoulders. "I don't know how to say this without being cruel."

"Go ahead. It'd never get back to her. You know that."

He nodded. "With Nicole . . . cute and nice is all you get. There's nothing else there. The same reason you don't want her as a new best friend is the same reason I don't want her as a girlfriend. I know you think maybe that would be good for me—someone who won't demand a lot—but I'm okay." He looked at me. "It's you I'm worried about."

I turned away to toss my muffin in the trash. "I'm fine."

"I know why you want to talk to Mina Lee," he said. "You want to find out if she knows anything about Serena's death."

I stopped, hand still over the garbage can.

His voice dropped. "You want to know how she died. Why she died. You want answers."

I dropped the muffin. "I know it was probably a freak accident. I know I'll never get a *why*, because there isn't one. I know that this reporter almost certainly doesn't have any answers for me. I just want—" I faced him. "I *need* to ask."

He looked like he wanted to say something. Even opened his mouth. Then he snapped it shut and nodded. "Let's check out that book first, so we know what her message meant before we confront her."

Reference books were on the second floor of the library. We found the one Mina Lee put on the card and took it to my favorite spot, a lone table on the far side of the stacks where light streamed through the window.

The book was an old text on agrarian cults that hadn't been checked out in years. Big shock there. Satanic cults, sex cults, drug cults—I'm sure they all get their share of interest. But agricultural cults? I didn't even know there were such things.

Daniel turned to the page as I looked over his shoulder. One word caught my eye.

"Witches?" I said. "Shouldn't this have been sent to me?"

"Not witches," he said, pointing. "Witch-hunters. An Italian cult of witch-hunters."

"Okay, so what's the connection to you? Your parents are Italian and you like fighting. Oh my God. You're a witch-hunter. I'm a witch. Hate to break it to you, Daniel, but if you're a witch-hunter? You're doing it wrong."

He gave me a sidelong smile. "Maybe it's not that kind of hunting."

"Then you're *definitely* doing it wrong."

He laughed and we continued reading, trying to find something—anything—that would tell us why Mina wanted Daniel to see this. The whole two-page spread was about this cult. The benandanti, which translated to "good walkers." Apparently, they believed that, on certain nights of the year, their spirits left their bodies and went out to protect the crops by fighting evil witches.

This wasn't just a myth, either. Like some people claimed to be skin-walkers, some claimed to be benandanti. Or they did before the Inquisition, when they were rounded up and executed as witches. If they insisted they had supernatural powers, then they were also witches, and it didn't matter that they were supposedly using those powers for good and for the benefit of the Catholic Church. They were evil. So they were hunted and killed.

It was only when Daniel turned the page that we figured out why Mina directed him to this book. There, written at the end of the section on the benandanti was a note. "If you want to know the truth about Salmon Creek, call me." A phone number followed.

Daniel flipped over the card Mina had left him. The number was the same as her cell.

"Okay, does this make any sense at all?" he said. "Why not just write the message on the back of the card?"

"Two possible reasons. One, she was afraid someone else would find the card. So she found a book no one was likely to check out. Two . . ." I looked around the library. "She's waiting for you to show up, hoping to talk to you away from town."

"Okay, but . . . the truth about Salmon Creek?"

I snorted. "She wants *you* to tell *her* the so-called truth. Proof of animal testing, horrific medical experiments . . ." I shook my head. "Call her again. I'll skulk around, see if she's here."

Mina wasn't at the library or outside it. Nor was she answering her phone.

Before we left, I wanted to look up skin-walkers. No, I

wasn't obsessing—I had my answer and I was happy with it. But I was curious about the paw-print birthmark connection. The more information I had, the easier it would be for me to mentally file the whole thing and forget it.

Most of what we found on skin-walkers was fiction. We only dug up a few brief references in books on Native beliefs and occult mythology. The Navajo don't like to talk about them. Like I said, some believe skin-walkers really exist. Treating them lightly invites trouble.

Those references did confirm what I told Daniel. Skin-walkers are evil witches who cast curses and take on the form of animals, usually canines. When we checked the internet, we did find one reference to them also shifting into bear form, but not cat, and no mention of them bearing any kind of mark, let alone a paw print. Clearly just an old woman's ramblings.

I was ready to pay a visit to Mina Lee. Daniel wanted food. Now, I know teenage guys like to eat. Teenage wrestlers really like to eat. Well, unless they're trying to get into a lower weight class, but Daniel never does that. So, it wasn't surprising that he'd want to grab food.

"I feel like fish," he said. "Let's swing by Pirate Chips."

"Hard to eat fish and chips while you're driving," I said. "We'll dine in."

He started toward the sidewalk. When he realized I

wasn't following, he turned.

"You don't need to talk to her about Serena," I said.

"What?"

"I'm the one who wants answers, not you. I get that. I can do this alone."

"I'm not—" He cut off the word with a snap. "I'm tired of playing the grieving boyfriend, okay? It's been a year, and still everyone makes me feel like—"

He stopped and turned his back.

"Makes you feel like what?" I moved up beside him.

"Just . . . stop doing that, okay? Stop pussyfooting around the subject of Serena. Stop treating me like I'm dying of a broken heart. Stop making me feel like I *should* be." He rubbed his mouth. "That didn't come out right. I don't mean . . . Of course, I miss her. She was a friend. A really good friend. I'm just . . ."

"Tired of being treated like the heartbroken boyfriend when you want to move on. Is that why it's not working with Nicole? You feel guilty because you want to date again?"

He threw up his hands and let out a growl of frustration that made passing tourists decide the other side of the street looked much more interesting. As he watched them cross, his growl turned to a laugh.

He shook his head at me. "The only thing holding me back from dating Nicole is a complete lack of interest, okay? As for Serena, I want answers, too. I've wanted them for a while, but since we weren't discussing it—and, yes, that's partly my fault, not wanting to upset you—I've never said so. I do want to talk to Mina Lee and see what she knows, and the only reason I'm stalling is because I've got something to say first. It's going to piss you off, and I'd really rather be sitting in a public place when it happens."

"So I won't storm off?"

"Exactly."

"I'd never do that, Daniel." I stepped closer and looked up at him. "You have the keys, and it's a very, very long walk—"

I snagged the keys from his pocket and took off. I easily darted around a gaggle of senior citizens nearly blocking the sidewalk. Daniel didn't have as much luck, and I heard him apologizing amid gasps and harrumphs. I raced toward the harbor. I was rounding the local theater, planning to circle back, when Daniel's shout pulled me up short.

I turned. He barreled toward me, his eyes wide with alarm. Right, like I was falling for that one.

I started to run again. I should have been able to outpace him easily. I always could. But the next thing I knew, I was being tackled. He knocked me into an alcove, both of us hitting the wall, then collapsing to the ground.

"Stay down!" he said.

Not much chance of doing anything else with him on top of me. But when I glanced up into his eyes, I saw that the panic wasn't fake. He looked around as if expecting a posse of armed gunmen to round the corner at any moment. When footsteps sounded, he tensed, muscles bunching, prepared to leap up and defend us against—

Two preteen boys passed the alcove. One of them saw us and whispered to his friend. They grinned our way and shot Daniel a thumbs-up.

When they'd gone by, I pushed him off me.

"Okay, I might have overreacted," he said as we sat up.

"You think?"

He pushed to his feet and looked around. "I thought I saw someone."

"Where?"

"I—I—" He looked around. "I don't know. Down there maybe?" He pointed along the wharf. "I was running after you and it happened so fast, I didn't get a good look."

"Was it a man? Woman? Young? Old?"

"I'm . . . not sure." He exhaled and leaned against the wall. "Okay, that sounds nuts. I'm not even sure I saw someone."

"You *sensed* someone?"

He made a face. "Now that really sounds nuts."

"Hey, if you're okay with me imagining myself as a pine marten, I'm okay with you sensing unseen assailants."

He laughed. "Mina Lee was right. The isolation is driving us crazy. We just hadn't realized it yet."

"Not the isolation. The mad science experiments. They've spiked the water with hallucinogens." I headed back to the sidewalk. "Your instincts are usually pretty good, though. Maybe Mina *is* lurking around here and you caught a glimpse of her. Let's wander a bit, see if we spot anyone."

TWENTY

W E ROAMED THE DOCKS and side streets for a while, but Daniel didn't pick up any more hints of danger. Had there ever been a threat? I don't know. Daniel's always been protective, but it's gotten worse in the last year. Since Serena's death.

Maybe this was his way of dealing with the guilt. He couldn't save her, so now he was on hyperalert with me, and being outside Salmon Creek only made him more anxious.

Finally, we headed to Pirate Chips on Commercial. It's a tiny place—seven counter seats and barely room to turn around. The best spot to sit is on the bench out front, near the wooden pirate. It's usually filled with teens, but today, maybe because it was Sunday, we had it to ourselves.

I got pierogies and poutine. Daniel ordered his usual:

fish and a deep fried Aero bar with ice cream. I didn't comment on the bar. I used to . . . until he pointed out that it was no worse than my poutine—fries with gravy and cheese curds.

"You wanted to talk to me," I said when we were halfway through our meal. "Or have you decided you'd rather not incur my wrath?"

He grinned. "Sorry, Maya, but your wrath isn't all that frightening." He leaned back on the bench and let out a sigh. "You are going to be mad at me, though." He spooned off a chunk of his bar before continuing. "When Corey said the reporter asked about Serena, it reminded me of stuff that happened right before she died."

I stopped in midbite, stomach clenching.

"Serena was going to talk to you about it, but she didn't get a chance. After she died, I was afraid it would seem like she'd confided in me and not you, and you didn't need that."

"What about?"

"She'd been feeling off," he said. "Not sick. Just . . . off. Run-down no matter how much sleep she got. You were prepping for that Labor Day track meet, and Brendan had just sprained his ankle, sidelining him. You were under a lot of pressure to cover for him, and she didn't want you worrying about her. She had that singing competition coming up, so she was stressed and she figured that was the problem. She only told me because we were supposed to go to Nanaimo to catch a movie and she had to beg off. Her mom and dad were making her go to the clinic."

He set his spoon down in the bowl. "They gave her meds, but they were too strong. She went from feeling tired to being hyper and restless. Her mom called the clinic, and they told her Serena should stop taking them and come back in on Monday morning. Only by Monday . . ."

"She'd drowned," I murmured. "When did her mom call about it?"

"Saturday, when Serena was getting ready to go meet you at the lake."

"So she'd probably already taken them for the day. You think that had something to do with her death."

"Not at first. Sure she was hyper, like she'd had a couple of energy drinks, but if I didn't know about the meds, I'd have chalked it up to a good mood. I wouldn't have suggested she skip swimming. It was only later that I started to wonder. What's always bugged me most is how it happened to *her*. How does a champion swimmer drown in a lake she's swum in all her life? The obvious answer is a cramp, of course. But Serena never got them."

"You think the medication did something."

"I think it's possible. They said it was new."

Around here, "new" meant it was a drug they were researching at the lab. They only use those with us if the drugs are at the very end of the testing regime. They're convinced it's safe, and they're giving it to us because it's the best around, not because we're guinea pigs. But that won't fly in court.

Daniel continued, "If a side effect caused her death, they'd be ruined."

"So they hush it up. They jump at the chance to let Serena's parents relocate. Now this woman is in town, a reporter or a spy, cozying up to the kids and asking about Serena."

"We need to talk to her."

Mina Lee was renting a cottage outside town. That wasn't unusual. There were no motels, no inns, no bed-and-breakfasts. All part of Salmon Creek's attitude toward tourists in general, which was kind of like their attitude toward wildlife within the town limits. Treat them with civility and respect, but don't give them any excuse to stick around.

The Braun place was the nearest rental property. We knew exactly where it was. Knew how to get in, too—there was a key in the shed. The cottage was Salmon Creek's version of Make-out Point, and was a whole lot more comfortable than the backseat of a car. Not that I'd know. Bringing a summer guy to a place with beds sent a message I was nowhere near ready to send. For town kids, though, while I'm sure some of them had sex there, most just used it as a place to get some privacy. Not exactly fair to the owners, but kids made sure they left it the way they found it, so the Brauns never caught on.

When we'd driven up, there was a rental car in the drive, which suggested Mina Lee was there. We knocked, but no one answered. We peered through the windows. All the lights were off and there was no sign of her. We walked over and shouted by the path leading into the woods. No answer. Either she was out for an evening hike or she'd walked into town, hoping it'd be easier to sneak around without her car.

I mentioned the key to Daniel, but he didn't like the idea of snooping through her stuff, and I had to agree that, no matter how badly I wanted answers, that crossed a line. We'd just have to keep phoning her. We could see that her stuff was still inside, so at least she hadn't left yet.

Daniel and I tended my animals, then did homework at my place until nine. I didn't stay up long after that. I was exhausted, and fell into a nightmare-free sleep. I'd solved the mystery of the old woman. I hadn't seen a cougar all day. I was taking steps to find out what happened to Serena. And as for Rafe, well, I was pretty sure that door was closed, so apparently my subconscious wasn't going to worry about it. I slept and I slept well.

Slept a little too well, actually. I woke to a text from Daniel asking if he could pick me up early and we'd swing by the Braun place, talk to Mina before school. By the time I got his message, it was already too late, especially since I didn't want to ask Dad to feed the animals again.

I called Daniel. He said that was fine—after he sent the

189 🙾

text he realized an early morning visit might not be the best way to get on Mina's good side. We'd go later.

I got to school with no expectation that Rafe would speak to me. No expectation that he'd pay any attention to me at all. Yet as often as I told myself it was over, I hoped it wasn't. As often as I told myself I was happy if it was over, I wasn't.

So when Daniel and I walked from the parking lot and saw Rafe there, I was sure that meant something. And apparently, it did. It meant he knew everyone thought he'd dosed me at the party and he was there to meet his accusers head-on.

We were both disappointed. Rafe made no attempt to speak to me. No one made any attempt to confront him about Saturday night. Daniel had gotten the word out yesterday that as far as we were concerned, Rafe hadn't done it.

If Rafe had totally snubbed me, then I'd know he was still mad, which meant he felt something. But he acted like he would have a week ago. It was as if that connection between us never happened, which made it clear that it had just happened for me. The only thing that hurt worse was the humiliation of knowing I'd fallen for him, just like every other girl, and ended up like them, mooning over him.

I wanted to curl up in a hole. I didn't. I had to face the problem, which meant I had to face Rafe.

Despite what Daniel had said, there were still rumblings. Corey and Brendan shot Rafe a few glances that suggested he'd better not be caught alone with them in the locker room. Trouble was brewing. To prove that I didn't think Rafe had dosed me, I needed to suck it up and be seen talking to him.

Easier said than done. He wasn't avoiding me, but when I tried to find him on our ten-minute break between morning classes, he was nowhere to be seen. The same couldn't be said for Hayley. When I turned into an empty hall, she cornered me.

"I didn't appreciate that stunt you pulled at the party," she said. "Walking in on me and Corey so Rafe could see us together."

"It was a mistake."

"The door was closed—"

"And I didn't hear anyone inside. An honest mistake. More honest than, say, spiking someone's drink, hoping *she'll* get caught with another guy. Only she gets caught with *the* guy, which kind of ruined the whole thing."

Hayley stared at me, then said, "You think I'm the one who dosed your drink? Hoping what? That you'd let Brendan finally get a shot at you? You'd discover you have the hots for Daniel? Please. I don't think anyone put anything in your drink. I think you faked it."

"*Faked* it?"

"Sure. You get all slutty with Rafe. You freak out. You cry date rape drug."

"Excuse me?" said a voice behind us. We turned to see Sam bearing down on Hayley. "Did you just say what I think you said? You'd better be damned sure of your facts before you accuse *any* girl of that. What if someone slips you a roofie? Worse yet, rapes you while you're dosed? Would you want anyone even suggesting you faked it?"

I expected Hayley to tell Sam to go to hell. She didn't. She actually flushed, gaze dropping as she muttered, "I didn't mean it like that."

"I bet you'd never have said it if it wasn't Maya. What's your problem with her, anyway? Some kind of clichéd popular girls rivalry? Cheerleader versus valedictorian? News flash, Hayley—rivalries only work if both sides *realize* they're rivals."

Hayley walked away.

"See," Sam said, "that's why I don't want to be popular."

I laughed, and we headed to class.

I decided to track Rafe down after lunch, when everyone had gone outside to play basketball. I excused myself from the game and went in search of him, planning to repeat my offer to visit Annie. I suspected he wouldn't take me up on it, but I'd make the effort.

It took me a while to find him. Finally, I rounded the back corner of the school to see him there, hidden in a doorway.

He was leaning back, smiling his fake sexy smile—not at me, but at the girl standing in front of him. He leaned toward her, talking, his fingers resting on her arm, enrapt in conversation . . . with Hayley Morris.

TWENTY-ONE

I BACKED AROUND THE corner so fast I stumbled into one of the little kids. I apologized, then broke into a fast walk and didn't stop until I was in the bathroom. I would say my humiliation was complete at that point. But it wasn't. The end of lunch bell rang, we went back to class, and there were two empty seats in our class—Rafe's and Hayley's—and they stayed empty for the rest of the afternoon.

I was looking forward to my visit to Mina with Daniel, which I hoped would slap thoughts of Rafe out of my head. Then, in last class, the boxing coach came by and told the guys that he needed to reschedule tomorrow's early morning meeting for four thirty today. So no visit.

Daniel knew something was bugging me and insisted on driving me to the park gates. He promised to call me later so we could pay Mina a visit that night.

Kenjii had been waiting at the gate and walked home beside me as usual. Otherwise, the woods were silent and still. I caught a whiff of what could have been smoke. I hoped not.

Last night Dad had said a small outbreak of fire had been spreading inland. Luckily, that's mostly uninhabited wilderness, and they hoped to have any blazes under control soon. Salmon Creek had once been evacuated for wildfires—before we moved here—but it had just been a precaution. Still, it worried me. Nothing is more devastating to a forest than fire. It was enough to make me wish for our typically rainy fall weather.

As I approached the house, I heard someone sawing wood. Had Walter—Dad's seasonal assistant—come back to Salmon Creek to help Dad because of the wildfires? Was he working on Fitz's tree house in the meantime? It would be a good ending to a lousy day, but when I didn't see Walter's truck in the lane, I figured Dad was cutting up firewood.

When I rounded the house to say hi to him, I saw a figure in the yard, using a handsaw on a small stack of boards. Fitz was stretched out in a sunny patch by his feet. I stopped and stared. Stared so long that Kenjii whined and nudged my hand.

Rafe turned and saw me. He brushed his hair back and smiled, the crooked "real" smile that made my breath catch.

He waved at the pile of wood. Beside it was the blueprint for Fitz's tree house. "I owe you a birthday present. You mentioned this yesterday. I asked your mom, and she said it would be all right if I gave it a shot. Can't promise anything, but I'm pretty good with a hammer and saw."

"Oh." A stupid thing to say, but all I could think of.

The smile fell. "Or if you'd rather I didn't . . ."

"No, that's . . . Thanks. It's just . . ." *It's just that I have no idea where this came from, and what you're doing here, and why you're doing this.* I looked at him. "You didn't say a word to me at school today."

"You didn't say a word to me."

"I was going to. I wanted to talk to you about visiting Annie, but you were with Hayley."

"Yeah, I heard the rumor that she'd been the one who dosed you. I figured if I could prove it, that might help. She thought I was mad at you, so I used that, chatting her up, trying to get her to admit she'd done it. Nothing, though."

"You didn't come back after lunch."

"Came here to see if I could work on this. Surprise you."

"Hayley left, too."

"Yeah, she's, uh, over by McGill Lake waiting for me. Or she was. I said I was cutting out early, heading there for a swim, hinted she was welcome to join me. I was hoping that would get her to spill about the drugs. Not the nicest thing I've ever done, but if she did dose you, she deserves it, and if she didn't, maybe she'll decide I'm a total jerk and back off." He stepped toward me. "I *was* a jerk yesterday, Maya, and I don't blame *you* for backing off. But you said you were confused, and so was I."

"Because of the drug thing."

"Not just that. I wasn't sure about the party, if you were inviting me because you wanted me there or you just wanted to be nice after meeting Annie. I finally decided to go and I wasn't expecting anything, but then it started out good. Really good. The climb and us talking. And then you went back to your friends, which I totally understood. But I figured maybe it was a hint, too—you'd played good hostess, and your job was done. So I took off for a while. Checked in on Annie. Came back and, bam, everything was good again. We go up to the roof and things are really good, even after I made an ass of myself confessing all that stuff. But then I find out you were drugged, so I don't know if you *do* like me or it was the dope. I spend the night worrying about it. I talk to you. Everything seems cool again . . . only it's not cool and I get the feeling you'd be a whole lot happier if I just went away and stayed away."

He wasn't wrong. About any of it. Even the last part. But happier wasn't the right word. More like relieved. Whatever was happening between us, it was too much, too fast, and I worried I was going to get hurt. I'd never been hurt before, not like that.

When I went out with guys, I liked it fun and casual. I had a good time while they were around, and when they left, I was okay with that. But if Rafe said he was leaving, I *wouldn't* be okay with that and it scared me.

"So . . ." he said when I didn't answer. "I'm here doing something to apologize, because I know that I handled yesterday badly. I pushed too hard, too fast, and stormed off in a temper when you needed me to slow down. It won't happen again. I'd like to turn back the clock to Saturday night, when we were talking, hanging out. I promise not to try to get you back into the woods." He paused. "For at least forty-eight hours."

I laughed. "So you *are* on a schedule."

"No, I'm impatient. But I will wait."

"For forty-eight hours. And if there's no make-out session by then, time's up."

"No. I said I won't *try* for forty-eight hours. What happens after that is up to you." He met my gaze. "It always will be."

My cheeks heated. I glanced over at the pile of wood and tools. "You don't have to do that."

"I want to." He picked up the saw as I crouched to pet Fitz. "Like I said, Mom was a carver. Annie got her creative talent, but I learned the woodworking stuff."

He placed another plank on the saw boards.

I straightened. "I should probably say hi to my parents. Can I get you a drink?"

"Water would be good."

I picked up my backpack and went in the rear door. My parents were in the kitchen. Mom was chopping vegetables at the sink and Dad was sitting at the table, both facing the window with a clear view of the backyard . . . and Rafe.

We did the usual "how was your day" stuff, but it was awkward, like we were all trying very hard not to be the first to mention the new guy in our yard. Finally, I thanked Mom for letting him take a shot at the plans.

"He seems to know what he's doing," she said. "And it is a nice gesture. Very sweet."

She said *sweet* in a weird way, like it surprised her or like she wasn't sure what to make of it.

Dad said, "I'd be a lot more impressed if he wasn't skipping school to do it." His tone told me he wouldn't be impressed at all, school or no school.

Neither seemed particularly thrilled to have him in our backyard. I wondered what they'd heard about him. No, strike that. I didn't need to wonder. If anything negative was being said about "the new boy," they'd heard it. My parents weren't as involved in the town as others, but that only meant they heard gossip the next day rather than within the hour.

"So . . ." Mom said, chopping a pepper from the garden. "I didn't know you were friends with Rafael."

I shrugged as I added ice to an empty glass. "It's recent."

She pushed the peppers into a bowl. "That tree house is a big undertaking. More than I'd expect from a new friend."

"Are you seeing him?" Dad cut in. "Dating?"

"I don't know."

"How can you not know? Either you are or—"

"Rick," Mom said.

I filled a glass with water and took a couple cans of pop. Grabbed granola bars, too. Then I said, "It seems to be heading that way. Is it a problem?"

Dad looked like he wanted to say "Hell, yes," but only pressed his lips together and looked at Mom. She took a cucumber from the pile of vegetables, and I knew I'd hurt her feelings. Normally, I'd come home and say, "Hey, Mom, I met this guy," and tell her all about him. But this was different. I wasn't ready to talk about Rafe until I had it worked out myself.

"If you have a concern . . ." I didn't finish, because I wasn't sure how to. Was I saying I *wouldn't* go out with a guy if they were worried? Normally, yes. With Rafe, no. It wouldn't matter what they thought or said. I had to make my own choices here, pay the price if I made the wrong ones.

"Just be careful," Mom said.

"I always am." I kissed her cheek and gave Dad a hug, and I'm not sure if that helped or not.

Rafe and I talked for over an hour as he worked. Once we started, the conversation just kept going, from one topic to another. I sat on the grass, dividing my attention between Fitz and Kenjii.

It was after five when he looked up at the blazing sun,

wiped his forehead and said, "I was just thinking about this afternoon, when I mentioned that swim to Hayley. I could really go for one now, if you're game."

When I didn't answer, he glanced over, squinting as he tried to see my expression.

"I don't really swim."

"Me neither. Just paddle around, cool off. We could—" The sun went behind the clouds and he got a good look at my face. "That's not what you mean, is it?"

"I just don't swim much lately, and the only lake in easy walking distance is the one—"

"Where your friend drowned last year." He put down the hammer and shook his head. "I'm sorry. That was really inconsiderate."

"No, it wasn't." I got to my feet. "We could, but I'd just rather not. If you want to do something, there's a place I can show you. For climbing. Not exactly the break you had in mind, but there's an overlook at the top. It's a great view."

"Sure."

I had to tell my parents. I stepped just inside the screen door and said we were going for a walk, which got a long moment of silence.

"Just to the overlook," I said. "We'll take Kenjii."

"And your cell phone," Rafe said, coming up to the door. "Don't forget your cell, because if I fall, I'm screwed. I don't have one."

Smooth. He obviously knew my parents weren't impressed with him. If he took any offense at that, he didn't show it, just added, "I'll have her back by dinner."

"Would you like to join us, Rafael?" my mom asked. "Or do you go by Rafe?"

"Usually." A disarming grin. "Unless I'm in trouble."

I opened the door and motioned him in as he continued, "About dinner, I appreciate that, but my sister will be expecting me."

"Another night then," Mom said. "Maybe on the weekend we can have a barbecue, and invite your sister."

"Or," I said, turning to Rafe, "if you want to skip the whole awkward meet-the-family social event, you could just submit your life story, including your views on politics, religion, and every social issue imaginable, along with anything else you think they might need to conduct a thorough background check."

Mom sighed. "I really don't know why we even bother trying to be subtle around you."

"Neither do I. It's not like he isn't going to realize he's being vetted as daughter-dating material."

Rafe grinned. "So we *are* dating?"

"No. You have to *pass* the parental exam first. It'll take you awhile to compile the data. They'd like it in triplicate." I turned to my parents. "We have Kenjii. We have my cell phone. Since we aren't yet officially dating, I'm sure you'll agree that's all the protection we need."

Dad choked on his coffee.

Mom waved us to the door. "Go. Have fun. Dinner will be at six thirty."

TWENTY-TWO

THE CLIFF WAS ONLY a ten-minute walk from the house. There was no easy way up, so Kenjii had to stay at the bottom. She was used to that and just staked out her customary spot. I left my jacket with her. Rafe did, too.

This was tougher than the wall—natural cliffs don't come with conveniently spaced holds and holes. I'd done it hundreds of times, though, so I knew the easiest path and showed Rafe.

It didn't matter that this wasn't a race. When we started climbing, it was like the first time—a heart-pounding, palms-sweating, adrenaline-pumping dizzy runner's high.

I didn't deliberately check my speed, but when we neared the top, Rafe was still beside me. I slowed and he was right there, his face inches from mine. He grinned, that blazing grin now, hair plastered to his face, eyes glittering.

I leaned over and kissed him. He hesitated for about a nanosecond, like he really hadn't expected that, and I laughed. Then he kissed me back, a light kiss, almost teasing, making me shiver.

"Probably not the safest place to make out," I murmured, pulling back to glance at the ground, fifty feet below.

"I don't care if you don't," he said.

We kissed until he tried to shift closer and nearly lost his foothold. I pulled away and scrambled up the last few feet. When he reached the top, I was standing there. He grinned and stepped toward me. I stepped back. His grin widened. I glanced over my shoulder. The cliff topped out on a hill, with forest stretching behind us, the mountains a distant backdrop.

"Uh-uh," Rafe said. "If you run, I'll chase. You know how much I like that part."

"All the more reason to do it."

His breath hitched and the look in his eyes made me *want* to run. I didn't care how silly or childish it was, I wanted to run so badly I could imagine it, the smell of the forest, the wind rushing past, the pounding of his feet right behind me.

Suddenly he was right there, his mouth on mine, my arms around his neck. Then he stopped. He caught my arms and backed up, studying my face.

"Has anyone had access to your drinks recently?" he said. "Any strange allergic reactions? Bug bites?"

"Shut up."

He ducked out of the way as I took a mock swing at him. Then he realized we were closer to the edge of the cliff than he thought, veered fast, and stumbled, toppling into the brush.

"Sorry," I said, hurrying over to him. "Are you—?"

As I bent, he tried to snag my leg and yank me down, but I danced back out of reach.

"Did you really think I'd fall for that?" I said.

"Hoping."

I laughed. He got to his feet. I backed up and glanced over my shoulder.

"I'm warning you," he said. "You don't want to run."

"Why not?"

"Because I'm faster than you."

"Think so?"

"Know so, and when I catch you—"

I took off. I ran across the open field atop the cliff, and quickly realized that was a mistake. He might not be faster than me, but he was fast enough that I could hear him right on my heels. I swerved into the woods.

Normally, that's where my advantage lies. Runners are accustomed to open ground. I actually prefer the forest, and I can dodge and dart around trees with barely a hitch in my pace. That's why hurdles are my best event.

Rafe fell back a little, but then gained on me when I slowed to skirt thick brush.

As we ran, bits of my dream slid back, and everything seemed to get sharper, more vivid. The bright greens of the conifers and the yellows and reds of the rare deciduous trees became a blur of color. Our pounding footfalls muted into the rhythmic *thump-thump, thump-thump* of a heartbeat.

I could hear him right behind me. More than that, I swore I could feel his breath on my neck, and it made me run faster, the air slicing past me, that *thump-thump* filling my head, pulse racing, knowing that when he caught me—

A yowl stopped me short. Rafe's sneakers crunched dry needles as he slid to a halt behind me.

"Maya?" Rafe said. "Look up."

There, crouched on a branch ten feet above us, was Marv. Something lay at his feet. Something bloody.

Marv picked up his kill. Then he leaped. I stumbled back. Rafe yanked me against him, his arms around me, both of us still facing the cougar.

The cat looked at Rafe, yellow eyes narrowing. His lips curled. He dropped his meal and snarled.

"Step back," I whispered.

Marv paced to one side, gaze locked on Rafe, still growling.

"Step back," I said again.

"Are you sure?"

I nodded. Rafe hesitated and I could tell he didn't want to, but after a moment he said, "Okay," and carefully moved away.

The cougar stopped snarling and grunted, as if satisfied. Then he picked up what looked like a chewed and bloody deer haunch. As he walked toward me, Rafe whispered, "I've got you covered."

It wasn't easy to stand still as a huge cougar came toward me. To do anything else, though, would be stupid. His body language was casual, no sign of impending attack, and I had to trust that. Maybe he thought he'd rescued me from Rafe. I only know that I didn't sense a threat.

When Marv got within a few feet, he tossed the deer haunch into the long grass at my feet. Then, with a final snarl and glare at Rafe, he turned and ambled into the forest.

I looked down at the haunch, mostly hidden in the long grass. I managed a laugh. "I guess this is like a house cat bringing its owner a dead mouse?"

Rafe didn't laugh back. As I turned, I saw he wasn't even smiling, just staring after Marv.

"We should get back to the house," I said.

I expected him to make a joke about the cougar spoiling the mood, but he just nodded as he stared into the forest.

"Hey," I said, stepping toward him. "You still with me?"

"Sorry." He swung his gaze back toward me. "That's just . . . not good."

"He's too bold, I know. My dad's going to need to deal with—"

I stopped. He was staring again—this time at the ground behind me. I turned to see what had caught his attention.

"Don't—" he began.

Too late. Having stepped away from whatever Marv had

dropped, I could now see it more clearly through the long grass. Or see part of it. Fingers.

I stood there, thoughts stuttering. I had to be wrong. Of course I was wrong. I'd seen a deer foreleg—a hairless . . .

Oh God.

I stepped forward. Rafe didn't try to stop me, and we both crouched for a better look. There, in the grass, lay a human forearm. Only two fingers were still attached. The rest—and most of the arm itself—had been—

My gorge rose. I swallowed hard and closed my eyes. Rafe's fingers touched my elbow.

"Give me your phone," he said. "I'll—"

"I've got it."

I straightened and took a deep breath. Then I took out my cell phone, opened it, and swore, the words coming out shaky.

"No signal," I said. "We need to get back down the cliff." I glanced at the arm. "We can't leave that, though. A scavenger will get it. We need something to carry it in."

Rafe plucked the hem of his shirt, like he was ready to pull it off. He stopped, though, and said, "We can grab my jacket."

His shirt would have been easier, but it was white, and I guess he was thinking he couldn't afford a new one if it got stained. Yet our jackets were also at the bottom of the cliff, which didn't solve the problem. Finally, we agreed to have him stand watch over the arm while I zipped down the cliff, made the call, and came back.

That was the plan anyway. Only I couldn't get reception at the bottom either. So I tied our jackets around my waist and went up.

I should have only brought my jacket. If it was stained, my parents would buy me a new one. Rafe, however, insisted on using his. He did let me help get the arm on it, which consisted of one person holding the jacket and the other rolling the forearm with a stick, and, yes, it was as bad as it sounds. The only thing that made it bearable was that, if I didn't look at the fingers, it was chewed too badly to tell it was an arm.

On second thought, no, that didn't make it better. My nightmares would definitely have fresh fodder now. But I managed to help Rafe without puking, and he didn't suggest I let him handle it by himself. I appreciated that.

He carried it, though, which was fine by me. I took guard duty—armed with a stick and scanning the forest for any flash of fur.

It was a quiet walk. We knew we were carrying the remains of a person killed by a cougar. Someone was dead and we had no idea who it was. For now, it was easier to think this was an anonymous corpse from some other town, scavenged by the cougar.

We'd almost reached the top of the cliff when Rafe turned, his face lifting slightly, catching the wind.

"Do you smell that?" he asked.

I could smell the arm, that was for sure. That was another thing I was trying not to think about. When I turned, though,

I caught the same stink of decomposition on the breeze.

"We should take a look," I said.

The stink got stronger with each step. Finally, in the trees ahead, I saw a cougar cache—a kill covered with branches. I noticed something blue dangling from a branch. A torn piece of denim.

"It's . . . the rest," Rafe said, his voice low, respectful. When I stepped forward, his fingers closed around my arm. "That's close enough, Maya. Chief Carling can take it from here."

"If the cat comes back and smells us this close, he'll move the body. I need to get a look. See if I—" I swallowed. "Recognize the victim. I know everyone around here."

His fingers slid down to my hand, squeezing it, then he walked beside me as I approached the cache. I could see dark hair at one end, so I veered that way. It looked like a woman, but pine needles blocked the face.

I bent and pulled a branch back and I saw the face then, dark eyes open, staring into nothing.

It was Mina Lee.

TWENTY-THREE

WE LEFT MINA LEE there and climbed down the cliff. I got cell phone reception less than twenty feet from the base. I called Chief Carling, then my dad.

My dad got there first, driving as close as he could get. Then he bundled Rafe, Kenjii, and me into the Jeep, where Mom waited, anxious and worried.

Kenjii was worried, too, whining and watching me, sticking so close she was practically on my lap in the backseat.

Chief Carling arrived next with Dr. Inglis. They went up to look at the body, then came back and got our statements. Chief Carling couldn't tell us much. Dr. Inglis didn't know how Mina Lee died. I'm guessing that's because she'd been partly eaten, but of course no one was saying that. No one was saying much of anything—to us or to each other.

Dad took us back to the house after that. More people were there—the mayor, the principal, and some other members of the town council. They converged on my dad as we got out of the Jeep. I slipped away. Rafe followed. We sneaked off to the forest's edge with Kenjii.

I was about to say something, when the roar of an engine cut me short. Daniel's truck whipped around the corner, spewing clods of dirt. He pulled in behind the others and was jumping out almost before the vehicle stopped.

I walked toward him. "Hey."

He looked from me to Rafe and I braced, but he only nodded at Rafe. A brusque nod but not unfriendly.

"Corey called," he said as he strode over. "He got the news from his mom. Are you okay?"

"Shaken and spooked, but otherwise fine."

"I heard from Nicole, too, after her dad was called. She offered to catch a ride with her dad . . ."

He didn't finish, but I knew what he meant. Nicole had offered to come in his place and he'd told her no. Probably told her to stay home, too, figuring it'd be crowded and chaotic enough. Now he was asking if I'd rather he'd let her come.

"This is good," I said. Which was true.

"Corey said—" Daniel's gaze shifted to Rafe and he lowered his voice. "Can we talk for a second?"

"I'll be over there," Rafe said, waving, before I could answer.

Daniel gave him another nod, a little less curt this time.

He steered me off to the side.

"Is it really Mina Lee? That's what Corey thought his mom said, but she had to take off, so he couldn't ask."

"It is."

"Are you sure?"

I nodded. "The cougar . . . They usually leave the head alone."

"Oh," he said, like he'd just realized exactly what I'd seen. He stepped forward, arms going around me. I lingered there a moment, then backed away. I could see Rafe staring into the forest, giving us privacy to talk, but he looked like he expected to see a cougar at any moment.

"I guess that's why she wasn't answering her phone," I said. "It may explain why her car was at the Braun place and she wasn't. I don't know if I should tell Chief Carling about that, to give her a better idea about time of death . . ."

"That's what I wanted to talk to you about."

"Just a sec." I looked over at Rafe. He'd shoved his hands in his pocket, still watching the forest, clearly worried, fidgeting now. He glanced at his watch.

"Someplace he needs to be?" Daniel muttered.

"Actually, I think there is. Hold on."

I walked to Rafe. "You're worried about Annie."

"Kind of. Yeah."

"Go on."

He looked at me. "I didn't mean I want to—"

"Yes, you do and it's okay. I know Annie likes to walk in

the woods, so right now, you're freaked out. With good cause. Go. I'll see you at school tomorrow."

"Thanks." He started moving away, then paused. "Are we okay?" He looked toward the adults, huddled near the house. "I guess that's, uh, the wrong thing to be thinking about under the circumstances."

"No, it's fine. We're good. I'll see you tomorrow. And I'll get your jacket from Chief Carling." I'd wash it for him, too, but I had a feeling I shouldn't mention that or he'd refuse.

His hands brushed my waist. "I'd kiss you good-bye, but considering your parents and Daniel are watching . . ."

"Tomorrow."

A crooked smile. Then he took off, walking at first, breaking into a jog when he thought no one could see him.

"Supportive guy," Daniel said, walking up behind me.

"He's worried about his sister. She goes for walks in the forest and they can't afford a phone. I insisted he go."

"Oh." He looked in the direction Rafe had gone. "I could give him a lift."

"He's fine. About Mina, should we mention the calls?"

"I say yes. If they find her cell phone, they'll see I called and wonder why I didn't tell them. I'm going to give them the card, too. I won't bring up the library or the visit. But if they ask point-blank, I'm going to tell the truth."

"Can you leave out the part about visiting the old woman?"

He nodded. "I'll just say I found the book and basically got the same message. That's only if they ask, though. I don't want them . . ." He made a face, then shrugged.

"You don't want them thinking we took her message seriously enough to follow up on it. Because you don't want them thinking we'd betray the town to a corporate spy?"

A half shrug this time, which meant that was only part of the reason.

"Serena, then," I said, lowering my voice even more. "You're thinking about the drugs they gave her before she died. If those drugs had anything to do with Serena's death, you don't want them suspecting that's why we wanted to talk to Mina Lee."

He nodded as my dad and Chief Carling came toward us. The chief asked where Rafe was. When I explained, I think he jumped a notch in Dad's estimation, same as he had in Daniel's.

Next I got grilled. This time, the subject wasn't the victim but the killer. Or the supposed killer.

"I don't think M—" I stopped myself, knowing my argument would be stronger without using his pet name. "I don't think the cougar did it."

I lifted my hands as my dad opened his mouth.

"I know it doesn't matter, Dad. Whether he killed her or scavenged her remains, he's a man-eater now, so he can't stay. I just don't want to jump to the conclusion he's the killer and overlook the possibility she was—" Daniel's arm nudged mine. A subtle gesture that could be accidental, but when you've been friends this long, you know when you're being told to shut up. "Killed another way," I continued. "Maybe a fall. Or a hunter's bullet."

"Well, that's the good thing about having the best doctors around," Chief Carling said. "They'll find out what killed Ms. Lee, no matter what the condition of—" She coughed and hurried on. "My guess is you're not far off saying a fall. The way she was tramping around these woods? I don't think she'd ever been out of the city in her life. Lots of cliffs and ravines to stumble in around here."

Mom bustled me and Daniel into the house. Even if I couldn't stomach the thought of food, she wanted me to have something. So the three of us sat at the table, and ate toast and drank tea and talked about everything we could think of that had nothing to do with cougars and reporters.

Another rough night. My roller coaster of a day all jumbled together in dreams and nightmares. Rafe kissing me. Rafe kissing Hayley. Rafe laughing. Marv snarling. The climb. The run. The body.

The body should have taken center stage. It didn't. Instead, it was the run that played through every scene, like a thread tying it all together. Running with Kenjii, laughing, my hair flying. Then running with Rafe, grinning, my heart pounding. Then running from Rafe, giddy, my pulse racing. Then running with a cougar, seeing it out of the corner of my eye, keeping pace, and feeling, not fear but something incredible, like all the other runs rolled together, exhilaration and excitement and a weird kind of peace.

When I *was* running with Rafe, we found ourselves at the cache and I could see Mina Lee, her eyes wide, face streaked with blood, and I could smell that blood, and it didn't smell bad. It smelled—

I jerked awake. Sweat rolled off me. My bed was soaked with it, my camisole pasted to my chest. I went to the balcony door and threw it open. Cool night air washed over me, but it wasn't enough. My chest ached and before I knew it, I was on the balcony, leaning over the railing as far as I dared and breathing. Just breathing.

"*Mrrr-upp?*"

I jumped at the sound, as familiar as it was. I glanced over to see Fitz stretching on the railing.

"How did you get up here?" I said.

A baleful look, like he was offended that I'd ask.

"I'm not carrying you down," I said. "You're here until morning."

He lay down on the wooden rail, as if in answer. I patted him, then headed back inside. As I climbed into bed, I could see him, sitting now, a gargoyle watch cat. Yellow eyes peering into the night. I smiled, pulled up the sweat-damp covers, and fell back to sleep.

I woke up in a weird mood. A good mood, which was the weird part, all things considered.

After I finished feeding the animals, Mom offered me another "get out of school free card." I refused it. I needed to talk to Daniel about Mina's and Serena's deaths, and school was the best place for that.

I was getting my lunch ready. Mom had gone into the studio, leaving Dad on "watch our child for signs of an imminent breakdown" duty, sitting at the table, sipping his coffee.

"You really like that boy," he said. "Rafael."

"Sure. I like him."

A pause, as if that wasn't the answer he wanted.

"I thought you didn't date boys from school."

I shrugged. "There's always a first time."

More silence. I glanced over to see him studying me.

I sighed and turned to him, peanut-butter-covered knife in hand. "If you've heard something about him, just spit it out."

He sipped his coffee, debating, then said, "They say he's something of a Romeo."

"Romeo?" I sputtered a laugh. "Seriously?"

"You know what I mean, Maya. He likes girls."

"Which, all things considered, is good."

He gave me a look, and I sighed. "Okay. You mean he's a player. I'd point out that doesn't make him a Romeo—which would imply he sets his sights on one and sticks to her, 'til an early death do them part. But I get it. And you're right. He likes girls."

"That doesn't bother you?"

I shrugged. "If he had a reputation for sleeping around, I'd steer clear. He doesn't. He likes to catch and release. I get that, which is why I'm being careful not to expect too much."

He took another slow sip of his coffee, which meant more was coming. I licked the peanut butter off the knife as I waited for it.

"No one in town really knows this boy, Maya. He showed up with his sister, and moved into a cabin that doesn't even have electricity. People have been concerned about them, but he's made it very clear that he doesn't want anyone's help. It bothers some people, the way they just appeared."

My eyes rounded. "You're right. Do you remember the night they arrived? That big flying saucer hovering over the park?"

He shook his head and pushed his chair back.

"I know you're serious, Dad, but I'm okay. Really."

"I just . . . I understand you might want to start dating more seriously, and that means dating someone from town. But if you're going to do that . . ." This time he took a long drink of coffee, and the mug was still at his lips when he said, "I like Daniel. He takes care of you."

I blinked. "Oh my God. Did you really just say that? He takes *care* of me?"

Dad flushed. "I didn't mean it like—"

"Takes *care* of me? Did I go to sleep and wake up in the nineteenth century?" I looked down at my jeans and T-shirt.

"Ack! I can't go to school like this. Where's my corset? My bonnet?"

Dad sighed as Mom walked in with her empty teacup.

"What did I miss?" she said.

"Dad's trying to marry me off to Daniel." I looked at him. "You know, if you offer him a new truck for a dowry, he might go for it."

"Apparently, I said the wrong thing," Dad told Mom. "Again."

"Never hard with our daughter." She walked over and slid my sandwich into a bag. "Leave your father alone and get going before you miss your ride."

"They're still looking for next of kin," Daniel said as I climbed into the truck. "But they found her cell phone so I'm glad I came clean on that."

I nodded. "Last night, when I was about to raise the possibility she was murdered, you stopped me. Was it because of Serena and the meds?"

"Because the medication caused her death and Mina found out, so the St. Clouds killed her? No. That'd be crazy. But all it takes is one person to be a little crazy, decide the research has to be protected at all costs, decide to take matters into his own hands . . ."

We drove along in thoughtful silence before Daniel said, "So I might not be completely nuts?"

"Not yet. I think we need to break into the Braun place

tonight. They won't clear it out until her next of kin shows up, and it sounds like that won't be anytime soon. It'll be our last chance to find out if she knew anything about Serena's death."

TWENTY-FOUR

WE DECIDED TO VISIT the Braun place after dark. As we reached town, the truck bounced from the dirt road to the pavement, and something underneath made an ugly cracking sound.

"It's been doing that," Daniel said. "Just ignore it. Corey says he'll take a look on the weekend."

"Well, no matter how dire the situation, if my dad offers you a new truck, don't do it. There's a serious string attached."

"Huh?" he said.

I told him what my dad had said. That got him laughing and as we pulled into the school parking lot, even the sight of Rafe waiting for me only made him roll his eyes.

We got out. I glanced at Daniel.

He sighed. "Go on."

"You sound like you're giving a five-year-old permission

to play with an unsuitable friend."

"If the shoe fits . . ."

I flipped him off.

"Watch it or I won't marry you," he said. "Truck or no truck."

I laughed and jogged over to Rafe.

"Did he just say . . . ?" Rafe began.

"Yes. And don't ask. How's Annie?"

"She's fine," he said as we walked along the forest's edge, skirting school property. "I tried to convince her to stay indoors for a few days. She doesn't get it. A couple of years ago, *she* was the one always telling me . . . Well, you know."

I didn't have any experience with brothers or sisters, but I suppose it would be as if Daniel got into an accident and stopped watching out for me. It'd be like losing the Daniel I knew.

"If you can't get her to stay out of the woods, I've got something that should help. A present from my dad." I swung my backpack off my shoulder and rummaged. "One for you and one for Annie. He makes me carry it all the time. You guys should, too."

He took the cans of pepper spray. "Good idea. Thank him for me."

"I will. If you need to use it, aim for the face—not just the eyes but the nose. Oh, here—and my dad threw in a pamphlet on animal encounters, even though I told him you seem to know how to handle yourself in the woods."

"Make lots of noise so you don't surprise them. Make more noise if you meet one. Try to be as big and intimidating as possible. Don't drop eye contact. Don't turn away."

"You got it."

As we walked, he'd been looking around. I asked what he was looking for.

"Someplace private," he said.

"So we can talk more? That's so sweet."

He laughed. "Talking's good, but the bell's going to ring. Not much time for deep conversation."

"Not much time for anything else, either."

A wicked grin. "There's enough."

He scanned the building and the forest. I knew he'd never officially dated any of the girls at school, but I'd figured that didn't mean he hadn't slipped off to a quiet spot with one. Obviously not.

"There's a nook around back," I said. "It's an emergency exit, so no one ever uses it."

"I thought you didn't date guys from school?"

"Doesn't mean I don't know the make-out spots."

"Make-out? I thought we were talking. But if you insist . . ."

I tugged him into the nook, wrapped my hand around the front of his shirt, pulled him to me, and kissed him. He chuckled, the vibration buzzing through our kiss. I'm bold, but I'd never been *this* bold. With Rafe, I could be. He liked bold. If his return kiss was any indication, he liked it a whole lot.

We kissed until the bell rang, then he pulled back but only to glower in the direction of the bell.

I laughed.

He stayed put, hands resting on my hips.

"You're okay, then?" he said. "After last night?"

"Better than I should be."

"What do you mean?"

I shrugged. "I feel like . . . like I'm holding up too well. I mean, I feel awful about it, but I'm not having any trouble coping."

"Because you're tough."

"It feels insensitive."

He shook his head, fingers sliding into my belt loops, leaning toward me until we were eye to eye. "I was there last night, Maya. What I saw was strength. You were upset, but you knew what had to be done and you did it. I was impressed. *Seriously* impressed."

He kissed me again and my arms went around his neck and I didn't care about the bell, didn't care if I ever got to class.

A throat-clearing behind Rafe made us both jump.

"I believe that was the bell, Rafael."

I couldn't see the speaker but recognized the voice as Ms. Tate's, the primary grades teacher.

"Whoops," he said. "Guess we'd better get inside, then."

When Ms. Tate saw me, she gave a little "oh" of surprise. "Maya . . ."

"Sorry," I said. "We were just going in."

I could feel her gaze on my back as we walked away. When we got around the corner, Rafe whispered, "I think she's disappointed in you."

"She'll get over it."

He grinned and we headed inside.

If I'd felt insensitive earlier, it wasn't long before I was feeling downright callous. Everyone kept telling me they'd heard what had happened and how horrible it must have been. But inside, I was still buzzing, my pulse racing, as giddy as the time Serena and I sneaked champagne at her cousin's wedding.

Rafe didn't make it easy, either. During first period, he found an excuse to walk past my desk and drop off a note. It read, "Not dating classmates means you've missed out on an important part of fifth grade. Time to catch up." Below that, he'd drawn a heart with our initials in it. I'd laughed, added "2 be + 2-gether = 4-ever" and passed it back.

And so it went, all morning, the page getting filled up with doodles as it went back and forth. It was completely fifth grade and completely silly and I loved it, because he wasn't *afraid* to be silly. It was like kissing him first—I could do whatever I wanted, and not have to worry what he'd think of me.

Five minutes before lunch, he dropped off another note marked "Open at the bell," then excused himself to use the washroom . . . and didn't return. When the bell went, I unfolded it to find a rough sketch of the school, with a dotted line from our class to an X by the principal's office.

I stuffed the note in my pocket and took off. At the office, I found an X in marker on the floor beside the trash can. I moved it and found another note. Another dotted line, this one leading outside to another X. That one ended just inside the forest, where I found a third note under a pebble. . . . It was blank.

I looked up.

Rafe's laugh floated down from the trees. "Can't fool you, huh?"

I scaled the tree. When I reached his branch, he was sitting there, legs dangling.

"Will that branch hold two?" I said, looking at it.

"Maybe. The question is whether you're willing to risk it."

I swung onto the branch and started sidling out.

He grinned. "*Dumb* question, wasn't it?"

"It was."

"You can't resist me."

"No, I can't resist a dare."

I stopped. He looked at the distance between us and lifted his brows.

"This seems close enough," I said. "For safety's sake."

"Safe from the branch breaking? Or from me?"

He swung his leg over and reached for me, pulling me into a kiss. He started slow, shifting, checking my balance.

I backed up a little and swung my leg over, so we were both straddling.

"Better?" I said.

"Much."

He gave me a real kiss then, deep and hungry, and I think the branch could have snapped and I wouldn't have noticed until I hit the ground. Maybe not even then.

We kissed, barely coming up for air, until a giggle sounded below us. Then a singsong voice.

"Rafe and Maya sitting in a tree, k-i-s-s-i-n-g."

"Annie . . ." Rafe peered down at his sister, beaming up at us. "I thought I asked you to stay inside today."

"I was careful." She grabbed the lowest branch and swung up. "I wanted to see Maya. I wanted to make sure she was coming over for dinner."

"I haven't invited her yet."

Annie grabbed our branch.

"Whoa, no!" Rafe said as it dipped. "She can't come over if she falls and breaks both her legs."

"She won't do that, silly. She'll land on her feet. Just like me."

"Rather not test that theory," he said and leaned over me to unwrap her fingers from the branch.

I slid down onto the one below us.

"That's cheating," Annie said. "This is how you do it."

She crouched and jumped. My heart rammed into my throat, but she hit the ground as easily as if it had been two feet down instead of ten. I flashed back to the night of my party, when I'd leaped off the roof, Rafe following.

Rafe swung onto the branch beside me. "Ignore her. She's showing off ten years of gymnastics."

We climbed the rest of the way down as Annie bounced on the ground, impatient.

"So, are you coming over, Maya? Rafe has something he wants to tell you." She grinned. "A secret."

"Does he?"

Rafe shot Annie a look, then glanced at me. He waved Annie aside.

"We just need to talk," he said in a low voice, once she'd stepped away.

"Are you in trouble?" I said.

"No, nothing like that."

"Well, I'm not sure about tonight." Daniel and I had to check the Braun place before it was cleared out. "I have that English essay that I've barely started . . ."

"Can you get an extension? After finding that body, I'm sure they'd understand. I really need to talk to you."

"How about now?"

He shook his head. "It's . . . not that kind of talk."

I looked into his eyes. They were clouded with worry and something almost like fear.

"You're freaking me out here," I said. "What's up?"

"Nothing. Sorry. Go have your lunch. I'm going to take Annie home. I probably won't be back, but I'll meet you in the square after school and walk you to the cabin. You shouldn't be in the woods alone."

I could have said the same for him, and this struck me as odd, coming from a guy who hadn't tried to shield me from stuff because I was a girl.

I agreed, and he made me promise to wait at the town square until he arrived. I made him slip back into school and get that pepper spray. I waited with Annie until he came back, then went to find Daniel and the others.

If the morning had sped by, the afternoon slogged. When it finally ended, I told Daniel I'd catch up with him after having dinner at Rafe's. Then I took off for the town square.

Rafe wasn't there. I perched on the base of the monument, a bronze life-size figure of a guy in a lab coat. It isn't marked with a plaque, and we tell people it's to honor all scientists. I've heard, though, that it's supposed to be some guy named Samuel Lyle. I looked him up once on the Internet, but couldn't find any mention of him.

I'd been there about ten minutes when a guy strolled my way. A stranger with dark blond hair pulled back in a ponytail and the vague-eyed look of a drug addict. I could see the top of a badly done tattoo on his collarbone, the rest hidden under a golf shirt buttoned all the way up. A windbreaker topped the golf shirt. He wore white sneakers and jeans that looked like they'd been bought this morning.

As he approached me, he smiled, and if he'd brushed his

teeth in the last year, I'd be shocked. I could smell his wind-breaker—that stink of new plastic. Smelled his breath, too, as soon as he opened his mouth.

"Hey there, Miss," he said, stumbling over the *Miss* a lit-tle. "I'm looking for someone, and I was told you could help."

One look at the guy, and I knew exactly who he was look-ing for. I glanced to the side, toward the forest, the path I knew Rafe would take. It was empty. Good.

"I will if I can," I said, giving my best tourist-friendly smile. "Who is it?"

"Kid named Rafael Santiago. No, Martinez. Rafe Martinez. He's about your age and I just talked to someone who said you're his girlfriend."

I managed a laugh. "I wouldn't go that far, but sure, I know him. You're a friend?"

"I am. From way back. Lost track of him when he came up to Canada. Then I was in Vancouver, visiting a buddy and he said, 'Hey, you know who's over on the island?' Course, I couldn't go home without saying hi to my old pal. He's been tougher to find than I thought, though."

He laughed. "Hell, this town was tougher to find than I thought. Wasn't even on the map. Then I get here and find out he's living with his sister in some cabin in the woods. Out there." He waved north. "Seems there isn't even a road to fol-low. I was hoping you could take me to him."

"I would, but I've never been there myself. I'm waiting for my dad to pick me—" I took out my cell, as if it had been vibrating, and answered. "Dad. Where are you?"

I paused, then sighed. "Fine, I'll walk home then."

I hung up and slid off the monument. "Seems I'm not getting a lift and my mom needs me home right away. Why don't you try Chief Carling's office? They can give you directions to Rafe's place."

There was no way this guy was going to the police station, and the look on his face confirmed it.

"All right then," he said. "I'll keep asking. Thanks for your help."

He couldn't resist a sarcastic twist on the last word. I hoisted my backpack and headed out.

TWENTY-FIVE

RAFE HAD LIED. HE was in trouble. He should have warned me. Now I needed to warn him. Luckily, he was more than a few minutes late.

With the guy hanging around I couldn't head straight for the path leading to Rafe's place. Still, I needed to go in that direction, so I could watch for him. I circled out of the thug's sight, then veered back toward the path, picking up my speed until I was safely in the forest.

When there was still no sign of Rafe, I started worrying that he'd taken another route. I wasn't even completely sure that mine was the right one, because I rarely went out to the Skylark cabin. It was a twenty-minute walk from school, and in the opposite direction from the park.

It was thick forest here, the evergreens so close together they were as bare as telephone poles, trunks soaring into the air, finding sunlight and sprouting branches only near their tops. When the weather wasn't so dry, the ground was boggy. It had to be the crappiest piece of land in the area, which is why Ed Skylark picked it.

Skylark had been an antisocial old hermit who'd lived here before the St. Clouds bought the land. Everyone else had happily taken the generous packages the St. Clouds offered. Ed Skylark had set up traps around his cabin and told the town that if any local kids stumbled over them, it wasn't his fault—he was just trying to catch mink and martens. We didn't know for sure if there actually were traps, but we'd grown up giving the cabin a wide berth.

No one had been surprised when heirs didn't show up to claim his estate or when—five years later—the pair who did were very distant, very young relatives. The more I thought about it, the more I wondered if Rafe and Annie were related to Ed Skylark at all or had been in one of the nearby towns, heard about the abandoned cabin, and declared themselves heirs. It wasn't like anyone was going to challenge them for custody of the place.

I was thinking about that when a branch cracked beside me. I wheeled and peered into the forest. This deep in, the forest was as dim as twilight. Once my eyes adjusted, I could make out a pale white sneaker peeking from behind a tree.

Rafe had white sneakers.

So did the guy looking for him.

I took out my pepper spray. Then I backed up, hoping to get a look at a jacket or pants or anything that would tell me it was Rafe goofing around. But as I moved, so did the other guy, circling the tree to keep out of sight.

I fingered the pepper spray. If it was Rafe, then I could say he deserved it for sneaking up when he knew I'd be on high alert for cougars. Still, a blast of pepper wasn't something to take lightly.

"If that's you, get out here before I call my dad and tell him I've found Marv."

No answer. I adjusted my grip on the can, fingers clammy now. I kept moving backward, not taking my eyes off that tree.

I thought about calling for help. But no one could make it here in time, and if I was wrong, I'd only get Rafe in trouble—maybe even alert the guy looking for him.

I gripped the pepper spray, took a deep breath, and started toward the tree.

"Okay," I said, raising my voice. "Hide-and-seek is not a game to play in the forest. If a hunter's around—"

The guy lunged at me, and I sprayed him. He howled in pain, yelling, "You bitch!"

I ran. He was able to follow, meaning he'd only caught a spritz of pepper. I picked up speed. This was a race I knew I could win. My strength and my territory. I'd easily outpace—

"Stop!" he yelled.

When I kept going, a bullet whizzed past.

"I said *stop*, bitch, or next time I won't miss."

I dove for the ground. He fired. The bullet hit a tree, splinters raining into my hair. I heard him curse as he tromped through the undergrowth. I crept along the ground, and when he came around a nearby tree, I could see him, his eyes streaming tears. He peered into the forest and swore again.

I tugged out my cell phone and opened it.

No service.

Please no. Not now.

I held the phone at every angle and at arm's length. Nothing.

The guy kept stumbling around, clearly having no idea how to move in a forest. I crept on my belly toward him, ready to leap up and blast him again. Then I stopped.

He had a *gun*. This was the time to run, not fight.

I rose onto all fours and crawled away from him, sweeping aside dried sticks and dead leaves and anything else that might crackle. As I moved, I kept looking up into the trees. I couldn't help it. My gut instinct didn't just say to run, it said *where* to run. Up.

That was nuts. In the time it took me to find a suitable tree, he could shoot me. I fought the impulse and concentrated on moving slowly and quietly.

"Do you really think you can get away?" he bellowed, his voice echoing through the forest. "I've got a gun, you stupid bitch. It's a half mile back to town. You'll never make it."

I could do a half mile. Inch by inch if I had to. I continued forward without pause . . . until I reached a dry creek bed full of dead vegetation. No way I was getting through that without making a racket.

"I'm not after you, kid," the guy yelled. "Just tell me what I want to know and you're free to go."

I started along the creek bank. When it threatened to take me too close to the guy thundering through the woods, I stopped and looked around. A fallen tree crossed the streambed. Staying in the long grass, I crawled to it, got my balance and—

A hand clamped over my mouth, yanking me back as I started to tumble. My fists flew at my attacker, but he held me tight, pulling me against him, one hand over my mouth, the other around my waist.

"Shhh. It's me."

I twisted to see Rafe. He motioned for silence, then let me go.

"I heard a shot," he whispered, checking me over. "What's going on? Who is that?"

"You forgot to mention that the guys you robbed tracked you down."

"What?" He blinked in genuine surprise.

"Is your real name Rafe Santiago?"

"No, but it's one of the aliases my mom used."

Aliases?

The guy yelled again. "That's a limited-time offer, kid.

The longer you take to come out, the more you're going to piss me off. You have two minutes. Starting now."

Rafe took a deep breath. "I'll handle this. Get back to town."

"Like hell. Where's Annie?"

"She took off an hour ago. That's why I'm late."

For a guy who worried about his sister so much, he didn't seem to keep a very close eye on her. Soon, this guy was going to tire of looking for me and continue down the path, hoping it led him to their cabin. If Annie was there, she wouldn't know enough to run.

"Distract him," I whispered. "I'll get help."

I started to crawl away.

Rafe grabbed my leg. "If the town finds out about Annie, we'll have to leave." He met my gaze. "I don't want to leave."

"Do you want to die?"

He didn't answer, just put his hand against the back of my head and pulled me into a kiss that made my head swim. Rough and deep and desperate.

He wouldn't look at me after that, just turned his gaze forward and said, "Get help. I'll distract him."

I took off crawling. I'd gone about twenty feet when the guy yelled, "Fine. You don't want to help me? I'll find Rafe myself, and when I'm done with him, I'm coming back for you. No one disrespects me like that, especially not a little . . ."

He let loose a string of racial epithets, which I'm sure he thought would wound me to the core or at least piss me off enough to give myself away. I kept crawling.

"You looking for me?" Rafe yelled.

The woods went silent. I held still.

"Rafael?" the guy called after a moment.

"That's me. And who are you?"

I rose, staying hunched over, and moved as fast as I dared toward the path.

"You don't know me," the guy called, "but I've been paid to bring you back to the Jacksons."

Rafe laughed. "Bring me back? Right."

"You think I'm going to kill you? Oh, no. The Jacksons want to do that themselves, sending a message to every other punk who tries to rip them off. The only question, Rafael, is whether you come along willingly or you make me go after your girlfriend and your sister first. The Jacksons don't want them." He let out a nasty laugh. "But I think I could find some use for them."

"And if I turn myself in, you'll leave them alone?" Rafe's voice had moved farther in the opposite direction, drawing the guy away from me.

"That's the plan."

The guy didn't seem to be following Rafe, but that was fine. He'd made contact with his target. I was safe. I reached the path and—

A bullet flew over my head. I ran.

"Maya!" Rafe shouted.

A sharp pain in my hip made me stumble and I went

down. My hip felt like it was on fire. There was a scorched track through my jeans, the skin below it grazed and burned.

I looked up to see the guy bearing down on me, gun pointed.

"Stay down, bitch, or—"

I rolled into the undergrowth. He fired. Missed. Fired again. In the distance, I could hear Rafe shouting as his footsteps pounded the path.

Another shot. Then a click and a grunt. I peered through the brush to see him trying to unjam the gun. I steadied my breathing, then scrambled along the ground until I was a few feet from him.

I leaped up and blasted him full in the face with pepper spray. He screamed and tried to fire, but the gun was still jammed, and I was already diving away.

He fell back, fumbling with the gun as tears streamed down his face. I ran toward him and grabbed the gun. I didn't get a good enough grip on it, and when he let go, it sailed into the forest.

The guy grabbed me by the arm. I wrenched free and tore off. He tried to follow, stumbling blindly after me. Rafe was no longer shouting, just running full out in our direction. His face was taut with anger, and when I heard the growl, I thought it came from him.

Then a tawny blur charged through the trees, snarling and snapping. It was the cougar from the night of my party, the female. She planted herself between me and the guy, who'd stopped swiping at his eyes and now stared at her like he was sure he was seeing wrong.

The cat crouched. Rafe skidded to a halt.

"No!" he said sharply.

The cat kept snarling, crouched and ready to spring.

"We're okay," Rafe said, his voice firm. "I'm okay. Maya's okay."

I looked at him. His gaze was fixed on the cat. He was talking to the *cat*.

I took a slow step, sidling toward the gun. I kept my gaze on the cougar, and when I moved, I could see her left flank and the mark there—dark fur in the shape of a paw print.

I swallowed. I knew what I was looking at. I knew what it meant. But I couldn't let the thought form. Not now.

Rafe was still talking, sharper now, telling the cat we were okay. She crouched, hindquarters shifting, the tip of her tail twitching.

"*No*," Rafe said, jumping forward. "Don't—"

The cat leaped just as the guy wheeled to run. He managed to dodge her, stumbling slightly as she brushed him. Rafe took off after the cat, yelling, but she tore after the guy. I followed.

The guy ran full out, knowing he was running for his life, but the cat was faster. As the gap between them narrowed, the cat hunkered down for a flying leap. Rafe shouted something I couldn't quite make out. Or maybe I could—I just wasn't ready to believe what I was hearing.

Just before the cat leaped, the guy's arms windmilled, legs buckling as he skidded to a stop right at the edge of the ridge we'd climbed the afternoon before. He turned, hands going up, and shouted "Okay! Okay!" as the cat crouched, tail flicking, amber eyes fixed on him.

"Call it off!" the guy yelled as Rafe raced toward them. "Call that thing off and I'll go away, okay? I never found you, okay? Just call—"

The cat jumped. Rafe shouted and this time I heard exactly what he said.

"Annie!"

The cat hit the guy, and they flew over the cliff. Rafe kept shouting her name, running toward them so fast I thought he was going to fall, too, and I lunged, screaming, but he stopped right at the edge.

I raced up beside him. Below, the cat lay on the guy, who was sprawled on the grass, his eyes open. Open and unseeing. The cat lifted her head and whined. We started climbing down.

At first, the cat just lay there, whimpering. When she tried to rise, she stumbled onto three legs, her left front one dangling.

"Stay there," Rafe yelled down. "Don't move. Just stay there!"

The cat made a noise low in her throat and looked up at us. I looked into her eyes and I knew what I saw—*who* I saw.

"Annie," I whispered.

Rafe looked over sharply. He tried to make eye contact, but I turned back to the ridge. Blood pounded through my veins so hard it hurt.

Annie. The cougar below was Annie.

As crazy as it sounded, I never once thought, "But that's impossible!" Because I knew it was true.

I saw that dark patch on her haunch and I knew when she was human, there'd be a birthmark in the same place. I knew what it meant for her. And I knew what it meant for me.

Yee naaldlooshii.

Skin-walker.

TWENTY-SIX

WHEN I REACHED THE bottom, I knelt beside the fallen guy. I checked for a pulse, but his staring eyes told me he was dead.

I thought of Mina Lee. Eaten by a cougar. Possibly killed by a cougar. I glanced over at Annie, then tore my gaze away. I couldn't think about that now. I couldn't think about a lot of things now.

Rafe noticed the hole in my jeans and realized I'd been shot. It was only a graze. Slap on a bandage and I'd be fine.

He crouched beside the cat as he checked her injuries, and if there was any doubt that it was Annie, it disappeared as I watched her letting him touch her hurt foreleg, only whimpering when he brushed a sore spot. I crouched beside them, and she stretched her head back and nudged me, giving a chirp of greeting, eyes closing as she rubbed her head against me.

"Is it broken?" Rafe asked me.

I ran my fingers along her leg.

"It doesn't seem to be," I said. "I think it's just a sprain. It should be wrapped, though. Can she . . . ?" I swallowed. "Can she Shift back? To human?"

"She will, but it's not really . . ." He paused. "It isn't under her control. She just will." He looked at me. "I know you have a lot of questions—"

"All of which can wait. Give me your jacket. I'll wrap her leg and see if she can stand on it."

He stripped out of his denim jacket. Underneath he was wearing the same sleeveless tank top he'd had on on Saturday. When he twisted, once again I saw the dark edge of what I'd presumed was another tattoo. I remembered yesterday, when he hadn't wanted to take off his shirt to wrap the arm.

I caught the armhole of his shirt and pulled it away before he could stop me. There, below his shoulder, was a paw-print birthmark.

For a second, I couldn't breathe. I just stared at that mark until he tugged the fabric from my fingers.

"Maya . . ."

I turned back to Annie. "Hold her still. This will hurt."

He leaned down, trying to catch my gaze. "Maya . . ."

"Hold her," I snapped. "We need to get her to safety and take care of—" I glanced at the dead guy and couldn't bring myself to finish, so I just looked over at Rafe and said, "I'm guessing you don't want to take this to Chief Carling?"

He shook his head. "I can't."

"Then we have work to do."

I didn't need to splint Annie's foreleg. I'd just set to work when she started her Shift back, and I don't know what I expected—a screaming, tortured transformation, I guess—but instead she started to twitch and quiver and whimper, and Rafe told me to get back, then she was human again.

It only took a couple of minutes as she morphed in a process that looked more like something from a sci-fi movie than a horror flick. It took a lot out of her, though, and she lay there, curled up in a ball, gasping and panting, naked and covered with sweat.

Then she sat up, looked around, saw me, and crawled over. She curled up, half in my lap, like a scared child, shivering, her heart pounding, snuggling against me for warmth. After a moment's hesitation, I hugged her and told her it would be okay as Rafe draped his jacket over her. Within minutes, she was asleep.

"We need to"—I glanced at the dead guy—"move him."

My second body in as many days. I should be horrified. At least with Mina Lee, I'd felt a hint of grief. Even then, though, my response had felt wrong. Cold.

Now it was even worse. I felt nothing. This guy had come for Rafe, and he'd been willing to kill me to get him. He'd died by accident. If he'd had his way, he'd have done a lot worse to us. Still, to feel nothing didn't seem right. Too sensible, even for me.

"I know a place," I said after thinking for a moment. I carefully slid from under Annie, lowering her to the ground and adjusting the jacket over her. I stood and looked down at the body. "Is anyone going to come looking for him?"

Rafe shook his head. "The Jacksons must have put out a bounty on me. He wanted to collect it himself, which means he wouldn't risk telling anyone else where he was going." He stepped toward me, fingers closing around my arm. "I'm sorry, Maya. I never would have gotten you involved—"

I pulled from his grasp. "Don't lie to me. Not now. That's why you're here. To get me involved. Not in this"—I motioned to the dead guy—"but *this*." I tugged my shirt away from my jeans, showing off the top of my matching mark, and as I did, I watched his expression, praying for a look of surprise and knowing I wouldn't get one. I didn't.

That's what you wanted, isn't it? You said you were looking for something special in a girl, and that's what it was.

I didn't say the words. Even thinking them made my gut clench, made me want to run as far from him as I could get, but I couldn't do that. I needed answers.

"I can explain," he said.

"I expect you to," I said. "But first, we have to get rid of him."

We carried the body to a narrow cave farther down the

ridge, where erosion had eaten away at the cliff side. We took his ID. He didn't have keys, so he must have hitched a ride. We put him in the cave, then stuffed the opening with rocks and branches, to keep scavengers away.

By the time we got back to Annie, she was awake again and ready to walk to the cabin. She was still exhausted, though, barely saying a word, leaning against her brother. When we got there, it was exactly as I remembered it—the kind of place so rundown that hikers would use it for shelter in bad weather, presuming no one lived there.

The cabin was barely larger than my bedroom and had an outhouse. A new generator supplied electricity and a propane stove provided heat for cooking. As rustic as you could get. Clean, though, I saw as I followed Rafe inside. Probably a lot cleaner than it had been when Ed Skylark lived here.

There were two beds, little more than bunks. One was original. The other was made of new wood, as was the table and two chairs. Add a tiny fridge, and that was it for furnishings. The bed linens and plates and other stuff all looked new but were discount store quality. Clearly Rafe was making the drug dealers' money last as long as he could.

Rafe helped Annie to the new bed, which was piled with colorful pillows and blankets. She snuggled in, saying something about being hungry, but she drifted off to sleep again before she could finish. Rafe got a health bar from a crate of groceries and a juice box from the fridge, and left them beside her bed. Then he motioned me outside.

He didn't say another word until we were standing beside the fire pit, and even then he only said, "So . . ." before lapsing into silence. I lowered myself onto the log they'd been using for a fireside chair. He sat and tried sliding closer, but when I tensed, he stopped and leaned forward, elbows on his knees, staring into the forest.

"You said your mother was Hopi," I said, pointing to the tattoo on his forearm.

He rubbed it and nodded.

"They have the skin-walker stories, too, don't they?"

He looked over sharply, blinking.

"Yes, I know the legend," I said. "But I'm guessing it's more than a legend."

"It is." His hand came down right beside my leg, not touching. He looked down at his hand, like he was hoping I'd slide closer, give him some sign everything was okay. When I didn't, he said, "This isn't how I imagined it. Telling you."

"Did you imagine telling me at all?"

His gaze shot to mine. "Yes. That's why I asked you to come out here tonight. I knew I couldn't wait. Shouldn't wait. Things were happening, and you needed to know the truth, if you didn't already."

"Okay, so you were going to tell me tonight. Well, it's tonight. Go on."

He squirmed and I knew the timing didn't matter—he'd expected this to play out differently, probably on a cliff top after a climb, sitting together, his arm around me, as he casually said, "Hey, you know how those mountain lions have been hanging around you a lot lately? Well, there's a reason . . ."

"Skin-walkers," I prompted.

"Right."

Silence.

"I've only read one reference to them turning into cougars," I said. "It's usually wolves, coyotes, even bears."

"It's there, if you dig deep enough. That's what my mom said, anyway." He cleared his throat and sat up straighter. "What you read—that was about witches, right? Cast curses? Wear animal skins and change form?"

"Right."

"Well, that's not us. Mom said we probably shouldn't even call ourselves skin-walkers, because of the confusion, but we had the name first. *Real* skin-walkers, like us, go back to before Columbus 'discovered' America. It's a kind of supernatural race. We're born into a family of skin-walkers. We can change into mountain lions. We get our energy from nature. We have healing powers and some control over animals." He met my gaze. "Sound familiar?"

He reached over to put a hand on my arm, and I realized I was covered in goose bumps.

I pulled away. "Go on."

He hesitated, then continued. "Mom was told the new kind of skin-walkers started out as assistants to the real ones, who were tribal healers and protectors. Our kind— Well, it's a long story and I'm sure you're not that interested yet. I can give the history lesson another time. Point is that we aren't the skin-walkers they believe in these days. Our kind went extinct."

"Annie doesn't look extinct to me."

"That's because—" He stopped, wincing, then stretched out his legs and rubbed his calves.

"You okay?"

"Muscle pains. I'm getting them a lot lately. I think it's close. The first Shift. Are you—?" He exhaled. "Later, right? Keep explaining. Okay. Skin-walker families lost their powers. Mom said it was a survival mechanism. They were being killed off by the new human kind of skin-walkers, and so all of a sudden, they started having kids without powers."

"Those kids weren't a threat, so the others left them alone."

"Right. But some families still passed along the old stories. Like Mom's. It was like telling your kids that your family used to be famous warriors. It didn't mean anything anymore, but it was cool. Then these people got in touch with her. People from other skin-walker families. They said scientists had figured out a way to reactivate the gene."

"Reactivate a skin-walker's powers?"

"Right."

"Why?"

He shrugged. "If we don't have them, we feel it. Mom said it's like being born a blind artist or a deaf musician. There's this . . . drive. This itch you can't scratch. There were people in her family who went crazy, and everyone said that was the reason. She worked her frustration out in art, but she said it was never enough. Something was always missing."

"So they reactivated the gene. For you and Annie."

"And others."

"Like me."

He nodded. "Annie was the first. When everything seemed to go fine with her, they did a full first wave of trials. They were in it together, our mothers. Of course, they worried about what might go wrong. Whether they'd done the right thing. They started getting paranoid. Then one of the mothers said she'd overheard the scientists talking about taking the babies away after they were born. So they ran."

"All of them?"

Another nod. "They split up because they thought that would make them harder to find. Later . . . well, later, Mom started thinking they'd overreacted. The woman who said she overheard the scientists had already wanted to leave."

"So maybe she made the story up. If they all went together, any efforts to find them would be split. It made it easier for her to get away."

"Right. But when people talk about taking kids away from their parents . . ." He shrugged. "It brings up bad memories."

Residential schools, he meant. I didn't know a lot about it in the United States, but I knew it was a big issue in Canada, where, for over a hundred years, Native kids were taken from their families to live in state-funded, church-run schools.

From inside the cabin, Annie yelled, "Rafe?"

"Right here!" he called back. He got to his feet, then turned to me. "Hold on. I'll be right back."

TWENTY-SEVEN

"THERE WASN'T AN ACCIDENT with Annie, was there?" I said when he came back. "It's not brain damage. Not really."

"No." He stared at the cabin, looking so sad that I had to resist the urge not to slide closer. "It started soon after she began Shifting. Just small things at first. Not interested in her art anymore, not interested in school, getting restless, wandering off and staying away until she was hungry. I figured it was just a combination of the Shifts and our mom's death."

"But it wasn't."

He shook his head. "It kept getting worse. She's not . . . She's not Annie anymore. I mean, she is, in some ways, but she's . . . simpler."

"More animal than human."

He nodded. "She still takes care of me, but in a different

way, protecting me, like with that guy today. But now I'm the parent. I make sure we have clothes and food and a place to live. I'm not complaining—she did it for years, and it's time I took some responsibility. But . . ."

"You want your sister back. You think she'd want to *be* back."

"I know she would. I mean, if that happened to me . . . If it happened to you . . ."

My heart started thudding so hard I struggled to breathe. Shifting into animal form, running and experiencing life as a cougar—that part sounded amazing. But truly becoming an animal, giving up all my dreams, my future? I felt sick just thinking about it.

"She's getting worse," he said in a low voice. "She Shifts more and more. One day, maybe she won't Shift back."

"But that's not normal, right? Obviously skin-walkers were still human. Something went wrong with the experiment. That's why you're here. You came looking for another subject, hoping to find leads to the group that did this, to see if they can fix her."

He nodded. "When Mom found out about the cancer, she started searching for the other subjects. She contacted someone who really didn't want to tell her anything but finally said he knew where one girl was. You. Here. When Mom was dying, she said if anything went wrong, to come here and look for you. She knew the name of the town and what your mom looked like, but that's all I had."

"Only my mom is my adopted mother. So you started going through all the girls, trying to find the one with the birthmark. If you were looking for a Native girl, though . . . kind of obvious, wasn't it?"

"I wasn't. Your mom's white."

"W-what?"

"That's what my mom said. It's how your mom's family hid. Intermarriage. She had Native blood, but she looked Caucasian—hazel eyes and light hair."

"And my dad?"

"I don't know. It was all in vitro fertilization."

My guess was that the sperm donors carried the gene, too. That would make sense, if you were trying to resuscitate a genetic trait. My dad must have been full Native, then. Not that it mattered now. Well, it *did* matter. I was half white. Or close to it.

For genetic shocks, that didn't quite match finding out I could change into a cougar, but it was close. I felt a weird squeezing panic in my chest, like waking up one day and looking in the mirror to see a stranger.

"So you figured I wasn't the girl you were looking for. You gave it a shot, but halfhearted, just in case."

"It wasn't like—"

"You thought it was Hayley, didn't you? Hazel eyes, blond hair, right age."

"Kind of. But not really. I was—" He exhaled, gaze dropping to his hands, folded in front of him. "Hayley liked me.

Enough to tell me anything I wanted without asking why I wanted to know it. She was on the swim team, and she'd have seen just about every girl here in a swimsuit . . ."

"She could tell you if anyone had a birthmark. She's seen mine, but she didn't mention it."

"No, and I got the feeling she wouldn't even if you had one."

So he had to see for himself. That was why he'd wanted to go swimming yesterday. To confirm his suspicion.

He continued, "I thought maybe it was Sam. Hayley wouldn't have noticed if she had a birthmark. Mom wasn't completely sure that you'd be here with your mother. She knew she'd given up one of her twins."

"Twins?"

"A boy and a girl. Multiple births are common with skin . . ." He trailed off. "You really didn't know, then."

"That I'm a skin-walker? That my mother is white? That I have a twin brother? No, apparently there's a lot about myself I didn't know."

"I'm not doing this right. I . . ." He slid closer, arm going behind me, but I jumped away so fast I almost fell off the log.

"Just tell me the rest," I said.

"My mom knew that yours gave up one of her kids to make them both harder to find—the scientists would be looking for twins. When she heard that you surfaced up here, she presumed you were the one your mom . . ." He looked over, like he'd just realized he was telling me that my mother chose to keep one of her children, and it wasn't me. "Maya . . ."

"Go on."

He swore and shifted position, giving me a look like he wanted to make this easier.

"So you figured it was Sam," I said. "She came here alone, so that fit, too. Only she didn't want anything to do with you, meaning there was no way you were getting close enough to check for a birthmark."

"No way I wanted to either," he muttered. "I asked her out. She said no. When I tried taking the slow route, getting to know her, she told me to take a hike, and when I didn't, she went after Annie."

"What?"

"Annie came by to get a look at her. Like with you, because I thought she was the one. Sam wanted her to tell me to back off. Annie laughed. Sam was about to take a swing at her when I got there. She stopped and she said she wasn't going to hit Annie. Doesn't matter. It completely freaked Annie out. And completely pissed me off. She could tell Annie was slow. It was like kicking a puppy that wants to play."

Sure, Sam was quick with her fists, but she was never cruel. My guess was that she'd just raised her hand in anger. An instinctive reaction with Sam.

Yet she'd had a few run-ins with other girls at school. Was I defending her because she was nice enough to *me*?

I said, "And that's when the cougars started taking an interest in me and you realized you'd been chasing the wrong girl."

He nodded, calm, like he had no idea what he was admitting.

I continued. "But I'd already made it clear I wasn't impressed by the bad boy routine, so you had to figure out what *would* impress me. Honesty. Let me see past the bad boy front and make me feel special, as if you liked me so much you'd let down your guard for me."

I wanted him to say no, I was wrong, that wasn't how it happened at all.

He didn't even try. I supposed, when this was over, I'd be grateful for that. But right now, it hurt. Hurt so bad. After everything I'd just found out, you'd think this wouldn't matter, but the rest of it was too hard to wrap my head around. I needed time for it to sink in. This sunk in. Like a dagger.

"So I guess you found what you were looking for," I said. "The girl you were looking for."

My words twisted with a bitterness I wished I could suck back in, and his lips parted in a curse, as if he'd just realized what he'd admitted.

"It isn't like that."

"Yes, it is. You chased me for the same reason you chased all the rest. You thought I was the one. You chased me harder because you were pretty sure I was. That's why you came to my party. That's why you took me up on the roof. It was you who dosed my drink, wasn't it? Hoping I might be willing to shed some clothing, so you could look for a birthmark."

"No! I did *not* drug you, Maya. Yes, that's why I hit on

you. That's why I hit on every girl. But you were different."

Because I was the one. I got to my feet.

"I don't know anything about my mother or skin-walkers or scientists. But if everything else you said is true—and I have no reason to think it isn't—then I need to find these answers as much as you do. So I'll help you. Right now, though, I need to go home."

"Maya." He took my arm.

I shook him off. "I need to go home, okay? I have a lot to think about. We'll talk tomorrow."

I walked away. He didn't try to stop me.

My relationship with Rafe was a lie. He'd chased me for a reason. He'd kissed me for a reason. Even when I'd looked into his eyes and thought I'd seen something special, it was there for a reason.

He'd tricked me. Lied to me. And the worst of it? I'd seen it coming.

I'd watched him go after half the girls at school. I'd rolled my eyes and said I couldn't believe they fell for it. When he made a run at me, I shot him down and I was so pleased with myself. I could see through the guy when no one else could.

Yeah, right.

Sure, I'd fended off his interest easily . . . because he wasn't all that interested at the time. Once he decided I might be who he was looking for, all he had to do was change tactics and I fell harder than any other girl.

Still, I'd suspected that he had a goal I couldn't see. But I didn't care. I didn't want it to be true, so I told myself it wasn't.

As much as I hated Rafe at that moment, the person I was most upset with was myself. As I trudged through the forest, I wallowed in that pain because it kept the rest at bay. Focus on the guy who played me for a fool, and I didn't need to think about being a skin-walker, having a twin brother, having a white mother who chose my brother over me. I didn't need to think about Annie, about becoming like Annie. Nope, just concentrate on the jerk that I'd really liked. Much easier that way. For now, at least.

I realized that my hip hurt a little, but when I stopped for a better look, the bullet graze was already scabbing over. Already healing. I shivered.

As I tugged my shirt down to cover the hole in my jeans, I thought about getting shot, which made me think about the dead guy. If being a skin-walker explained my healing powers, did it also explain my reaction to his death? And Mina's? I'd met Mina, so I felt sparks of pity. The other guy, though, had been a threat, so I felt nothing. Reacting as an animal would. Like a predator would.

I shivered again.

When my cell phone blipped, telling me I had a text message, I almost didn't answer. It wasn't Rafe—he didn't have a cell. But there wasn't anyone else I particularly cared to speak to. I wasn't even sure what I'd do when I got home. Tell my parents I'd eaten dinner at Rafe's? Pretend everything was okay? Or walk in and say "Hey, remember what that old woman at the tattoo studio said? Well, it turns out she wasn't crazy after all."

No, I wasn't saying anything to my parents. At least not until I was sure Rafe was telling the truth. In my gut, I knew he was. But informing my parents that I was, apparently, a member of a formerly extinct race of supernatural beings? Not until I knew more.

When I did check my phone and saw the text came from Daniel, my gut plummeted. I was supposed to meet him tonight. But how could I act like everything was okay? Keeping a secret from him was even worse than keeping one from my parents. Harder.

I checked his message.

Come over whenever you're done with dinner. My dad's not home yet.

As I read it, I realized I did want to go over. See Daniel. Tell Daniel. Get advice from someone I could trust, *really* trust.

I texted back saying I hadn't stayed for dinner so I had to grab something to eat.

Come anyway, he texted back. *I'll make spaghetti.*

TWENTY-EİGHT

TWENTY MINUTES LATER, I turned the corner to see Mr. Bianchi's car in the drive and knew there wouldn't be any spaghetti tonight. Cooking any of Daniel's mom's Italian recipes was forbidden when his dad was home. I was about to text to ask if he still wanted me to come over, when I saw him, out back in the boxing ring he'd made with Corey years ago.

I crept up behind him. I was good at that. Some of my friends joked it was my Native blood. But it wasn't, was it? Quiet as a cat.

The guys had made log benches for spectators, back when they were twelve and had visions of every girl in class lining those benches, swooning as they showed off in the ring. Never quite worked out that way—if there were spectators, they were more likely to be heckling than swooning—but the memory made me smile as I lowered myself quietly onto the bench behind Daniel.

He was shadowboxing, throwing punches and dodging an imaginary opponent. He was dressed in his usual gear—sweatpants and a tank top, both emblazoned with the school logo. I sat there and watched him, muscles flexing, sweat dripping from his dark blond hair, spraying with every swing, the silence punctuated by soft grunts when a blow seemed right and frustrated snorts when it didn't.

As I watched him, I started to relax. This was familiar. The sight, the sounds, the feel of the bench under my fingers, even the faint smell of perspiration—it was familiar and it was real and it made the last few hours drift away, wisps of a nightmare disconnected from reality.

Finally, he sensed me there and danced in a circle, fists falling to his sides, feet still moving. His face lit up in a grin so big it chased away the last of my worries.

"I'm guessing spaghetti is off the menu?" I said, nodding toward the house.

"Yeah. We're going out instead. My treat."

I didn't want to go out, but I would. Right now, I just wanted to be with him.

He looked over at me. "What's wrong?"

"Nothing."

"Liar. Is it Rafe?"

When I hesitated, his hands clenched, jaw clenching with them.

"That son of a bitch," he muttered.

"This is the part where you get to say 'I told you so.' "

He swore and came over to sit beside me. "What happened?"

He meant with Rafe, but I didn't want to tell him about Rafe. Instead, I thought of everything Rafe told me, everything I desperately needed to share. But I couldn't see any way to start.

So I settled for, "It just didn't work out. Big shock, I'm sure."

"He wasn't who you thought he was."

True, yet not in the way Daniel meant. Rafe really was the person I'd seen the other night on the roof, a decent guy thrown into a hellish situation, forced to grow up fast, be strong, take responsibility.

Even now, as much as I despised being part of his solution, I understood why he'd had to find me, whatever it took. He wasn't a bad person. He wasn't even someone I could hate. That made it all the harder.

"You liked him," Daniel said softly.

I forced a smile. "Fell for the wrong guy. Every girl has to do it once in her life. At least it was a quick lesson." I got to my feet. "I could really use that dinner."

He plucked the front of his sweat-soaked shirt. "I should have a shower and change. Guess I wasn't thinking this through too well."

He glanced toward the house, and I knew he wasn't eager

to go in. For the same reason he'd been out here boxing.

"You'll dry," I said. "And if the smell doesn't fade, I'll just sit at another table. Now come on before I starve."

We started circling wide around the house, heading for the road. The Blender was only a ten-minute walk, so we didn't have to bother with the truck. We made it about ten steps before the front door banged open and his dad yelled, "Where the hell do you think you're going?"

Daniel hunched his shoulders, as if against a blast of icy wind and mumbled, "Just keep walking."

Footsteps pounded behind us. A hand grabbed Daniel's shoulder and whipped him around. I could smell the booze.

Even before Daniel's mom left, I'd never seen his father much. If he was around, he'd joke with us in that awkward way grown-ups sometimes do with kids—a little too loud, trying a little too hard—and there'd be the smell of beer on his breath.

Daniel would get embarrassed and herd us outside to play. We all knew something was wrong, but everyone's parents had a drink now and then, and everyone's parents did embarrassing things. So no one thought about it much until his mom took off, and we realized his dad wasn't like every other parent, and maybe he never had been.

In the old days, his dad was always dressed up—shirt and tie, pressed pants, shiny shoes, dark hair slicked back, clean shaven, smelling faintly of cologne. Now, he still wore the shirt and slacks, but they were rumpled and stained, the shoes scuffed, his hair slick with oil, face covered in stubble. The only thing he smelled of was booze, so strong he seemed to have showered with it.

"I asked where you're going. You tore the kitchen apart trying to cook dinner, and now you're going to leave me with the mess?"

"No," Daniel's voice was low and calm, like he was talking to a child. "I said I'd clean it before bed. Maya and I are going out for dinner."

His dad blinked at me, like he hadn't seen me there. Then he scowled. No awkward joking for me these days. He didn't have much patience for any of Daniel's friends, but he seemed to like me the least, I suppose because I was the one Daniel stayed with when he needed to escape.

"Maya," he said. "Can't stay away, can you? Always coming around, teasing the boy."

Daniel's fingers wrapped around my elbow "We're leaving, Dad. There's a casserole in the—"

"You like teasing, don't you, Maya?" His dad stepped closer as Daniel pulled me back. "Just like all the girls. Tease and flirt and keep the boys running after you, spending their money building a climbing wall for you. Maybe get a kiss on the cheek for it. Holding out to see if he makes something of himself, because that's what counts for you girls. Is he going to be a hotshot lawyer? Olympic wrestler? Or just a lowly public defender? Or washed-up gym teacher?"

"That's enough." Daniel eased me behind him, while casting glances at the surrounding houses. He wanted to get out of there, but he didn't want to make a scene. "I'll be back—"

"Of course you'll be back. Got nowhere else to go. You're a parasite, boy. Just like your little not-yet girlfriend here. She's waiting to see what you'll make of yourself first, so she can live off you. That's what all women want. Find a good man. A stupid man who'll keep paying the bills even when she brings home a brat that doesn't look anything like you. She'll tell you he's yours, and you'll believe her until one day she finds someone else, and off she goes, leaving you to raise the bastard brat."

"See if they'll give you another job in the company," Daniel said. "Leave me here and go."

His father laughed. "You think they'll allow that? I'm trapped here, looking after a freak who isn't even my son—"

"And wishes to God that was true," Daniel muttered.

His dad swung. Daniel caught his arm and yanked it behind his back, spinning his dad around.

"If you don't think I'm yours, test it," he said. "You've got access to everything you need. But you won't, will you? You know I'm your son. You just like to torment me. You think that's getting back at her somehow. Well, it isn't." He wrenched his father's arm up until his eyes bulged. "I'm tired of it."

Daniel thrust him out of the way. They faced off. It didn't last long before his dad spun and walked away, spitting curses.

"I'm sorry," Daniel murmured to me. "He's just—"

"Drunk. And angry and bitter, and taking it out on you." I looked up at him. "Come stay with us."

He nodded. "Yeah, I'd better not go home tonight."

"I mean for good."

"It's only another couple of years, until I can escape to university like my brothers."

"Can they help? I'm sure there's something—"

"No. They're gone and happy to be gone. When they come home, they see things are worse and just pat me on the back and tell me to hang in there."

"Will you think about it? Staying with us full-time? Please? We've got the room, and my parents have always said you're welcome for as long as you want."

"I'll . . . think about it."

As we walked, I knew I wouldn't be telling him what Rafe had said tonight. He had too much else on his mind. It could wait. Let me work it out for myself first.

We reached the Blender—a soda shop owned by the Morrises. It looks like something out of the fifties, and sells burgers and ice cream. There's even a jukebox in the corner.

We walked in as Mayor Tillson and his wife were walking out, Nicole dawdling behind them, Sam even farther back.

"Maya. Daniel." The mayor gave us an election-poster

smile and thumped Daniel on the back. "Practicing for regionals? Good to see it." He winked. "Even if you could already win it with one hand tied behind your back."

Mrs. Tillson rolled her eyes, murmuring, "Leave the kids alone, Phil," and smiling as she prodded him past us.

Nicole frowned at me as her parents left. "Daniel said you were eating at Rafe's."

"It didn't work out."

"Nicole," her mom called. "Dad has a town meeting tonight."

"What's this with you and Rafe?" Sam said as she walked up.

"Nothing." I turned to Nicole. "I'll talk to you later."

"Tonight," she said. "Call, okay?"

"I'll try."

She looked hurt by that, so I said I *would* call. She left, Sam trailing after her, casting glances back at us, like she was trying to figure out what was up.

When we sat, Daniel said, "Do you want to talk about it?"

"No, I want to talk about our plans for tonight."

While we ate, we quietly made a list of things to look for. As we left the Blender, Dr. Hajek drove by. She honked and waved. Then Chief Carling passed and did the same.

"Looks like the whole council is going to that meeting," Daniel said. "Aren't they usually the last Tuesday of the month?"

271

I nodded. My dad went if there was anything on the agenda about the park.

"So why call a special . . . ?" He stopped walking.

"Mina Lee," I said. "They're meeting to discuss her death. Guess we have a stop to make."

TWENTY-NİNE

THE TOWN COUNCIL MET at the school. That meant we knew exactly how to sneak in. There was a window in the guys' locker room that never closed right. Well, it didn't after grade eight, when Corey and Brendan broke in to set up a video camera in the girls' locker room. No videos were ever taken. Daniel had caught them and said if the camera wasn't gone by Monday morning, he'd give us photos from the last time they went skinny-dipping, when the lake had been really cold and . . . well, the photos wouldn't have been flattering.

Corey had busted the window frame trying to get in to set up the camera. Daniel had fixed it, but only good enough so the damage wasn't obvious from the outside. Now we all had an after-hours entrance.

The hardest part about getting in was waiting for a break

in the traffic flowing into the parking lot. A seven o'clock town council meeting in Salmon Creek means "come by when you're done with dinner," so at seven-thirty, cars were still driving into the lot—right beside the broken window.

As we watched from the bushes, a minivan pulled in, headlights illuminating the far side of the lot, where one lone vehicle sat apart from the rest. My dad's Jeep. Seeing that made my heart give an extra thump. Even if I thought the town was involved in Mina's death—which I didn't—I knew my dad had nothing to do with it. But why *was* he here? If the meeting was about dealing with the cougar problem, they didn't need the whole council for that.

Finally, Daniel boosted me through, then vaulted in himself. We stepped out of the locker room into the pitch-black hall.

"Lead the way," Daniel said.

After taking a moment for my eyes to adjust, I led him to the classrooms at the end.

"Hear anything?" he whispered.

I nodded. "Do you?"

He shook his head. He didn't question why I could and he couldn't. That's the way it has always been, like me being able to see better in the dark. Serena used to say it was because I lived in the "middle of freaking nowhere," so I was used to the silence and the dark. Only now I knew that wasn't the reason at all.

Improved night vision. Improved sense of smell and

hearing. Improved agility. Improved stealth. Signs that something more than human blood flowed in my veins. Signs that I was—

I shivered and Daniel rubbed my shoulder. "We can turn back if you're not sure about this."

"I'm fine. We'll need to get closer. I'm just hearing voices, not any words."

I crept along the hall. When Daniel's shoe squeaked behind me, I winced. No one came racing from the meeting room, though. They were deep in a heated discussion.

I led Daniel into the intermediary grades classroom. It was beside the meeting room and there was a vent joining the two. When we'd been in that class, Serena and I had figured out that if I took a seat at the back, I could hear who was getting in trouble. That's a lot less useful than it sounds—at our school, there was never anything interesting going on or anyone getting in trouble who we didn't already know was in trouble.

Daniel moved a desk under the vent. He motioned me up, but I whispered that I could hear fine where I was.

We'd only needed to listen for a minute before realizing there was another reason why the town would call an emergency meeting tonight, one that had nothing to do with Mina Lee, but that explained why my dad had to be there.

"Okay," Dad was saying. "So far, the fires are all to the west and the wind is blowing in the same direction, meaning we aren't in its path."

"*Yet*," Chief Carling said.

"Exactly. At this point, the fires are under control, but we all know that can change. So can the wind direction. We've been lucky enough to have wet autumns for the last five years. That means, though, that our evacuation plan is designed to deal with children, and, as we all know, teenagers are a bit tougher to manage."

"Like herding cats," Mayor Tillson said. "Annabelle's thinking we might need to slip a GPS in Sam's running shoes, just so we can *find* her if we need to evacuate."

"And we now have Rafael and his sister," Dr. Hajek said. "We may want to consider offering them a place in town until the threat passes. At the very least, we need to get them cell phones."

The others agreed and so the conversation went—plans for a potential evacuation. All very important. And very dull. I motioned to Daniel that we should leave, but he shook his head.

After a half hour more of evacuation strategy, Mayor Tillson said, "And now, as long as we're all here, I've asked Dr. Inglis and Chief Carling for an update on our recent tragedy."

Daniel nodded in satisfaction.

Chief Carling spoke first. "The young woman's name, as most of you know, was Mina Lee. Or that's the name on her ID, which appears to be fake, as we discovered when we tried to notify next of kin. That would seem to confirm our suspicion that she was a corporate spy. I have her description out to my contacts, and with any luck, we'll find out her real name so we can notify her family. Her death hasn't been ruled a homicide, so my main priority is identifying the victim. But I have, of course, started a case file, should the situation change."

"And, at this point, I don't think it will," Dr. Inglis said. "Cause of death was exsanguination. Fatal loss of blood. The damage to the throat tissue makes it impossible to determine whether it was homicide, misadventure, or predation. For now, I'm going to say it was most likely predation, given the rising number of cougar encounters and the obvious signs of feeding. When we find the young woman's family, if they want to get a second opinion, we can do that."

Everyone agreed this was fair. My dad excused himself to get home and resume tracking the fires. After he left, they continued talking about the murder but only boring stuff like moving the body to cold storage at the medical lab. Daniel agreed we could leave now. Time to check out the Braun place.

We parked down an old logging road, then walked back, sticking to the woods. We got the spare key from the shed and went inside.

The cottage had already been searched. It wasn't a rip-the-place-apart kind of search, just kitchen and dresser drawers opened and stuff inside left piled on top, like Chief

Carling had been looking for anything that might help her find Mina Lee's family.

We'd hoped to find a laptop, but there was no sign of one.

While Daniel searched more thoroughly, I checked caller ID on the landline. It said she'd had five calls since yesterday, presumably all after her death. Three came from unlisted numbers. The other two had the same number attached with an area code I didn't recognize. I wrote it down. Then I played her messages. There was only one, and it must have come in after Chief Carling searched the place, because no one had listened to it yet.

"Hey, it's me." The voice was male. "You did get my text messages, right? The Nasts paid me a visit. They're starting to think we're holding out on them, that we found something and we're seeing if the Cortezes will pay more. I told them we aren't stupid enough to try that."

A pause. "We aren't, right? Double-cross a Cabal and we'll be paying the price into the afterlife." Another pause. "You know that, right?"

The man swore. "I can't believe you'd ever be that stupid, but if I don't hear back from you soon, I'm bolting—and taking everything we have so far with me."

Daniel walked in, frowning as the message finished. "When did that come in?"

"Tonight. If anyone else left messages, someone erased them. This one's from the only number on caller ID." I lifted a scrap of paper. "I wrote it down."

"Can you play it again? I missed the beginning. Someone drove by on a dirt bike and drowned it out."

I did. As he listened, his frown grew.

"Could be corporate espionage," he said. "A drug company wants to buy stolen research. Sounds like that guy's really afraid of them, though. I imagine it'd be a shady company, if they're willing to buy that information. Maybe that's what *cabal* means. Industry slang."

"It doesn't explain what she wanted with *us*," I said. "How would cozying up to local teens help?"

"I don't know."

He walked over to the desk and started moving stuff around, looking under the phone and the answering machine, searching drawers. I kept thinking about the message.

We'll be paying the price into the afterlife.

It was probably just an exaggerated phrase, like saying "kick our asses into the next century." But put it together with that book on witches and the stuff on skin-walkers and it just . . . It bugged me.

"Daniel?" I said.

He bent to run his hand under a drawer. "Hmm?"

When I didn't continue, he straightened. "What's up?"

"I found out something today, and it's going to sound crazy—"

The back door clicked. I waved Daniel to silence and mouthed, "Someone's here."

He opened the folding door to the closet. I hesitated.

Even thinking about being in such a small place made my skin crawl. I glanced at the window instead, but he shook his head. No time for that.

The closet was even smaller than it looked. Daniel went in first and I had to back in. To get the door closed, he had to put his arm around my waist and pull me against him.

"Just relax," he said, his breath hot against my ear.

His hand slid to rest against my hip. He stayed bent over my shoulder, as if trying to see through the slats in the door, his breath ruffling my hair. When I shifted, he put his other hand on my other hip. I shifted again.

"Stop squirming," he said. "I didn't wear my steel-toed boots."

I stepped off his foot. "Sorry."

"I know you hate small places. Just close your eyes and relax."

I did and focused on the light footsteps. Chief Carling?

Drawers opened and shut. Papers rustled.

The intruder finished in the living room and went into the bedroom. More searching. Now Daniel was the one getting restless, fidgeting and shifting. When I tried to pull away to give him room, he jumped like I'd startled him, then murmured, "Just relax," like I'd been the one fussing.

Finally, the intruder came into the study. Through the slats, I could make out only a dark figure, but I picked up a faint smell of—

A day ago, I'd have told myself I was smelling perfume

or hair gel or fabric softener, something that would identify a person. Now I realized I was smelling the person's scent.

I leaned forward. Daniel tried to stop me, but I waved him off. I bent, putting my face to the slats. It was a far from perfect peephole, but I could see enough to confirm my guess.

I pushed open the folding door and stepped out. "What are you doing here?"

Sam spun.

Her eyes narrowed when she saw me. "What am *I* doing here? I'm not the one hiding in—" Her gaze lifted over my shoulder. "Daniel?"

She looked from me to him.

I realized I was in a notorious make-out spot with Daniel. "We're not—"

"What are you looking for, Sam?" he said, stepping toward her.

"Looking for? N-nothing."

"You were really interested in Mina Lee," I said. "You thought she was here because of you."

"What? No."

"Why are you going through her things?"

"None of your business."

She brushed past me. As she walked away, I saw papers sticking out of her rear pocket. I snatched them. She yelped and spun, swiping at me as I backed out of reach.

"That's mine," she said.

"No, it's not." I held the papers up for Daniel to see.

"Recognize the handwriting?"

He nodded. "It's Ms. Lee's."

"You don't know that." Sam lunged to grab them, but I backed up again.

"She left a note for Daniel," I said. "That's her handwriting."

Sam went still. "A note about what?"

I scanned the first page. "Not about you. This one is, though. Background notes. Where you're from. What happened to your—" I looked up at her. "Your parents didn't die in a car accident. They were—"

"Give those back," she said, advancing on me.

"Your parents were murdered," I said. "Why does everyone think—?"

She hit me. A right hook to the jaw. I flew off my feet. Daniel knocked her out of the way before she could hit me again. She grabbed the pages and took off.

Daniel started to go after her, then saw me and ran back, grabbing tissue. I tasted blood. As I winced, blood gushed from a split lip. Daniel pressed the tissues to my mouth.

He moved me back to sit on the edge of the desk. "Hold that. I'm going to find some ice."

I shook my head. "Sam. Those pages—"

The roar of a dirt bike stopped me. I tried to get up, but he tugged me back onto the desk.

"She's gone," he said. "We need to stop the bleeding and

get some ice on that." He paused. "Are your teeth . . . ?"

I ran my tongue over them, ignoring the sharp tang of blood. "Present and accounted for."

"Good. Hold on then."

THIRTY

I DID HOLD ON—TO the tissues. I didn't stay put, though. With my free hand, I mopped up drops of blood from the hardwood floor. If this turned into a murder investigation, I definitely didn't want my blood found in the victim's house.

When Daniel came back, he had some ice wrapped in a dishcloth. As he exchanged it for the bloody tissues, he said, "I can't believe she did that. I mean, Sam is way too fast with her fists, but to *deck* you? Over papers?"

I'd been thinking the same thing. I felt weirdly hurt—and not because my jaw ached. I always thought Sam and I got along okay. In the last few days, she'd even been friendly. Now I realized that was only because she thought I might have more information on Mina Lee.

I told Daniel that, then said, "I'm still shocked that she

hit me. I know she took a swing at Rafe's sister—" I stopped, realizing what I was saying, then continued. "She's . . . brain damaged. That's why he's away from school a lot."

"Looking after her." Daniel wadded up the bloodied tissues inside clean ones, then stuffed them into his pocket. "I hadn't heard that."

"No one knows. And no one can know. She's his guardian, and if people find out . . ."

"They won't from me. You know that." He leaned beside me, against the desk. "So, what happened? Sam didn't realize Rafe's sister was brain damaged and lashed out when she provoked her?"

"Not unless being extremely friendly can be considered provocation."

Daniel shook his head. "The girl's definitely got some loose wiring, and it seems to be getting looser." He glanced at me. "Steer clear, okay?"

"I intend to."

"So those sheets said her parents had been murdered? What else?"

"That was as far as I got. Her parents were killed in a home invasion, and it said Sam 'survived,' which must mean she was there. I guess that might explain some of the loose wiring. And why the Tillsons told everyone her parents died in a car accident."

"Less traumatic."

I nodded. Made sense, but it still bugged me. Why had

Sam still been determined to get those papers before I read more? What else was in there?

"Bleeding's stopped," I said, taking the makeshift ice pack. "We should keep looking around. Sam found something. Maybe we can, too."

We discovered where Sam had found the pages—under the mattress in the main bedroom. We hadn't looked there earlier, and we wouldn't have now if we hadn't noticed the bedcovers were wrinkled.

Under the mattress was a file containing background info on every kid in our class. Parents' names, date of birth, hobbies. Mina had put a lot of emphasis on hobbies, underlining some of them, like wrestling, boxing, and law for Daniel. The emphasis on sports and extracurricular interests would make sense . . . if you were filling out applications for a dating service. Why would a corporate spy care what local teens liked to do in their spare time?

"It's a cover," Daniel said. "If anyone gets close, she can pull out these, and the hobbies and stuff make it seem like she really is doing a general interest story." He flipped through the pages. "She's got everyone here. Even Rafe, though his is filled with question marks and notes for follow-up. Seems she wasn't having much luck getting background on him. Weird."

I kept my gaze on the pages, so he wouldn't see that I knew it wasn't weird at all. "Where's my page?"

"Right—" He flipped through again. "Huh. Seems someone *is* missing."

"Me?"

He didn't answer until he'd laid out all the sheets on the bed, in alphabetical order. Everyone was there except Sam and me.

"I bet she grabbed yours, too," Daniel said. "Sam, I mean. They weren't in any kind of order, and she had a bunch of pages. Yours was probably behind hers." He folded the sheets and stuck them in the backpack we'd brought. "Let's keep looking."

We didn't find anything else. When we were done, I went back into the study to make sure we'd left it the way we found it.

"We should double-check that number you wrote down." Daniel clicked through the recall list. "Hey, it tracks calls out, too. The last five."

"Grab those." I handed him a pen.

He started writing down numbers, then stopped and stared down at the display.

"Daniel?" I peered over at the number.

"It's my mom's cell." He blinked and pulled his gaze away. "Or it was. Dad got it from the lab files, and he used to call it when he was drunk. She changed it a few months ago."

I didn't ask how he recognized the number. I could picture him, writing it down from redial, then sitting in his room, phone in hand, preparing for a call he'd never make.

Daniel didn't get emails from his mother. Didn't get calls. Didn't even get birthday cards. I don't think he ever got an explanation either. She just left.

I don't know how anyone could do that to a kid, but I especially don't know how anyone could do it to Daniel. We used to joke that he was so good he made the rest of us look like brats. I'm sure he wondered what he'd done to make her leave and not look back. I think that about my birth mother, who'd never had a chance to know me, so he must think it about his mom.

"You okay?" I said.

"Course." He shrugged it off as he put the phone back. "But I'm wondering how Mina Lee got that number, and more important, why she'd be calling it. At least twice."

"Because, other than Serena's parents, your mom is the only employee who ever left Salmon Creek. Serena's parents still work for the St. Clouds. Your mother doesn't. Which might make her more willing to talk about problems."

"And if there were problems, she might know." Dr. Bianchi had been a chemist at the lab. "We could check her old computer. My dad's probably passed out by now."

"Let's do that."

Daniel's father wasn't passed out. We could tell that as soon as we rounded the corner and heard the TV blaring through the open kitchen window. But he was too engrossed in his TV show to notice us as we sneaked inside. Daniel waved me to his mom's study while he closed the window. The neighbors never complained about the noise, but it embarrassed him anyway.

His mom's office looked exactly the way it had when she'd taken off. Although the company had left her desktop computer for Daniel, his dad wouldn't let him use the office, making him do his homework at the kitchen table.

I slipped in, waited for Daniel, then closed the door behind him. He turned on the computer. He knew her password—she'd given it to him once when his laptop was acting wonky. It was 19Curie11, after the scientist Marie Curie's 1911 Nobel Prize in chemistry. That password said a lot about Dr. Bianchi and what mattered in her life.

"We probably won't find anything," Daniel said as he logged on. "I know she had to do all her work on the company network and save the files on their servers. They shut that connection down after she left. I'm hoping she saved something to the hard drive, though. Dad told them he wiped it so I could use it, but since I never got to, I don't think he bothered. He doesn't come in here."

Someone had cleared the hard drive, just not very well. Whether it was his mother before she left, quickly deleting files, or his dad doing a cursory wipe in case the St. Clouds checked, I don't know. The documents and email folders had been emptied, but not wiped from the trash.

Most of what was in it was garbage. Family schedules.

Shopping lists. Personal emails to college friends and colleagues. Then an email from a colleague that wasn't personal.

It was a chain of messages that ended shortly before she left. The last one told Dr. Bianchi to do what she wanted with the information, just make sure she printed the correspondence, then deleted it.

Daniel scrolled down to the previous message.

"Perfect," his mother had written. "They won't try to hold me to my contract now."

Beneath that, her correspondent had written, "Fine, here's the list. Good enough? It better be. Don't ask me for anything else. We're even now."

A list of names followed. Under that was the beginning of the email chain.

I need more, Mike. Damn it, you owe me. Telling them I know the experiment went wrong won't help. I need proof. Give me the names of the failed subjects. They screwed up in Buffalo and I'm not sticking around until the same thing happens here.

I reread the emails in sequential order, figuring it out aloud as I did. "Your mom discovered that the St. Clouds were hiding a failed project in Buffalo, where Dr. Davidoff works. Whatever research they're doing here, she expected the same thing to happen, and she wanted out before it blew up in their faces. She blackmailed them with the details in order to get out of her contract."

Ever since Mrs. Bianchi left, people in Salmon Creek had whispered about how she broke her contract. The most popular theory was that her husband had been abusing her. Wouldn't it have made more sense to get rid of him, though? He was in the business office; she was the valuable scientist.

We searched for the earlier emails, where she'd gotten the details about the failed study. They were gone. She must have been careful about permanently erasing them but got careless with the last messages, eager to leave.

Daniel scrolled the email back to the list of names.

"Project Genesis," he said. "Have you ever heard of it?"

"No, I—" I stopped and stared at a name on the list. *"Elizabeth Delaney."*

Daniel frowned. "Is that a relative?"

"Not that I know of."

"Well, no one in your family works for the St. Clouds, so it must be a coincidence. Common enough last name, isn't it?"

I nodded.

"Make a note of it, then. We should write down all—"

A crash made us both jump.

"Daniel?" His dad called from the kitchen. "You here, Danny? I need some help."

Daniel let out a puff of breath. The nickname and the plaintive tone told him his dad was at the far end of a drinking bout, past the anger.

"Danny?" Footsteps approached the study.

Daniel swore as we realized the light was on. He motioned

me back, then opened the door and slid out. I took out my house keys and plugged my key chain thumb drive into his mother's computer.

"Hey, Dad. Did you drop a plate? Let me clean that—"

"What were you doing in your mother's office?"

"Looking for a stapler."

"You know I don't like you in there." An edge seeped into Mr. Bianchi's voice.

"It's okay, Dad. Everything's all right."

"I don't—"

Daniel's voice took on the same tone that had convinced the old woman to tell us what *yee naaldlooshii* meant. "Everything's all right. You can go lie down. I've got it under control."

I turned off the computer, then peered through the door crack. Daniel stood eye to eye with his father. Mr. Bianchi shifted uneasily, like he was trying to break eye contact but couldn't.

"Just go watch TV, Dad. Everything's all right."

Mr. Bianchi nodded, then shuffled back into the living room. Daniel waited until he was gone before coming back to me.

I lifted the thumb drive. He nodded and waved me out.

"Close one," I said. "Thank God for your amazing powers of persuasion."

"Yeah, if only they worked when he was really pissed. And really pissed off."

"Still, you need to teach me how to do that sometime, so I can use it on *my* dad, get whatever I want."

"Like you don't already."

"Maybe. But I'm always looking for ways to fine-tune the process."

He shook his head and waved me to the truck.

An unintentional side effect from Serena's medication must have killed her. We were almost certain of that now. The St. Clouds were already covering up the failure of this Project Genesis, and they didn't dare admit that they were responsible for Serena, too. It didn't matter if it'd been a freak side effect and they honestly thought the drugs were safe. They had to cover it up.

So what had happened when Mina Lee came snooping around? Did she find something and confront them? Did they kill her?

The problem with that theory was the "they." *Who* killed her? Chief Carling? Mayor Tillson? Dr. Inglis? No way. Daniel agreed. His theory was that the St. Clouds had sent someone to murder her and no one in town was involved.

I was good with the no-one-in-town part, but the other half of the explanation seemed a little Hollywood to me. Hired assassins in Salmon Creek? This wasn't New York or even Vancouver. You couldn't just sneak in here unnoticed. The bounty hunter who'd come after Rafe had barely made it to town, but I bet people were already talking about him, wondering who he'd been, what he wanted with Rafe.

Damn. I hadn't thought of that. People would have noticed him. He'd spoken to someone who knew me. There would be questions. We needed—

No, Rafe could handle that. My problem right now was Serena—or that was the problem I was focusing on, to keep from thinking of Rafe and Annie and skin-walkers and—

Serena.

We thought we knew how she died. So what would we do about it?

I suppose the obvious answer would be "expose the failed research to the world and bring down the St. Clouds." Or that would be the obvious answer if we thought they were mad scientists about to unleash unsafe drugs on the world. But they weren't. They were the people who gave us a great life and took care of us, and if they were responsible for Serena's death, we couldn't ignore that, but nor could we do anything drastic until we were sure it hadn't been a freak accident that they'd learned from.

We needed to know more.

THIRTY-ONE

WHEN I GOT HOME, my parents noticed my lip right away—kind of hard to hide. I said I'd been sparring with Daniel, who played along, teasing me about not ducking fast enough.

Dad was on the computer, tracking the wildfires. I wasn't eager to retreat to the silence of my bedroom, so I suggested we keep Dad company. The four of us played poker until Dad decided he could stop monitoring the situation and grab a few hours of sleep.

That night I lay in bed for hours, thinking mostly about what Rafe said. I tossed and turned, but I could smell the forest through my open window, and it was like trying to sleep when I was starving and could smell steak grilling outside.

Finally I got up to close the window. I stood there, looking out. Moonlight flooded the yard. Scents washed over me. Even the sounds of the forest seemed to call to me, and I told myself I was just reacting to what Rafe said, but that wasn't true. I'd felt this way for the last three nights. Only now I knew what it meant and that made all the difference.

I wanted to go out. I wanted *so* badly to go out. Even Fitz, stretched on the railing again, watched me as if to say, "Well, are you coming?"

When I stepped out the balcony doors, he chirped, rising and stretching. Then I climbed onto the railing and crouched there, and he chirped again, glanced over, and leaped. He landed awkwardly, then looked up at me, yellow eyes glinting.

I jumped. I hit the ground in a crouch. Pain darted through my legs, but I'd instinctively landed right, without injury. Just like Rafe and Annie. Just like a cat.

Fitz's chirp pulled me from my thoughts. He started toward the forest, then glanced back to see if I was coming. I followed.

After a few steps, a cold nose brushed my hand and I looked down to see Kenjii, seeming worried as she nudged me. I patted her head and told her I was fine and she followed at my side. Fitz trotted along at a distance, as if he was simply heading the same way.

The forest was like a warm wave washing over me. My muscles relaxed, my heart rate slowed, and quiet energy pulsed through me.

I glanced at Kenjii and Fitz, then over at the recuperation

shed, the animals inside stirring, as if they sensed me nearby.

We get our energy from nature.

Control over animals.

Healing powers.

Sound familiar?

I shivered, and Kenjii licked my fingers, whining. I patted her absently and gazed around, as if I expected to see something.

See what?

I don't know.

Yes, you do. You're looking for what drew you out here.

I searched the darkness.

"I'm over here."

I spun to see Rafe on the edge of the clearing. He stepped back, hands raised.

"That was a warning, so I wouldn't spook you." A wry smile. "Not much chance of that, I suppose, finding me outside your house at two in the morning."

"What are you doing here?"

"I'm *not* stalking you, as bad as it looks. I wasn't going near your house. I just . . . I couldn't sleep, and I thought maybe you couldn't either, so I walked over, in case you came out."

"That's quite a hike."

He shrugged and stepped toward me, then stopped short. "Your lip."

"Sam."

He swore. "What happened?"

"Daniel and I bumped into her, and . . ." I shrugged. "It's not important. I—"

"It's Daniel," he said.

"What?"

"She likes Daniel. Along with every girl in this town except you. He's the local equivalent of the high school quarterback." He stepped closer. "But if she's got you in her sights, watch out, Maya. She's got problems. And she has a crush on Daniel."

"I don't think it's like that."

"Then why'd she flip out when Nicole went to your party with him?"

"What?"

"Hayley said she heard them fighting next door before the party. Sam found out Nicole was going with Daniel and lit into her. That's what Hayley was talking to me about after the climb. Saying how surprised she was that Sam showed up, and that Nicole better watch her back."

He met my gaze. "I'd say the same to you. I know you and Daniel are just friends, but Sam . . ."

"She's unstable." A memory flashed, something Serena said about Sam. While I tried to recall it, Rafe took another step forward.

"How are you doing?" he said. "Other than that?"

What do you think? You told me I'm a shape-shifter. That

I'm going to change into a cougar. That someday I might not change back.

"Just . . . not sleeping well these days."

Another step closer, but still keeping his distance. "Is it the dreams?"

I looked up at him.

"Dreams of the forest," he said. "Of running. You wake up with a fever. You need to get outside."

I nodded.

"Me, too. It started a little while ago. Annie went through it just before . . ."

"She started to Shift."

"It's the Calling. The start of the transformation."

"So it's coming." I tried not to shiver. "How much longer?"

"A couple of weeks with Annie." He paused. "We need to talk about all that but . . . later. Let's just . . ." He looked out at the forest, then at me. "Let's just go for now. Run. Work it off. It'll help you sleep."

He backed into the forest, and his eyes shone like amber.

"Come on," he whispered. "I know you're still mad at me, but I won't try anything. Just forget that for now and come on."

Forget that for now and come on.

God, how I wanted to. I wanted to forget everything he'd done. Just go with him, be with him, run with him, and let it be the way it was before, the way it was in my dreams. I looked at him, half hidden in the shadows, watching me, waiting for me, and I wanted it so badly tears prickled my eyes and I blinked hard.

"Maya?" He stepped back into the clearing.

"I can't. I just"—I sucked in cool night air—"can't."

He exhaled, a loud sigh that made Kenjii slip over and nudge his hand.

"Do you want to talk?" he asked.

I shook my head.

Kenjii returned to my side and whined. At a chirp from overhead, I looked up to see Fitz watching from a tree branch.

"You've got this whole power-over-animals thing down a lot better than me," Rafe said, trying for a smile. "They like me well enough, but that's about it. And the healing part, too. You—"

"You don't have to make nice, Rafe. I know you want my help finding the people who did this to us. But I need those answers, too. I'm not stupid—"

"God forbid," he muttered.

"What's that supposed to mean?"

"Just agreeing. You're not stupid." He sat on a tree stump. "You think you could have handled this better, don't you?"

"What?"

"You understand why I needed to find you, but you

disagree with the way I did it."

"Uh, yeah. Hitting on girls you don't care about, pretending to be someone you're not, pretending you like them . . . Sure, guys take that road all the time, hoping for a shortcut to sex. But that doesn't mean it's okay."

"Whoa, wait a minute. Are you saying I'm no better than guys who—"

"You think it's okay to hurt people to get what you want, just like they do. Yes, I think you could have found another way to do it. I just don't think you wanted to bother."

"Or maybe I didn't have the brains."

"I never said—"

"You would have thought up a better way."

"I'm not going to fight with you about this." I turned to go. "You think you did the right thing. I think you didn't. No amount of arguing is going to change that."

"Hayley's right," he said. "You don't give an inch to anyone."

"What?"

"You heard me."

"Seems Hayley's telling you a lot. A word of advice? She's not the most reliable source of information in Salmon Creek."

"Because she tried to cheat on her math homework in seventh grade?"

"That was a long time ago."

"Exactly her point. You caught her breaking into your

locker to copy your math homework. One screwup that you've never forgotten."

"If she says I squealed on her, she's lying. The teachers never found out."

"Because you handled it your own way. You started ignoring her. And if you ignored her, then your friends did, too."

"So I turned her into the school outcast?" I laughed. "Seriously, does she seem like an outcast to you? She's got her crowd. It's just not my crowd. She hangs out with us when she wants to. Nicole doesn't ignore her. Corey definitely doesn't ignore her."

"No, he'll make out with her when he's had a beer or two and there's no one else around. But if you and Daniel can't stand her, then she's not dating material."

"That's crap. Yes, I don't trust Hayley, and, yes, it started with that homework. But if she's telling people that I've made her life miserable for five years because of it?" I shook my head and started to turn away.

Rafe stepped in front of me. "I'm sure she's the one still holding a grudge. I also think she's the one who dosed your drink. But the point, Maya, is that you don't give anyone a second chance. One strike and we're out."

"So I'm inflexible and intolerant."

"Maybe."

"Well, then it's a good thing you're done with me, isn't it?"

I headed for the house. Rafe let out a curse. I heard a

thump and a gasp of pain. I glanced back to see him cradling his hand, the small tree beside him quivering from a blow. He looked up and caught me watching. Then he spun and strode into the forest.

THIRTY-TWO

AS I APPROACHED THE house, I could see Mom on the porch, her feet bare as she tugged on one of my dad's jackets and peered anxiously into the forest. When she saw me, she let out a sigh of relief.

"I heard voices," she said. "Was that Rafe?"

"Yes."

She pulled the jacket around her and lowered her voice. "I know you really like him, Maya, but you can't be meeting him—"

"I wasn't. It's over."

"Oh." She waited until I was on the porch. "Did you just break up now?"

I shook my head. "Earlier. He came by to see if I'd talk. Maybe work things out. We couldn't."

"I'm sorry."

She gave me a hug, then ushered me into the house, Kenjii following. She led me to the kitchen and started fixing a snack. I wasn't hungry, but I wasn't eager to go to bed either.

Kenjii lay at my feet and I petted her as Mom put crackers on a plate. As she was slicing cheese, she said, with her back still to me, "Your lip. Does that have anything to do with . . . ?"

"Did Rafe hit me? One, I wouldn't sneak into the woods to talk to a guy who split my lip. Two, if something like that happened, Daniel would never help me cover it up."

"Sorry," she said, bringing the plate to the table. "I had to ask."

"I know."

She sat across from me. I nibbled on a cheese-covered cracker.

After a minute, she said, "He wasn't what you thought he was."

Exactly what Daniel had said. I nodded, then I asked, "Do you think I'm intolerant?"

She frowned. "In what way?"

"If someone screws up, I won't give him a second chance. I've made up my mind about him and I won't trust him again."

"Is that what Rafe said?"

"Something like that."

She leaned back in her chair and watched me for a moment before she responded. "He wasn't who you thought he was, and you're angry with him for tricking you."

I nodded.

"If I'm right, though, you're even more angry with yourself for not seeing it."

I put down my cracker. "But I *did* see it. That's the problem. I saw what he was before anyone else did."

"A player."

I nodded. "He knew I wasn't going to fall for that, so he showed me . . ." I picked at the cheese on my cracker. "He showed me something else."

"Another part of himself," she said softly. "And you fell for him."

I wanted to deny it. Salvage my pride and say, no, it wasn't that way, I only liked him a little. But it *was* that way.

So I nodded, and she reached out for my hand.

"That's what you're really upset about. Being tricked. Yes, you set high standards for people. Too high sometimes. But you set higher ones for yourself and that's what worries me more, Maya. I want you to have big dreams, big goals. I want you to strive to achieve them. But I don't want to see you beating yourself up every time you make a mistake."

I nodded.

"I don't know the whole situation with Rafe, and I'm not going to pry," she said. "But if he's trying to talk to you,

you should hear him out. Maybe you can forgive him. More important, forgive yourself."

As Mom was cleaning up, I thought about what Rafe said, about the experiments.

I was genetically modified. And I was living in a medical research town. Again I pictured that list of names.

"Does Dad have a relative named Elizabeth Delaney?"

Mom paused. "Isn't that his cousin Greg's wife? No, that's Bethany, I think. You should ask him. God knows he has plenty of relatives. Did you meet someone online?"

I shook my head. After another minute, I asked, "How exactly did Dad get this job?"

"Hmm?"

"Someone at school said the St. Clouds just offered him the job."

She laughed and sat down again. "I wish it'd been that easy. If someone's implying that he had connections and was handed his position, the answer is no. I'm sure that applies to some people here, but not us. The St. Cloud Corporation wanted a new park warden, so they hired a headhunter. Do you know what that is?"

"A company that looks for people matching a job description."

"Right. The St. Clouds wanted a specific kind of person. They preferred a young warden with a young family. And, if not Canadian, then with a Canadian connection, to make the transition easier."

"Someone who'd put down roots and stay. Become part of the community."

"Exactly. When we arrived for the interview, there were a half dozen other applicants. We suited the profile better than most. I'm Canadian, with family nearby, and, as much as I loved Oregon, I wanted to come home. You were the same age as a lot of the kids here. And your dad came with glowing recommendations. Still, we almost missed out. A woman got the offer first but ended up turning it down."

What did I expect? That my family was linked to the St. Clouds by this Project Genesis? That they just happened to be living in Oregon when I was found and were approved to adopt me? Or that the St. Clouds were the scientists who'd genetically modified me, and they'd found me and lured my parents here?

If I thought about it more, I'd have realized there couldn't be a connection. The research going on here was drug related, not genetic. The St. Clouds weren't mad scientists; they were a legitimate corporation. You could find them on the internet and find links to the drug companies they owned.

It might seem coincidental—being genetically modified and living in a medical research town—but I couldn't see any connection beyond that. My parents obviously knew nothing of my past and neither did the St. Clouds.

ꖶ   ꖶ   ꖶ

When I got back to bed, I fell straight into a nightmare about Serena. Saw her disappearing under the water as if yanked down. Swam out and felt someone yanking *me* down.

When the hand released me, I started to swim up. Then pain sliced through my legs, so sharp and strong that I howled. Water filled my lungs.

I jolted awake. My legs seized and I had to jam my pillow against my mouth to keep from screaming. It felt like a dozen charley horses hitting at once, excruciating cramps that brought tears to my eyes.

If I could have cried out, I think I would have. But the pain clamped my jaws shut and all I could do was lie on my side in agony until, slowly, my muscles began to relax.

As I massaged them, the knotted muscles felt like golf balls under my skin. I inhaled and exhaled as deeply as I could, remembering all my runner's tricks for dealing with leg cramps.

Only these weren't from running. I heard Rafe's voice.

Muscle pains. I've been getting them a lot lately.

When I could stand, I walked to my mirror. I lifted one bare arm and made a fist, watching my muscles bunch and imagined them bunching more, changing, fur sprouting as my upper arm became a thick foreleg, my fist turned to a paw, huge claws sheathed. I shook my arm and turned away.

People couldn't turn into animals. They just couldn't.

But you saw it.

And that was the reason I hadn't protested, hadn't

questioned. I'd watched Annie Shift.

If I really wanted to, I could find an explanation, however lame—I was overtired from sleepless nights, I'd hallucinated, I'd been drugged. Only I hadn't considered any of that. I'd accepted it, maybe even more easily than I accepted the news that my mother was white, not because I'd rather be a skin-walker than Caucasian, but because this *felt* like the truth.

All my life I'd felt like I didn't quite know who I was. I'd chalked that up to the adoption, not knowing my family, not knowing my tribe. But that wasn't the missing piece. This was.

I could stand in front of the mirror and mentally refuse to believe a person could change into an animal, but in my heart I knew it was true. One day, like Annie, I'd be running through the forest on all fours, smelling, seeing, hearing, and feeling the world as a big cat.

One day? No. If Rafe was right about the dreams and the muscle cramps, that day was coming fast. The thought of it made my stomach seize. In relief, excitement, or downright terror? Probably a little of each.

When would it happen? *How* would it happen? What would it be like? Could I prepare?

And the rest—the part of "becoming like Annie"—that I was trying so hard not to think about. The part where I lost my human reason and began a true descent into animal. How long after the first Shift would that start? How much time would I have to find answers and make sure that didn't happen to me?

No, how much time would *we* have. Rafe and I. As much as it hurt to be around him, I needed him. We wanted the same answers, and he had a lot more of them already than I did.

Maybe I *had* screwed up with Rafe. What mattered was that he was the guy with the facts and, I hoped, a plan.

When I got downstairs the next morning, Daniel was already up, sitting with Dad, looking over his shoulder as he monitored the fires.

"So what's the latest word from the flaming frontier?" I asked as I poured myself an orange juice.

"It's not flaming enough to cancel school," Dad said.

"Damn." I glanced at the map on the computer. "I'm guessing those red spots are fire. Looks safe for now, but what about the animals?"

"I'm driving them to the refuge this morning," Mom said. "They'll keep them until the fire watch ends."

I gave her a hug. "Thank you."

She handed me her teacup for a refill. I took it and ignored Daniel's outstretched empty coffee mug.

He arched his brows. "You want a ride to school or not?"

"If you don't drive me in, Dad will have to. There are dangerous predators on the loose."

Daniel sighed and got up to fill his mug.

"You okay?" he whispered as he stood beside me at the counter.

I nodded and turned to Dad. "Speaking of predators, any luck finding Marv?"

Dad shook his head. "Right now, the focus is on this fire."

Good. I hoped any cougar hunts were postponed for a while. Otherwise, with Annie roaming the woods in cat form, we could have another problem to deal with.

Daniel and I took care of the animals and got them ready for transport. When we arrived at school, I left Daniel with Corey and Brendan, and went off in search of Rafe. I checked the smoking pit first. Hayley was there. She glanced at me, and I nodded, then moved on, rounding the school to start down the path he'd take to get here.

"Looking for Rafe?" a voice said behind me.

It was Hayley. Her expression was guarded, and I thought of what Rafe had said. She was right—I'd never gotten past that incident with the math homework. I hadn't consciously held it against her, but it had changed the way I saw her. I'd backed off, and maybe others had, too. I should have noticed, and I hadn't.

That didn't justify all the crappy things she'd done to me and said about me since, but it did make me look at her a little differently as she came down the path.

"I heard you guys broke up," she said.

"We did."

"Did you decide he wasn't good enough for you?"

If I had, I wouldn't be looking for him, would I? I didn't say that. Didn't have the energy to fight back. Just shook my head and kept walking.

"Maya?"

I glanced over.

"What happened to your lip?" There wasn't any nasty snap in Hayley's voice now.

"It wasn't Rafe," I said.

I started to turn away again.

"He likes you."

I looked at her.

She shrugged. "I'm just saying, if you didn't want to break up, he'll come back. He really likes you." A sardonic twist of a smile. "Everyone does."

She walked away. I wanted to go after her, but I didn't know what to say.

I carried on along the path again and didn't get far before someone else hailed me. When I saw Sam jogging along, I tensed and glanced around. We were still within sight of the school. Safe enough.

She stopped in front of me. For a minute, she just stared at my lip. Then she pulled her gaze up to my eyes and said, "I'm sorry."

I remembered what Rafe said and what Mom said, and I resisted the urge to say "whatever" and walk away. But I wasn't going to say "It's okay," either, because it wasn't.

"Why'd you hit me?" I said.

"I didn't mean to. I just—" Her gaze shunted to the side. "I get mad sometimes, okay? Like Daniel does, only he can control it and I—I can't."

"Like with Rafe's sister?"

Her cheeks colored. "I wouldn't have hit her. I could tell she was, you know, slow. But I was mad at Rafe for not taking a hint, and when she laughed at me for wanting him to stay away, I blew up. I stopped, though."

"You didn't with me."

"I wanted those pages."

"Why? Because they said your parents had been murdered? How come that's a secret?"

I waited for her to explode. *How come that's a secret?* Would I want everyone knowing my parents had been murdered? Would I want them asking questions? Looking at me funny? Wondering what exactly I'd seen?

She didn't say any of that, just scowled and started to walk away.

"What else was in those pages?" I called.

She stopped, her shoulders tensing.

"There was more, wasn't there? Something you didn't want me to see."

She turned, then, and gave me this look that made me shiver. A figure appeared around the bend, bearing down fast.

Sam opened her mouth, as if to say something, then wheeled to walk away—and smacked into Daniel.

"D-Daniel."

"You going to take a swing at me, too, Sam?"

Sam stammered denials and Daniel told her off, but I wasn't listening. Last night, I'd started to remember something Serena said about Sam before she died. Now seeing her with Daniel, it came back.

Serena had been at my place, holding down a rabbit while I changed its dressing.

"I had a run-in with Sam last night."

"Sam?"

"Yeah. I was at the Blender with Nicole, when you and Daniel were taking this little guy to Dr. Hajek. There were a couple of summer boys there, college guys hiking the island. They came over and flirted with us. Nicole got shy, like she always does, and I was trying to show her how it's done."

"Uh-huh."

She laughed. *"Okay, I was kind of flirting back. But you know me. I don't mean anything by it. Even Daniel only gives me hell for teasing the poor guys. Anyway, I'm flirting and Sam stops in to grab a burger. Acts like she doesn't know us, of course. I talk to the guys a bit more, then Nic and I leave."*

"Okay."

"I cut through the woods to Daniel's place. I'm by the ridge, and who pops up? Sam. She tears a strip out of me for flirting with the summer boys. Says it's disrespectful to

Daniel. I tell her to mind her own freaking business. She gets really pissed. Calls me a blond twit who doesn't appreciate what she's got. She said someone needed to teach me a lesson. I laughed, which was the wrong thing to do, because she gave me this look, this really . . . scary look."

Serena tried to laugh, but it came out shaky. "I know that sounds dumb, but it spooked me. Then Daniel got there. He heard us fighting. I told him what she was mad about— that I'd been flirting with summer boys. He just shrugged and said, 'So?' but Sam gives me that look again and stomps off."

Was Rafe right that Sam had a crush on Daniel? I'd never thought so, but maybe she just didn't express her feelings the way most girls did. Sam didn't do anything the way most girls did.

I remembered my dream, about Serena being pulled under. She had gone down so fast she did seem to be dragged. And I *had* felt something grab my leg.

How angry had Sam been with Serena? How jealous over Daniel? Jealous enough to "teach her a lesson" that had gone very, very wrong?

But how would she do it? Slip into the water at the wooded edge, then swim under it and hold Serena down long enough to drown her?

That was crazy. No one could hold her breath longer than Serena.

Daniel brushed past Sam like she wasn't there and came to me. He leaned down to whisper, "She do anything?"

I shook my head as the bell rang. We started back toward school.

"You need to stay away from her," Daniel murmured when Sam was out of earshot.

"I know."

THIRTY-THREE

RAFE DIDN'T SHOW UP that morning. With every passing minute the questions weighed heavier, until by the time the break bell went, I was so distracted, I didn't hear it, just sat there, pretending to listen to a lesson long over.

Fingers tentatively touched my shoulder. I looked up to see Nicole. The classroom was almost empty. Daniel stood at the door, as if he'd just realized I hadn't left my seat. Nicole mouthed, "I've got it," and waved him on.

"Daydreaming, I guess." I stood.

She cleared her throat. "I know I'm not the person you want to talk to about this. About Rafe. That's why you didn't call last night. I'm not Serena."

"No, that's not—"

"It is. I get that. You guys were best friends. Except, well, there are things you can't talk to Daniel about, right? He didn't like Rafe, so he's happy you guys broke up. If you're *not* happy about it, you can't talk to him."

She was right.

"You like Rafe." She led me from the classroom, voice lowered as we walked into the crowded hall. "I don't need to be Serena to see that. I've watched you with other guys, summer boys. That's just for fun. This is different."

Right again.

"Is it because of the party?" she asked. "You think maybe he *did* drug you? Because I'm sure it was Hayley. If you want, we could try to prove it—break into her place, look for the dope."

I stared at Nicole.

Her cheeks colored. "What can I say—I'm a closet rebel. But if it's not the party thing, is it because he came on strong when you were drugged? I could help with that, too. You guys arrange a date and I'll be close by, so there's someone you can call if things get out of hand."

"You'll be my secret bodyguard?" I grinned at her. "You really *are* a rebel."

She flushed more. "Hardly. I just think you guys are good for each other."

I looked at Nicole. I'd misjudged her. Just like I'd misjudged Sam. And maybe Hayley. And Rafe? I didn't even want to think about that one.

I'd always considered myself such a good judge of

character. The last few days, it seemed I was finding out I didn't know anyone except Daniel.

"Do you want to come over this weekend?" I asked. "Mom's taking the animals to the refuge in Victoria today, and I plan to go on the weekend to see the fledglings get their first flying lesson."

Her eyes lit up. "Seriously? I'd love that. I've always wanted to go there."

"I'd have invited you before, but I didn't think you were much of an animal person."

"I am. Smaller animals anyway. You can keep your cougars. But, well, animals were your thing, yours and Serena's. And yours and Daniel's. I didn't want to intrude."

"We'll go together, just you and me."

She smiled and we headed off to our next class.

When we broke for lunch, I caught up with Daniel outside the classroom. Corey and Brendan took off, saying they'd meet up with us at our table.

"What's wrong?" Daniel said.

"Noth—"

"If those guys can tell something's wrong, then it is, Maya."

I led him to a corner and waved to Nicole that I'd catch up with her later.

Daniel and I stepped out the side door into the empty yard. I caught the faint smell of smoke on the wind and turned, frowning. I was about to mention it but decided not to. If I hinted the fires were getting closer, he'd never let me do what I was about to ask.

"I need a huge favor," I said. "And you know I wouldn't ask this if it wasn't important."

"Okay."

"Can I borrow your truck?"

He lifted one brow. "That's a huge favor? You can borrow it anytime. You drive just fine."

"I need it to go see Rafe. Now. Over lunch."

"Oh." His gaze shuttered.

"No, I'm not asking for your truck because I want to get back together with him. I'm worried about him and his sister being out there with the fire threat. They should be in town."

He relaxed. "Good idea."

"Under normal circumstances, I'd run there, and try to make it back by the end of lunch period but—"

"Not when we might have a man-killing cat roaming around. Come on. I'll drive you."

He started toward the lot.

I jogged up beside him. "You don't have to do that. Go eat your lunch."

"I've got some energy bars in the glove box."

I jostled him. "What, you don't trust me to drive your baby? Go on. I can handle it."

"It's not that. She's been acting up lately, remember? I don't want you stranded and walking back through the forest."

Getting a lift from Daniel was going to make it a whole lot tougher to ask Rafe about skin-walkers. But I'd have to work with it. The important thing was checking on him and Annie.

It took nearly as long to drive there as it did to walk. We had to travel out of town on the main road, then find the rutted lane Mr. Skylark had used for his truck. It was clear enough for Daniel's pickup to make it through, but it wasn't a trip he'd want to do daily.

When we got to the cabin, it was dark inside. I told myself they were just careful about using the generator—fuel costs money. Daniel parked twenty feet away and said he'd wait there for me, maybe get out and stretch his legs.

I knocked, then opened the door and my breath hitched. It wasn't just empty, it was *empty*. The crates that stored their clothes and food now held only an item or two.

I knew Rafe might leave when I couldn't provide answers, but I never thought he'd just . . . go. As upset and hurt as I'd been, I'd held onto the scrap of hope that he really did care about me, that he wasn't just trying to make nice to secure my help. Wrong again. The moment he realized I didn't have any information that would help his sister, he'd left.

I was backing out of the cabin when I noticed a piece of folded paper on the floor weighted down by a rock. I nudged the rock with my foot and saw my name.

When I picked up the note, something fell out, and

dropped beside the rock. I ignored it and took the note to the window to read it.

Left this AM. *We'll come back when I have answers.*

There was another line, so scratched out I couldn't decipher a word. I stared at the note for a second, then remembered the fallen object. I squinted at the floor but saw only the pale rock. I patted around until I found something, then rose, lifting it to the light.

It was the rawhide band with the cat's-eye stone, Rafe's bracelet, the one his mother gave him.

I clutched it in my hand. My breath hitched again, heart pounding.

Don't read anything into it, Maya. You know you can't read anything into it.

I opened the note again. Just those two lines. Cool and emotionless. Left. Will return.

I held the page up to the window, trying to see what he'd crossed out.

Okay, now you're just being pathetic. Get a grip, Maya. The guy is gone.

I looked down at the bracelet in my hand.

"No sign of them?" Daniel said from the doorway.

I jumped and stuffed the bracelet into my pocket.

"Sorry. I know I said I'd stay outside, but I didn't hear you talking to anyone." He stepped inside. "I don't want to freak you out, Maya. I'm sure they're just out in the woods, but there are signs of a cougar all over the place. I know your dad's busy with this fire threat. We need to get him over here, though, just in case—"

"They're fine." I lifted the note. "They left."

"Left?"

"Back to the States or whatever."

He didn't look convinced. "I still think we should call your dad. There are prints, scat, clawed trees. Even fur. A cougar has been here and been here a lot, and that's—"

"Small tracks?" I said. "Like a young female?"

"I guess so . . ."

I need to tell you something.

I wanted to say that. God, I wanted to say it. Here was the perfect segue. But the words wouldn't come. Instead I said, "Okay, we should go, then. We need to get back to school."

"Actually, I thought maybe we'd head into Nanaimo," he said as we walked out. "There's something I need to look up. And, apparently, I can't do it here."

He reached into his pocket and handed me a piece of paper. "I found that in the Braun cottage. I was going to show it to you, but then with Sam turning up and the stuff about my mom . . . I decided it could wait. I wanted to find out what it meant before I brought it to you. I tried this morning, but my laptop wouldn't let me search for it."

"What?"

"The nanny software kicked in. No idea why."

I unfolded the sheet to find four words written on it. The top one we'd already seen. Benandanti.

"That's the word—" I began.

"From that book. So Mina didn't just pick a random page for her note after all. But the word below it, isn't that the one the old woman used? Navajo for skin-walker?"

It was. So Mina was here investigating *me*? Was that what this meant? So why send us to that book about the benandanti?

I need to tell you something, Daniel.

I clutched the note and took a deep breath as we walked out of the cabin. "There's something I—"

As we stepped out, the smell hit me like a slap on the face, knocking every other thought out of my head.

Daniel stopped in his tracks. "Is that . . . ?"

"Fire," I said.

He swore and prodded me toward the truck.

I dug in my heels and shook my head. "It's just someone burning trash. The forest fires wouldn't have reached this far this fast. My dad would have called me."

I took out my cell phone and opened it.

"No service?" Daniel said.

I looked over to see him staring down at his.

"In the truck," he said. "Now."

I was hurrying around it when a crashing in the undergrowth made me spin. A stag barreled into the clearing. Spotting us, it froze, and I didn't need to see its rolling eyes or flaring nostrils—I could *feel* its fear, a stark terror that made the hair on my neck rise.

It thundered off, crashing through the trees in blind panic. Fire was coming.

THIRTY-FOUR

I YANKED OPEN THE truck door and jumped in. Daniel jammed the key into the ignition and cranked it. Nothing happened.

"No," he whispered. "No, no, *no.*"

He turned it again and again, twisting it back and forth, then letting go, slamming his palms against the steering wheel.

I opened my door. "We'll walk. The fire can't be that close—"

"No. Just hold on." He took a deep breath, then tried again, calmer now.

My dad always said that when the wildlife started to flee, it was time to take cover. By that point, you can't outrun it on foot.

On the second twist, the engine caught, faltered, then

roared to life. Daniel nodded, slammed it into drive, hit the gas and . . .

The tires spun.

"No way. No goddamn way."

He threw open the door. "Slide over. When I yell, hit the gas."

He pushed. I accelerated. The tires spun, refusing to take hold. Ash settled on the hood. I hit the gas harder. Finally, the truck jolted from the rut and sped forward. I hit the brakes.

"No!" Daniel yelled. "Keep her rolling."

I glanced in the mirrors to see him racing along the side of the truck. He grabbed the door and yanked it open. I turned my attention back to the road. Daniel swung in, then slammed the door shut and collapsed in the passenger seat, panting.

"Always wanted to do that, haven't you?" I said.

He laughed and struggled to catch his breath. Ash frosted his hair and shoulders.

"Just keep going," he said. "It's rough, and if you slow down, she'll get stuck again."

Rough was right. I hadn't noticed it as a passenger, but now I felt every jerk, every roll. Another deer raced past us. Then a fox, so panicked it almost ran under the wheels. The animals were heading toward town. That meant the fire was in the other direction. Good.

When we reached the road, I could see a wall of smoke over the distant treetops.

"I see it," Daniel said, before I could speak. His voice was low, and calm now. "Do you want me to take over?"

I shook my head and hit the gas, driving as fast as I dared on the winding road.

The ash stopped falling. When I looked in the rearview mirror, though, I could still see the smoke.

"How can it be coming in so fast?" I said.

"You know the saying. Spreads like wildfire."

"Sure, but this seems *too* fast."

He shrugged. It didn't matter. Just get to safety. As I drove, Daniel checked his cell phone.

"Still no service?" I said.

"Don't worry about it. We'll be there in—"

A huge shape leaped from the bushes. I hit the brakes as Daniel shouted "Don't swerve!" I knew better—out here you learned that lesson as soon as you got behind the wheel. Then I realized it was a massive Roosevelt elk, its antlers nearly as wide as the windshield.

"Duck!" I said.

I hit the brakes as hard as I could and steered to the right, away from the elk. The rule "don't swerve" doesn't apply with a creature that big. We ducked—another tactic we'd been taught, though elk herds rarely ventured this far east. When an elk hits a car, it'll crush the roof—and you under it.

A thump as the truck hit the animal, but it was a glancing blow and the elk only stumbled, then—

Crash!

Something hit my door. Then a doe scrambled right over the hood.

"They're running into the truck!" Daniel shouted. "Drive!"

I hit the gas. Another thud. I looked over to see the huge elk charging. Its antlers hit and the truck rocked, threatening to tip right over. The animal backed up. Its eyes rolled in rage and panic. It charged the door again. The glass smashed. Daniel grabbed me, but I was caught in my seat belt. He fumbled with it as I braced for the next blow.

Calm down, I thought. *Please, please, please, calm down.*

The elk hit the door but seemed to check itself at the last second. It snorted. Hot air blasted through the window. I could smell the beast, smell its panic. It backed away, head lowering, those huge antlers swinging through the window, one prong brushing my cheek as I ducked.

Just calm down. Please calm down.

"Got it!" Daniel said.

The seat belt flew loose and he grabbed me as the elk charged again.

"Hang on!" Daniel shouted.

I clutched the steering wheel, but at the last second, the elk swerved. Then it stood there, sides heaving, looking faintly confused, as if it had forgotten what it was doing.

Daniel threw open the passenger door, and we tumbled onto the road. The elk snorted again and nudged the truck. It rocked. I scrambled out of the way, tugging Daniel after me.

"Hey!" someone shouted.

I caught the distant pounding of footsteps.

"Hey! Yeah, you! Get out of here!"

I knew that voice. Knew it, but couldn't believe I was hearing it.

I turned to see Rafe running toward the elk, waving his arms. The rest of the herd stood on the side of the road, milling about in confusion, waiting for their leader.

"Go on!" Rafe shouted. "Move it!"

The elk snorted. Then, with a dismissive flip of its tail, it bounded across the road and into the forest. The herd followed.

I tried to stand, but Daniel made me sit on the ground as he checked me out. He squeezed my shoulder and I winced.

"Just bruised," I said. "I can walk."

Rafe jogged over to us. "She was driving? Is she okay?"

"Yes, *she* is," I said, getting to my feet. I looked behind him. "Where's Annie?"

"She—" Rafe stopped and looked at Daniel.

"Took off?" I said. "Like she does sometimes?"

He nodded. "We set out this morning, but we didn't get far before she . . ."

"Ran away," I finished.

A glance at Daniel, then he went on. "Right. I sat down to wait. She comes back when she's done, and there's nothing else I can do until then. This time, though, she was gone longer than usual. I started getting worried, so I left our packs and headed down the path. That's when I smelled the smoke. I've been looking for her. I heard the crashing, came out to the road, and saw you guys."

Daniel anxiously eyed the smoky horizon as Rafe explained. He tried to start the truck, but it was too badly damaged.

"We have to go," he said. "That fire's coming fast."

Rafe shook his head. "Go on. I need to find her. She's probably just back at the cabin—"

"She's not," I said. "We just left there."

He rocked on the balls of his feet and I could tell he'd barely heard me.

I grabbed his arm. "Rafe."

"What?"

I lowered my voice as I pulled him away from Daniel. "She's a cat, right? She thinks like a cat now. She'll do what every other animal is doing—running away from the fire. We'll cut through the forest and try to find her on our way back to town."

He nodded. "I'll do that. You guys go on. The road's faster."

"If Annie's out there, I'll help."

"*We'll* help," Daniel said as he walked over. "Now let's move it."

We split up, staying within shouting range. Daniel veered off first. Rafe came over to me after Daniel was gone.

"You didn't tell him, right?" he said.

"No." *Not yet*, I thought. I was sure he'd insist that I never tell Daniel, and I had every intention of doing so, as soon as we were out of this mess. "If he sees her in cat form, he'll say something to warn us. If that happens, we'll . . . figure something out. But we'll find Annie. One way or another, we'll find her."

Maybe I'd been driving fast enough to put some decent distance between us and the flames. Or maybe the fire had shifted direction or hit a firebreak. Whatever the reason, as we searched we weren't running for our lives with flames licking at our heels.

We could smell it, and ash flakes still drifted down, so we moved at a steady jog, a few hundred feet apart, calling for Annie as we made our way to town.

Like us, the wildlife was on the move but not as panicked about it. I saw families of raccoons and a small herd of black-tailed deer making their way steadfastly toward town. When I caught a glimpse of tawny fur slinking through the underbrush, I picked up speed. Both guys ran over just as the cougar appeared around a hemlock and glanced over at me. Then I saw the grizzled fur and torn ear and let out a sigh.

"Marv."

He stopped and chirped.

"Go on," I said. "Find someplace safe."

Another chirp, like he understood, and he took off at a lope into the forest.

We'd gone about another twenty feet when a crashing in the trees had us all jumping. Something was running our way. Something big enough to make the saplings shake and the dead undergrowth crackle like gunfire.

"Bear!" I shouted.

THIRTY-FIVE

I GRABBED THE BOTTOM branch of the nearest big tree and swung up. Daniel followed. As I crouched on the branch, I looked for Rafe and found him where I'd last seen him, just standing there with this weird look on his face, like he wanted to run but couldn't. He glowered at the bear and his expression wasn't shock or fear. It was defiance.

"Rafe!" I screamed.

That snapped him out of it. He blinked and saw the forest flattening in a path heading straight for him. His lips formed a curse and he backpedaled. The bear shot up from the brush, rising on two legs with a roar.

It was just a black bear. I say "just" because we do get the odd report of grizzlies swimming across from the mainland, and that's a whole other level of predator. A black bear is no harmless teddy though, especially Vancouver Island black bears. When this guy reared up, he was taller than Rafe and twice as heavy.

"Go away!" I shouted. "Shoo!"

Daniel whistled and clapped. Usually that's enough to get rid of them, but this one just stood there, snarling and waving his front paws, huge claws flashing. Enraged by the smell of fire or the smell of another predator, he wasn't leaving.

Rafe glanced over his shoulder, looking for a closer tree, but nothing nearby would support his weight.

"Back up toward us," I said. "Keep eye contact, and don't turn around."

He nodded, impatient. He knew that. It was hard to remember he wasn't the city boy he pretended to be.

The moment he started retreating, the bear roared again, dropped to all fours, and charged. Rafe did turn his back then—to run for the tree. As the gap between Rafe and the bear narrowed, Daniel jumped to the ground, waving his arms.

"Hey!" Daniel shouted as he raced for the next big tree. "Over here. Come on!"

But the bear kept charging Rafe, tiny eyes blazing with rage. The overwhelming scent of musk filled my nose, making my brain shout mixed messages—to run, to stand firm, to help Rafe.

Then I remembered the elk.

Power over animals.

I closed my eyes and concentrated, telling the bear to

relax, that everything was fine; we weren't a threat; he had to leave, get away from the fire. But the ground kept quaking, and when I opened my eyes, the bear was right behind Rafe. The bear snarled and snapped, but Rafe shot ahead just in time.

I bent down to grab Rafe's hand. He waved me back, and with a flying leap, caught the bottom branch in both hands and swung up. The bear hit the trunk and I lost my balance. Rafe grabbed the back of my jacket and hauled me up, flailing, until I could grasp the branch again.

"Climb!" he shouted.

The bear backed away, shaking his shaggy head, dazed by the impact. He looked at me, and I froze and I knew then what had stopped Rafe from running. When the bear met my gaze, any thoughts of escape vanished. Instinct said to fight. This was my territory, and no bear was going to take it from me. Stand firm and—

"Maya!" Rafe grabbed my jacket again and nearly yanked me off the branch. "Climb!"

That snapped me out of it, and when I looked down now, all I saw was a very big, very pissed off bear.

As I scrambled up, pain ripped through my foot, and something wrenched my leg. I looked down to see the bear's jaws clamped around my shoe. Daniel was running toward the bear, shouting and waving his arms. Rafe grabbed me under the armpits and yanked. My shoe came off in the bear's mouth as Rafe hauled me up to the next branch.

The bear shook my shoe, growling, then tossed it aside. As it did, it noticed Daniel, standing only a few feet away.

"Daniel!" I shouted.

He backed up, looking for a suitable tree. The bear only snorted at him, then peered nearsightedly up at us. It rose on its hind legs, front paws hitting the trunk hard enough to make the tree quiver.

I swung onto the next branch as Rafe did the same on the other side. I felt the bear's hot breath on my stockinged foot and snatched it away as his teeth clicked together. He roared in frustration, then leaned on the tree and shook it again.

"Hold on!" Rafe shouted, like I was planning on doing anything else.

I clung to the tree, arms around the trunk, as it swayed. The bear swiped at us, but we were well out of reach. After a moment, he figured that out and backed down onto all fours. He eyed us for another moment, then, with a snort, lumbered into the forest.

"You okay?" Rafe said when the bear was gone.

I sat on a branch and pulled my foot up. My sock was ripped, but the bear's teeth hadn't broken the skin. I squeezed my foot and winced.

"Just bruised," I said.

"Maya?" Daniel called.

I tried to see him but couldn't through the thick ever-greens.

"We're fine!" I yelled. "You?"

He said he was all right, and I was about to climb down, when Rafe climbed over to my branch and crouched there.

"Seems that control-over-animals thing doesn't work so well with the animals we really need control over."

"No kidding, huh?" I said.

His head tilted as he scanned the forest. When he glanced back at me, I thought he was going to say something, but he only nodded toward the ground and said, "We should go. Fire's still coming. I can smell it."

I twisted to kneel on the branch, so I could lower myself to the next one. As I did, I glanced up and realized we were in the biggest tree around. Which gave me an idea.

"I'm going higher first," I said, "to look around for Annie."

"Good idea."

I called down to Daniel to say what we were doing. Rafe was already two branches above me. I scrambled up after him. The faster I went, the faster he did, and I thought it was just coincidence until he grinned down at me.

My heart sped up and I raced after him, trying to catch up, cursing when I couldn't. I forgot about Annie and the fire and the bear, and everything that happened before that—and it was just us again, climbing a tree, the bark rough under my hands, the sharp smell of pines surrounding me, the sound of his breathing pulsing through the air like a heartbeat. I didn't even notice I'd caught up until I was right beside him and he was leaning around the tree, smiling at me.

"Gotcha," I said.

"Uh, no. I stopped."

He waved overhead and I realized we were as high as we could safely go.

"Damn," I said.

He laughed and I looked into his eyes, then swallowed hard and turned away to look for Annie. As I did, my hip bumped the trunk and something jabbed into my hip. I pulled out his bracelet.

"You'd better take this," I said.

He shook his head. "I still need to take off, track down answers. Keep it."

"But it's important to you."

"Proving I mean it when I say I'll be back."

My cheeks heated and I pressed it into his hand. "Please. I don't want to lose it."

He took it. Before I could pull my hand back, he caught my wrist and tied the bracelet around it.

"Problem solved."

I tried to glance down at it, but his fingers slid under my chin, eyes closing as his mouth moved toward mine. Our lips brushed. Then his eyes snapped open and he pulled back fast.

I jerked away. "Right. Bad idea. We—"

"No." He pointed. "That."

I twisted to see a wall of smoke heading straight for us. Rafe started scrambling down the tree, shouting to Daniel below. I stayed where I was and got my first good look at the fire. To the north and south, the forest was clear and calm. There was just one huge swath of smoke heading our way.

"Maya!" Rafe tugged at my foot. "Come on."

I took one last look, making sure I was seeing right. One patch of fire heading straight for Salmon Creek. That didn't seem natural.

Rafe yanked again, but I was already coming down, calling for Annie as I did. There was no sign of her. Gone to safe ground. Or so I hoped.

Once my shoe was back on, we ran. Within minutes, the ash began to rain down again. We kept calling for Annie, staying close together now, running full out toward town.

Rafe heard the sound of an engine first and shouted, "Someone's coming. Where's the road?"

I waved to the north, but Daniel shook his head.

"We're too far from it," he said. "We should be almost in town now."

In other words, no time—or need—to detour. A few strides later, though, we hit a strip of empty land.

"Road!" Rafe yelled. "It'll be quicker than running through the forest."

It *used* to be a road, back when our town was just an empty space for logging camps. Then the St. Clouds came and the loggers left, and this road no longer led anywhere. The forest had crept in on either side, weeds stubbornly poking through the packed earth. But the diesel fumes I was smelling weren't fifteen years old.

As we stepped onto the winding road, I noticed a truck going the other way, barely visible through the trees.

Daniel followed my gaze. "We'd never catch it. It's heading away from town, anyway."

"But *why*? There's nothing over there."

"Doesn't matter. Just keep moving."

We'd just rounded the next curve when I heard the rumble of an engine behind us. I turned to see the truck heading back our way.

"They must have spotted us." Rafe started to lift his hand.

Daniel stopped him. "Let's be sure first."

We moved into the alder bushes at the side of the road. When I looked over at Daniel, he was focused on the truck like a hawk watching an approaching cougar. I'd seen that look before. When I touched his arm, he didn't respond. I knew he wouldn't.

"What are we—?" Rafe began.

"Shhh!" Daniel hissed, still staring down the road.

"Um, okay," Rafe said. "Maya, what are we doing? We've got a fire bearing down on us, and a rescue truck coming—"

Daniel hit my back so hard he knocked the wind out of me. "Down!"

I dropped. When Rafe didn't, Daniel pushed him to the ground, too.

"What the hell?" Rafe said, rolling out of his reach.

"Shhh!" Daniel met Rafe's glare with one of his own. "Something's wrong. I can tell."

"You can *tell*?"

"Cool it," I whispered. "Both of you."

I lay there, under the alder bushes, the branches poking into my back. Ash drifted down like snow now. Tendrils of smoke wafted over on the breeze. When I closed my eyes, I could hear the steady crackle and the occasional rumble and roar as fire consumed the forest.

I imagined the devastation, and my chest seized, tears springing to my eyes. My forest. My beautiful forest.

"It's getting closer," I whispered. "We need to go."

"Just hold on," Daniel said. "Let me figure this out."

"Figure what out?" Rafe looked at me for an answer.

When I didn't reply, Rafe turned away, tense and angry. I could feel that—bursts of anger that made me anxious, too, every muscle tight, telling me to run, just run, before the fire caught me.

The truck rounded the last corner. It was more like a cube van, yellow with some kind of crest on the side. I struggled for a better look. The air was getting hazy now. Invisible smoke stung my eyes.

"The fire department?" Rafe scowled at Daniel. "We're running from a fire and hiding from the *fire* department?"

I could see the insignia now—a red crest with a light-house in the middle. An auxiliary vehicle for Nanaimo Fire Rescue.

Rafe started getting up.

"Wait," Daniel said sharply, not a request but a command.

I swore Rafe's hackles rose.

"Just hold on a sec," I said.

"No. I'm sorry, Maya, but this is nuts. I need to get to town and see if Annie's there."

"Go on, then," Daniel said. "But don't expect me to come to your rescue if you do something stupid again."

Rafe stopped, crouching. "Stupid? What the hell did I—?"

"Standing up to a bear? Yeah, kinda stupid."

Rafe's face reddened.

"It wasn't like that," I cut in. "Rafe, just—"

The truck's brakes squealed. We were still beneath the alder, but they could have caught a flash of color through the branches.

The truck was idling, less than twenty feet away. I caught the muffled sound of voices. Then a click and a slam as a door opened and shut, echoed by a second.

Figures walked to the front of the truck. Anonymous figures in dark blue jumpsuits and gasmasks.

Rafe started to rise again. Daniel caught his arm.

"They're not from the fire department," he whispered.

"Right. In a fire truck, wearing fire—"

"And carrying automatic rifles? Maybe that's standard gear for rescue workers in the States, but *no* one carries those here. Not even the cops."

I saw the guns now, slung across the backs of the two figures.

"Fine." Rafe studied them, then said, "I still think they might be search-and-rescue, but we . . . shouldn't take the chance."

He stretched out beside us again, moving carefully to not make any noise.

The two figures still stood in front of the truck, looking around. Something stung my scalp and I jumped. Another glowing ember landed on my hand.

The ash was falling heavier now, flakes glowing with fire. When I turned to look over my shoulder, I caught a blast of smoke that filled my mouth and nose, and I clamped my hand over them, struggling not to cough.

"These guys aren't moving on fast enough," Daniel said. "We need to go. Back out slowly."

"Back?" My heart raced. "Toward the fire? We can't—"

I stopped myself. Struggled for calm. Glanced over at Rafe and saw him doing the same. He met my gaze, and mouthed, "It's okay."

Push past the instinct. That's all it was. Animal instinct telling me to get away from the fire at all costs. Human reason had to overrule.

I crept backward. As we got into the thicker woods, Daniel's foot slipped in scat. He stumbled. I tried to catch him, but he grabbed a skinny pine for support. The tree creaked and swayed. Dead needles rained down.

"Did you hear that?" a man's voice asked. "Someone's out there. I see white."

Daniel glanced down at his white tee and swore. Rafe yanked off his denim jacket and tossed it over. Daniel tugged it on as we moved.

We were running straight into the fire now. A curtain of red shone through the trees. The heat blasted us. Ash and smoke filled our eyes and noses. The roar sounded like an oncoming train. I could hear shouts, though, and what sounded like an ATV.

I swerved to the left, where the trees were thicker. When Rafe started to follow, Daniel caught his shoulder.

"Split up!" he shouted. "That way!" He pointed in the other direction.

Rafe took off.

"Maya!" Daniel yelled.

When I glanced back, he coughed, struggling to breathe. I veered toward him.

"No!" he said. "Go on! Head toward town! I'll stay close!"

I nodded and ran, circling back toward the road.

THIRTY-SIX

T HE SMOKE GOT WORSE with every step. Tears streamed from my eyes. Smoke seared my lungs and each breath burned.

Was I heading in the right direction? My gut told me home was this way, but I'd gotten off course. Between the smoke and the ash, I couldn't see more than a few feet in front—

I stumbled onto the road, nearly pitching face-first when the ground dipped. I stopped and bent, getting my head as close to the ground as I could, breathing in the better air down there.

"Maya!"

With the distant roar and crackle of the fire, I couldn't tell if that was Daniel or Rafe. I turned, still bent, hands on my thighs as I blinked to see through the smoke. All I could make out was a figure walking toward me.

At the last second, I saw the dark blue jumpsuit and wheeled toward the forest. Then I noticed the rifle pointed right at me.

I stopped in mid-twist. I gasped for air as my brain spun, trying to find a way out of this, but knowing I couldn't. He was less than ten feet away and that gun was aimed right at my chest.

"Please," I said, lifting my hands. "You're the police, right? You can get me back to town?"

A lame plan, but if he didn't want to kill me, this was a way out—he would pretend to be the cops and get me back to Salmon Creek.

He stopped walking.

"Our truck broke down," I said, words rushing out. "We saw the fire. Can you help me?"

He lowered the rifle. *Yes, oh please, yes!*

"Maya," he said.

No! Pretend you don't know me. Pretend you're just a cop. Please!

I glanced across the road, then at the gun. How fast could I get to the woods? Faster than he could aim and fire?

"It's okay, Maya," he said. "Everything's okay."

He pulled off his air mask and smiled at me, and I stood there, frozen. He was about my dad's age. Brush-cut black hair. Tall and lean. He was Native, but that wasn't what had me staring. It was his face—the cheekbones and the reddish brown eyes.

I'd seen those eyes and those cheekbones before.

I saw them every time I looked in a mirror.

Blood pounded in my ears. I could see him coming toward me, could see his lips moving, but couldn't hear anything except that rush of blood. Then a beep and a crackle and he pulled a radio off his hip and lifted it to his mouth.

"I've got Maya," he said, still smiling at me. "She's fine. She's going to come with me."

I inched backward, trying not to look at the gun. When he saw me moving, his smile faltered. His lips pursed, like I'd insulted him.

"Come on, Maya," he said. "We need to get you out of here."

"No." I stepped sideways toward the woods. "I can make it from here."

"That fire's coming in fast. Let me take you—"

I twisted to run. I heard him shout my name. Glanced back to see the gun rising. I tried to stop, skidding on the dirt. The gun fired.

"*Nooo!*" The shout came from behind us.

Daniel charged out of the smoke, his face flushed, even his eyes seeming to glow red. The man pointed the gun at me. Daniel shouted again, so loud it was like a sonic boom, more felt than heard. I staggered back. Then Daniel was there, grabbing my arm, pulling me, and the man was on the ground, struggling to get up.

We ran into the forest.

"Did you hit him?" I said.

"What?"

When I repeated the question, he just looked at me, confused. I thought he couldn't hear me, but before I could say it wasn't important, he said, "I guess so," like he wasn't sure himself and I thought of the other day, when he said he'd hit his dad, but couldn't remember doing it.

It didn't matter now. We kept running toward town. The crackle and bellow of the fire was so loud we couldn't hear if anyone was following us. It was like racing through endless fog, praying you're going in the right direction, knowing you are only when you can finally see the trees *before* you smack into them.

A shout behind us. An answering one. The crash of a vehicle mowing through the undergrowth. Then the whine of an ATV engine.

Daniel yanked me behind a huge Douglas fir.

The ATV engine died to a low idle. Then a woman's voice sounded, harsh, like she was talking into a radio.

"It's me," she said. "They're close by. Grab my coordinates and head over."

Pause.

"Already? Who have they evacuated?"

Another pause. The woman swore. "Yeah, well remind

him that forest fires are one thing he can't control, even if they're set by Aduros. He wanted chaos? He's got it. He'd just better hope when the smoke clears, we have what we came for."

She revved the engine. When I leaned out, trying to see it, I noticed a faint figure about thirty feet away, watching us. Before I could warn Daniel, the figure waved frantically, and I realized it was Rafe.

He pointed to show us where the ATV was. Daniel nodded and whispered, "About ten feet away in that direction."

"Too close," I whispered back.

"I know."

Rafe motioned that there were two ATVs. I waved for him to take off—he was far enough to get away safely. He shook his head . . . and stepped out from his hiding spot.

"What the hell is he—?"

"Hey!" Rafe yelled, looking in the opposite direction. "Maya! Daniel! Where are you guys?"

He stopped and slowly turned, as if just noticing the ATV. Then he took off, barreling through the brush. The ATVs followed.

Daniel caught my arm before I could run after Rafe. "He gave us a chance to get away. It won't do us any good to blow it. He's heading toward the main road anyway. They'll back off once he gets there."

Those people had guns. *Guns.* But Daniel was right. With

the fire closing in, we couldn't play cat and mouse. We had to get to town.

So we ran through the forest, me in the lead, cutting the path, struggling to see, my eyes burning so much I could barely keep them open. The pain had moved into my skull now, a pounding headache. I'd pulled my shirt over my mouth, but it didn't seem to help. When I coughed, I splattered my shirt with black.

Were we outrunning the fire? I was past noticing. The heat, the noise, the smoke, the falling ash—it was just there, all the time. Finally, I could hear the whoop of the town's emergency alarm.

"Almost there," I said, my voice hoarse. "Almost—"

I stopped and turned around.

"Keep going!" Daniel shouted, pushing me forward.

I ran toward the road, my feet moving, my brain refusing to wonder why.

"Go on!" I said when Daniel thundered after me.

"Like hell! What are you—?"

We reached the road. There, almost hidden in the long grass beside it, was a body.

"Rafe," I whispered. "Oh God. Rafe."

I ran over and dropped beside him. Daniel flipped Rafe onto his back and lowered his head to his chest.

"He's breathing," Daniel said. "But barely."

As he pulled Rafe up, I ran around him, searching for blood, a bullet hole, anything.

"It's smoke," Daniel said. "Grab his other arm."

I did and we carried Rafe, one arm over each of our shoulders. After a minute, I could see a house ahead. Then another. Headlights pierced the veil of smoke. They started to turn, then stopped, brakes squealing. The lights swung our way. I froze and looked around, ready to bolt. Then I saw the vehicle—a familiar SUV with familiar faces in the driver's and passenger's seat.

THÍRTY-SEVEN

NICOLE SCRAMBLED OUT BEFORE the SUV even stopped moving. She raced over to us.

"Oh my God!" she said. "Everyone's been looking for you. They're evacuating us. The helicopter's here and— What happened to Rafe?"

"Smoke inhalation," Daniel said. "My truck broke down."

"Maya, Nicole, get inside," her father said. "Daniel, help me get Rafe into the back."

"His sister's missing," I said as Nicole tugged me away. "Has she come back to town?"

"Not yet," Mayor Tillson said. "But I'll let the search team know to keep looking."

They laid Rafe across the backseat. I sat beside him, holding his hand and watching him breathe as Mrs. Tillson checked him out. She was a nurse at the clinic.

As Mayor Tillson got back into the driver's seat, I said, "There are people in the woods. They set the fires."

The mayor's head whipped around so fast his elbow knocked the steering wheel. "What?"

"Drive, Phil," his wife said. "Please. Just drive. We need to get the kids on the helicopter before the smoke's too thick for it to take off. They'll explain as we go."

We did, as best it could be explained. There were people in the forest, pretending to be Fire Rescue officers. They said the blaze was set by someone named Aduros.

"I think they're after stuff from the lab," Daniel said. "A fire means we'll all evacuate fast, leaving it unsecured. It's an extreme way to steal a project, but if it's important enough—"

"It is," Mayor Tillson said.

He called Dr. Inglis to tell her, and as he did, we asked Mrs. Tillson about everyone else. She said some of the families had driven out ahead of the fire, but most of the kids had been evacuated by helicopter. The last one was waiting for us now.

She called my dad and said we were on our way. Then I got on the phone and he said Mom had already gone to Victoria with the animals before the evacuation began. She was safe and staying at the rehabilitation center until we could meet up. Dad was on his way to the helicopter pad. He'd see me there.

Finally, we reached the laboratory. The pad was on top and I could hear the helicopter up there, the *whump-whump* of the propeller. We were almost to the front doors when Dr. Inglis came barreling out.

"Are they okay?" She hurried to Rafe without waiting for an answer and impatiently motioned for Daniel and the mayor to put him down.

"Can you give him something to wake him up?" Mrs. Tillson said. "That'll make it easier."

"No." When everyone turned to me, I hesitated. I knew what I had to say, and I knew Rafe might never forgive me for it. I took a deep breath, coughing slightly as I did. Dr. Inglis made a move to check me, but I waved her back.

"His sister," I said. "He won't let you evacuate him without her."

"She's right," Daniel said.

"That's settled, then," Dr. Inglis said. "We'll get a stretcher to take him up while we keep looking for his sister." She took out her phone and stepped away to make a call.

Mrs. Tillson bustled Nicole and me inside the building. When a third figure followed, I jumped, startled to see Sam there. I suppose she'd been in the SUV but I'd been so stressed out, I hadn't noticed her. She just brushed past me and started up the stairs.

When we reached the top, the helicopter pilot jogged over. Through the open doors of the aircraft, I could see Hayley and Corey. They looked as numb as I felt, staring into space, pale and anxious. Hayley lifted a hand in a hesitant wave. Corey unfastened his seat belt and leaped out.

"Is this the last of them?" the pilot yelled over the deafening thump of the helicopter.

"Two more," I said, lifting my fingers. "One's on a stretcher."

"Who?" he asked, as if the answer would make a difference.

"Rafe Martinez."

He pointed at the helicopter. "Get in."

"But my dad—" I began. The pilot was already out of earshot, running to the door to help with Rafe.

"I'm sure he'll be here, dear," Mrs. Tillson said, laying a hand on my shoulder. "Just go and get in. They need to lift off."

I thought of the people in the woods. I wasn't getting in that helicopter until I saw—

"Maya!"

Dad pushed open the door onto the roof. He ran over, Kenjii racing alongside him, and caught me up in a bear hug, the way he hadn't since I was twelve and he couldn't swing me off my feet anymore. He managed to lift me now, though, hugging me so tight my lungs hurt. I threw my arms around his neck and hugged him back.

"Everything's going to be okay," he whispered. "You're leaving now. The mayor is going with you. I'll follow on the next helicopter."

"Fitz—" I began as I patted Kenjii.

"He's in the Jeep waiting for me. He smelled the smoke

and hopped right in." He put me down and took out his phone. "Your mom wants to talk to you."

"We don't have time for that," the pilot said. "We have a narrow window—"

Dad waved at Rafe. "Get him loaded. We'll be right behind you." He handed me the phone.

Mom sounded like she was crying with relief. I assured her I was okay and Daniel was okay, and Rafe seemed fine, and we were getting on the helicopter now.

"We have to leave," the pilot said, "or that last chopper will never make it in for the rest of you."

Dad hugged me, tight and fierce. Then he helped me fasten my seat belt, kissed my cheek, and squeezed Daniel's shoulder.

As he backed out, Kenjii leaped in and laid down at my feet.

"Come on, girl," Dad said. "You're going with me."

When she didn't budge, the pilot reached in to grab her collar. She growled.

"Leave her," Mayor Tillson said. "She's a good dog. She'll behave."

The pilot looked ready to argue, but someone buzzed his radio, telling him he had to get going. He closed the door.

Mayor Tillson climbed into the front passenger seat and looked back. "Everyone buckled in?"

It was a big helicopter. Six passengers in the back, plus Kenjii at my feet and Rafe, stretched out on the floor, still unconscious. Daniel sat beside me, right behind the pilot. Sam and Nicole were adjusting their seat belts. Corey and Hayley were in the last set of seats. We'd run through the drill often enough, everyone being told who they'd evacuate with, no changes allowed. Except Rafe.

I looked over the seat at him. I thought of Annie. Had she managed to escape the fire? God, I hoped so. When he woke up, though, and found out I'd made him leave without her . . .

I took a deep breath. I couldn't think about that now. I'd made the only choice I could. He'd forgive me or he wouldn't.

When I shivered, Daniel reached over and squeezed my hand, whispering, "It'll be okay."

I nodded. We had a lot of questions that still needed answers, but for now, the biggest danger—the fire and the people who set it—were behind us. We were safe, and there would be plenty of time for questions later.

The helicopter wobbled once, then lifted off.